Veronica Stallwood was born in London, educated abroad and now lives near Oxford. In the past she has worked in the Bodleian Library and more recently in Lincoln College library. Her first crime novel, *Death-spell*, was published to great critical acclaim and became a local bestseller, as did the novels which followed, *Death and the Oxford Box*, *Oxford Exit*, *Oxford Mourning* and *Oxford Fall*. *Oxford Knot* is the fifth novel to feature Kate Ivory. The sixth, entitled *Oxford Blue*, is now available in hardback.

When she is not writing, Veronica Stallwood enjoys going for long walks, talking and eating with friends, and gazing out at the peaceful Oxfordshire countryside from the windows of her cottage.

Oxford Knot

Veronica Stallwood

HEADLINE

First published in 1998
by Macmillan London Limited

First published in paperback in 1998
by HEADLINE BOOK PUBLISHING

10 9 8 7 6 5 4 3 2 1

ISBN 0 7472 5990 9

Printed and bound in Great Britain by
Clays Ltd, St Ives plc

HEADLINE BOOK PUBLISHING
A division of Hodder Headline PLC
338 Euston Road
London NW1 3BH

For Deirdre
with love

Chapter One

The phone was ringing.

Upstairs, someone shouted 'Phone!'

Kate Ivory heard footsteps, a door opening, then another voice: 'Well, answer the thing, why don't you?' There were more heavy feet, a door closing, and the phone stopped in mid-ring.

Kate wondered whether to shut her workroom door. She used to enjoy the link with the outside world which the open door provided while she sat closeted with her word processor, but circumstances had changed. Once, the outside world lived on the other side of the wall dividing her from the neighbours; now it walked and talked all over her house.

'Kate, it's for you,' a male voice called down the stairs.

Oh yes, real life invaded her house. It tramped through her kitchen and colonised her sitting room.

'Kate!' The voice was louder and nearer. 'Phone! For you!'

'I should hope so, too. It is my phone, after all,' Kate muttered. She crossed the room and shouted up the stairs: 'Tell them I'll ring back later.' Then she closed the door. To hell with keeping in touch with real life. She returned to her imaginary one.

Izanna sat before her looking-glass and gazed deep into her own blue eyes, she typed. She changed the previous line, then continued to rattle out the last sentences of chapter four. She typed in the final full stop and instructed the machine to save the chapter. Twenty minutes to go. Yawning, she massaged the muscles at the back of her neck, stretched out her cramped legs, and wondered whether her new book was as awful as she feared. There was only one way to find out: she would have to read it all through. She scrolled back to the beginning of the chapter.

Could you have too much devotion from a man? wondered Izanna, seated before the looking-glass.

But now footsteps were actually descending the stairs to Kate's workroom. There was a pause as her visitor absorbed the novelty of the closed door, and she heard a light tap. He came in without waiting for an invitation to enter. She looked round. Male. Medium height, thinning reddish brown hair curling round his large ears; light blue eyes; soft white hands. Andrew Grove. Old friend.

'I'm not interrupting your work, am I?'

What could she say? 'No,' she answered, her thumb resting on the space bar and her little finger hovering over the return key. 'But how is the Bodleian Library managing without you? Shouldn't you be counting your books or searching readers' briefcases on this weekday afternoon?'

'I have to work until ten tomorrow, if you remember' – yes, she should have remembered, it happened on the same evening every week during the University term – 'so I have taken this afternoon off in compensation.'

'And you've been spending it in my kitchen, by the look of you.' Now that she had swivelled her chair right round so that she was facing him she could see that he was wearing an apron over his dark suit. Not, thank goodness, anything pretty, frilly and feminine, or even one of those plastic things with a facetious message on the front. No, he had acquired the plain white cotton twill worn by serious cooks. The tapes encircled his expanding girth and tied neatly in a bow in the centre of his chest.

'Well, I just thought I'd let you know that I shall be infusing Costa Rican coffee in near-boiling Thames Valley tap water in about ten minutes' time. I suggest that you come upstairs to drink it before it has time to form any unhealthy alkaloids.'

Kate sniffed. 'It smells delicious up there.'

'And I've made a couple of trays of biscuits,' he said. He smiled tentatively and his eyes twinkled. This, Kate reminded herself, did not mean that he was becoming more like Mr Pickwick, but because he had recently exchanged his glasses for contact lenses which glittered as they caught the light.

'The little crispy almond ones?' she asked.

'I've made a few *tuiles d'amandes*, yes. But I'm practising chocolate chip cookies as well this week,' he said.

'Wonderful,' said Kate, dreaming of soft-textured dough and dark, melting chocolate. 'Is this phase going to last, do you think?'

'What do you mean, *phase*? You make it sound as though I was always taking up new hobbies and dropping them again.'

'So this time it's true love? The real thing?' Her gaze returned unwillingly to the computer. She really must re-read what she had written this afternoon before she went upstairs to pig out on biscuits.

'Are you quite sure I'm not disturbing you?' asked Andrew, ignoring her last comment. 'You don't look as though you're in full flow, but one can never tell with authors.'

'No, no,' said Kate. 'I'm just reading through what I wrote earlier. And I'm really looking forward to trying the new biscuits, Andrew.' She noticed that his face had a light dusting of flour and his polished black shoes had acquired a few splodges of biscuit dough. It was as well that the undergraduates in the Theology reading room at the Bodleian Library couldn't see him now, or his authority would be gone for ever.

'Oh, and the telephone rang.'

'Yes, I noticed. Did you happen to answer it?'

'Luckily I had just bent the *tuiles* into shape before they got cold, and placed the cookies on the middle shelf of the oven. So I did respond, yes.'

'Who was it?' asked Kate patiently. 'What did they want?'

'It was some woman with a funny name.'

'Aisling Furnavent-Lawne?' she guessed. Names didn't come much funnier than that.

'That might have been it. Did she make it up herself, do you think? It can't be real.'

'On the other hand, nobody making up a name would choose something so awful. Did she leave a message?'

'It was something to do with Devlin.'

'Devlin? Never heard of him. If it is a him, that is. I suppose it could be a place, or a pop group. Or even a piece of kitchen equipment.'

'No, not kitchen equipment,' said Andrew seriously. 'I'd have recognised it.'

'Did you tell Aisling that I'd ring back?'

'I said you'd ring back when you emerged from the coal face.' He stood looking expectantly at her, but Kate hardened her heart. She wasn't leaving the coal face for a little while yet.

'Fine, I'll be up in a few minutes. I'm sure she can wait till then,' she said.

'I'll leave you to get on with your work.'

'Mmmh,' said Kate, starting to read and hardly noticing when Andrew closed the door behind him.

Could you have too much devotion from a man? wondered Izanna, seated before the looking-glass and gazing deep into the reflection of her own blue eyes. Ever since her fifteenth birthday she had schemed and manoeuvred to catch his attention. She had arranged her wayward curls and ordered her maid to lace her slender waist, she had practised her songs and fretted over her watercolours – even though her romantic landscapes often resembled nothing so much as a patchwork of dingy grey scraps – just so that she would strike Lord Arthur de Gascoyne as a suitable match.

Not that Andrew would ever make a suitable match for anyone, she mused. He was fonder of the Bodleian Library than he was of any woman, and he had dreadful taste in lovers. *Isabel*, remembered Kate. But Isabel was out of Andrew's life at last, just as Liam – her own nasty mistake – was out of hers. And now Andrew spent nearly every evening at her house in Agatha Street, practising his way through gourmet cookery books. One day he might remember that she was quite capable of producing her own meals, but she recognised that he needed company, and let him get on with it. The smell of cooking chocolate crept under the door: and he did make exceedingly good biscuits.

Upstairs, the front doorbell pealed. Surely Aisling wasn't calling in person? It seemed unlikely since she could rarely be tempted away from SW3, unless it was into SW1. Oxford was not on her visiting list. Kate heard sounds of the door opening, of a short murmured conversation and then the door closed again. She resisted the temptation to go upstairs and find out who it was. *Izanna's Secret* was all that mattered at present, though for a moment she wondered whether the title didn't sound suspiciously familiar.

Had all that effort been worth it? she read. For another five minutes she worked at her manuscript.

The back door slammed shut and heavy footsteps crossed the kitchen and thumped down the stairs towards her door. Her concentration shattered into small fragments. This time the intruder didn't stop to knock but barged straight in, flinging the door back to bounce off a filing cabinet. A small chip of cream gloss paint fell to the carpet.

'Hello, Harley,' said Kate without turning round.

' 'Ere, Kate!'

'Good afternoon, Harley,' Kate replied pointedly. 'Have you had a productive day at Fridesley Comp?'

'Wha'?'

'Never mind.'

Harley said: 'I thought you'd want to know I got 87 for me maths.'

Her coolness had hurt his feelings. She looked away from the screen and gave him a big smile. 'That's brilliant, Harley. It really is.'

'Yeah, isn't it.'

Harley, her teenage neighbour from the house next door, was growing long and gangling, and his bony shoulders were starting to broaden. His dark hair was cut very short – about five millimetres – but at least he no longer actually shaved his head. He was growing into his strong features, Kate reckoned, and he might one day remove the steel stud that he wore in one nostril. His prominent cheekbones were quite attractive, and he had been putting in some hard work on his spots, which now hardly showed at all.

'Was that the assignment that Paul was helping you with?' she asked.

7

'Yeah. He's brilliant at explaining things, that Paul. I understand it all now, those matrices and that.'

Mattresses? wondered Kate. What had they got to do with mathematics? Better not to enquire.

Harley was wandering round her room, examining the books that lined the walls, pulling out volumes at random. 'What's this then? *The Illustrated Pepys*? Why haven't you got nothing good?' He moved on. 'Shakespeare.' His voice said it all: hours in the classroom, being bored by *Julius Caesar*. 'Wilkie Collins. Who's he? Never heard of him.'

'You're welcome to borrow something if you want to,' said Kate. It seemed a good thing to encourage Harley while he was in a bookish mood, however negative his views on her own collection. 'The paperback fiction is over there by the window.'

'Nah, I've got a book, anyway.'

'You have? What book? I didn't think you read books unless forced to by a big, strong teacher.'

'I read books,' said Harley, affronted. 'Lots of 'em.'

'I'm glad to hear it. There are those of us who believe that they hold the key to all that is worthwhile in life,' said Kate pompously.

'Yeah, well, you have to say that, don't you, seeing as you're in the business, like.'

'So tell me about your book.'

'Jace give it me for me birthday,' he explained.

'Jace?'

'Mum's latest bloke.'

'Of course. Jason. The one with the receding hairline and the ponytail.'

'The one what don't like dogs,' said Harley.

'The one I can blame for Dave's presence under my kitchen table at all times of night and day.' Dave was Harley's red woolly dog, of indeterminate breed, who had come to stay for a day or two and had now been in residence at Kate's house for a number of months.

'Dog-hating fascist,' said Harley. 'He bosses us all around. He don't like the noise of Shayla's recorder, so he breaks it in two.'

Ah, that would explain the unusual silence from next door. Jace might be a man to admire, after all. 'And what about little Toadface – sorry, Tyler? I haven't heard him recently, either.' No thumps, screams, tantrums. Bliss.

'He does look a bit like a toad, now you mention it. Jace makes Mum send him to nursery school.'

'Really? How's he getting on?'

'There's a few complaints from the other kids, but he's all right.'

Harley's closed expression told Kate more than his words how unhappy he was at home since Trevor, his father, had walked out. Kate used the excuse that Jace insisted on a constant diet of high-fat take-aways and no fresh vegetables to invite Harley round to her place most evenings for a proper meal. What neither of them mentioned was that Kate's house was a haven of order and structure for him after the mayhem of his own home. Kate and her friends might be a funny crowd who used too many long words, but they didn't shout at each other or get fighting drunk.

'Let's see this book of yours then,' said Kate.

Harley produced a thick, brightly coloured paperback, its cover loud with gold and iridescent scarlet. Kate took it and examined the illustration: two women spilled their bosoms from skimpy bodices and pouted scarlet lips at a swashbuckling hero with windswept dark locks.

'A genuine bodice-ripper,' said Kate. 'I didn't realise they still existed. Who's the author?'

'Devlin Hayle!' said Harley. 'Do you know him?'

'Devlin?' Wasn't that the name that Aisling had mentioned? Could it be the same person? Once a name registered, you seemed to hear it everywhere. 'I don't think so. Let's have a look at him.' She checked the imprint: Fergusson – her own publisher. She turned to the black-and-white photo of the author at the end of the text.

Piercing dark eyes stared straight into hers, the pupils catching and reflecting the light from a carefully placed spotlight. He had a beard, also dark, and a mass of curly hair that tumbled artistically over his forehead. He looked to be in his early thirties, a sensitive and creative soul with a touch of the Don Juan about him. She looked for the name of the photographer and found it was one who was famous for his flattering touch with the airbrush. Add a wrinkle or two, and Devlin Hayle might look familiar.

'I could have met him,' she said cautiously, realising that her status in Harley's eyes was at stake here. She called up a vague memory of a loud man called Hayle with a misplaced belief in his attractiveness to women, whom she had encountered at some Fergusson authors' party.

'What's he like? What's he say? You got his autograph?'

'I'm sure he's very nice,' said Kate guardedly. 'I can't actually remember what he said, but I think it was some comment about the meanness of the person pouring the wine. And I didn't ask for his autograph, I'm afraid, as I didn't know you were a fan of his.'

'He's brilliant,' said Harley. This appeared to be his current and only word of approbation. 'Really brilliant.'

'He puts in plenty of sex and violence?' enquired Kate.

'Yeah. Brilliant. You want to write stuff like his,' he added kindly. 'Then you could get famous and make lots of money.'

'Possibly.' She tried not to grit her teeth.

'You working now?' asked Harley.

'Trying to,' said Kate, her eyes straying back to the screen.

'But it's easy, that stuff you write, isn't it? I mean, I seen you, sat in your chair with your eyes closed when you say you're working.'

'It's called thinking,' said Kate. 'It can be quite painful, believe me. Writers have to do it all the time, and we can do it just as well with our eyes closed as with them open. But I do need to work for a bit longer today, Harley.' Harley's expression told her that he was unconvinced by her argument. He shrugged.

'Oh, right. I'm on me way.'

'There are biscuits just out of the oven. Why don't you try some?' She added a smile to the suggestion.

'Already have,' said Harley, walking back through the wide-open door and leaving it that way. 'They're brilliant. I'll try some of the ones with nuts in now.'

'Door, Harley!' shouted Kate after his retreating back.

'Right,' said Harley, returning and slamming it shut for her.

'Thanks, Harley,' said Kate into the quivering silence. She stared at the screen.

Had all that effort been worth it? Now that he had declared his love, proposed marriage and been blushingly accepted, it appeared that he expected her to stay at home and attend to his comfort while he went off and enjoyed a full and interesting life. Her mother told her that this was the way that things were meant to be, but still the prospect made her uneasy. She could feel his love and concern for her in this very room, like invisible weights pressing down on her head, rooting her to the same spot on the carpet for the rest of her life.

Harley clumped upstairs and pushed his head round the kitchen door. Dave whimpered with excitement at the appearance of his master.

'Is me tea ready?' Harley asked Andrew.

'Another five minutes yet. Time for you to wash your face and hands before joining us in the dining room.'

'Nah. I'll take Dave for a walk,' said Harley quickly,

snapping a lead on to the dog's collar and opening the back door.

'Don't be late back,' Andrew called after him. 'You have no more than five minutes, remember.'

'Just going to the rec. and back,' said Harley. 'Dave needs a pee.'

'Have you done your homework yet?' called a voice from the sitting room.

That was the trouble with Paul Taylor, thought Harley, he had ears in the back of his head. Must be all the snooping he did as a policeman.

'I'll do it when I've had me tea,' called Harley, slamming the back door behind him and clattering down the path. The door shook in its frame.

'Just as well I'm not making a soufflé,' said Andrew to himself, watching Kate's pin-board sway on the wall. He rubbed his left eye, which was itching, and went over to the stove to stir a pan full of something pale, smooth and creamy. He licked the wooden spoon. 'Needs just a touch of sour cream, I think.' Te pom, pom te pom pom te pom pom te pom. *Traviata*. There was a lot to be said for cooking, especially here in Kate's kitchen, which was surprisingly well-equipped considering what a slapdash cook she was. She had recently painted the walls a cheerful yellow and hung a green and blue blind at the window. Her cookery books were displayed on a shelf, and there were bright new museum posters framed and hung on the walls. He liked the sounds of life going on around him in the house. It was like having a real family of his own. And now that Isabel had gone off to Phoenix, Arizona, and the lovely Marielle had returned to Brussels, his own house felt lonely. But he wouldn't look for another woman just yet. Cooking, and then eating the food he produced, was really just as satisfying as sex, and more so, on occasions.

He blinked. His vision had blurred. Blinking didn't help. Two saucepans wavered in front of him instead of one. A nasty thought struck him, and he turned off the heat under the broccoli soup. The trouble with losing a contact lens was that you couldn't then see well enough to find it. He ran the spoon through the soup, slowly this time, squinting into the thick stuff. Maybe he could pass it through a sieve. That would separate out any random lenses.

Something glinted amid the pale green. Andrew did something delicate with a teaspoon and recovered his lost lens. He didn't have all his cleaning paraphernalia with him, so he rinsed it under the cold tap, slid it back into his eye and hoped for the best.

There were more footsteps on the stairs down to Kate's workroom. Light, springy footsteps this time. A tap on the door, a pause, and Paul Taylor entered. A neat, self-contained person. If he grew his hair, would he have a riot of red-gold curls that tumbled over his forehead and gave him a look of the young Don Juan? She smiled to herself at the ridiculous idea. Paul's hair was cut to a military neatness and gelled into submission. His grey eyes were as unreadable as a poker player's and his off-duty clothes were clean and pressed. His jeans looked as though he starched them. She wondered whether it was because he was a policeman that he behaved like that, or whether it was this starched and pressed attitude to life that led him into his profession in the first place.

'Sorry to interrupt,' he said.

'That's all right.' This line was coming out quite fluently now, she felt, with all the practice she was getting.

'I really think you should phone back the publicity person from your publisher, Aisling Furnavent-Lawne.' My goodness, he had even got the woman's name right. 'She's been trying to reach you all afternoon, and last time she rang she said that she has to go out of the office in twenty minutes.'

'Off swilling champagne with one of her best-selling authors, I expect. Why doesn't she ever do anything for me?'

'I believe she's trying to, but you'll have to ring her back. You've got five or ten minutes left of the twenty.'

'Ten minutes,' said Kate. 'I'll come upstairs and phone her then, I promise.'

'What's wrong with you? Why are you crouching down here behind a closed door? There are people wanting your company upstairs and a publicity person longing to make you famous.'

'I'm trying to work.'

'You're sitting there, scowling at your screen. I don't believe you've written a useful paragraph all afternoon. So why don't you leave it for the rest of the day, and come and join us?'

'You're probably right. I'll just exit from this file and then I'll join you.'

'There's been some post for you, including a small parcel. And tea's nearly ready, too.'

'And after tea we have to oversee Harley's home-work,' said Kate resignedly.

'Our interest in Harley is showing results,' said Paul. Then he turned and left the room as unobtrus-ively as he had entered it. Kate stared at the door for a moment. A parcel? She loved parcels. And did she really wish her house to be empty, the way Andrew's was?

Would she perhaps be happier alone on a small island, remote from fashionable London? She could pack up all her new dresses, and set off with none but her maid and her dear cat, Pilgrim, to keep her company in her solitude. She would take a trunkful of books and concentrate on improving her mind. Who needed a man, anyway?

Kate read the same section through again, hoping that this time it would strike her as interesting and well-written. But no, it was still just as awful, and even worse than that, it would never sell. No one wanted to read a romantic novel about a heroine who had given up on men. Even her faithful reader would get no further than *Who needed a man, anyway?* before snap-ping the book shut and returning it forthwith to the library. Don't give me any more by that Ivory woman, Faithful Reader would tell the librarian, I don't like these aggressive modern feminists. Kate blocked the paragraph and deleted it, then scrolled back a page, read that through and deleted it as well. Then she exited from the program. She leafed through her note-book. What could she put down for today's word count? Minus three hundred.

She stared moodily out of the window at scrubby green grass rising steeply away from the concrete path that Harley called her patio. It was three minutes to four on a February afternoon. Sullen clouds dipped low over the city and concealed the sun. As the gloom intensified, mist crept along the Thames valley and clung to the windows of suburban houses. All over Oxford people dreamed of sitting down to tea and home-made biscuits in front of a log fire just like the one that waited for her upstairs.

The mist lapped against the door of her house and billowed round the grey slate roof. The lights were on in the house, the yellow glow trying to make its way outwards through the soft, enveloping cocoon. For a moment she thought of putting on her running shoes and making off across Port Meadow into the centre of Oxford. But she would have to come home again eventually.

She sat in her chair, chewing her mutilated pencil.

Chapter Two

In the kitchen, Andrew had put the tray ready on the table. Now he placed a white linen cloth on it and plates with small blue flowers and a single gold line. Milk jug to match. If he left it to Kate she would serve tea with the milk bottle on the table. Pom pom te pom te te da, he sang, to a tune that might have come from *The Marriage of Figaro*. He found a large blue plate and covered it with a white napkin. Then he arranged the various biscuits in rows upon it. They were still warm.

The kettle boiled and he poured the water into the heated pot. Strainer, cups, saucers, sugar for Harley. Oh, and the coffee for Kate. He still hadn't managed to prevent her from drinking coffee in the afternoon, although he found the habit quite uncivilised. He knew that she would prefer to drink it from one of her mugs, but this afternoon she could use a china cup and saucer like the rest of them.

He took the tray through into the dining room. The room was chilly with disuse, so he switched on the electric wall heater. It would be nice to add flowers to the table but he didn't fancy wading through the drenched grass in the back garden in search of the scruffy snowdrops and crocuses which were all it would offer at this time of year. He brought in the plates of sandwiches he had prepared, and the sliced fruit cake from yesterday. Really, Kate should use this room more often. It was small, certainly, but the walls were painted a deep bluish green and the low pendant light made the table into a sunlit island set in a tropical sea. He would get some table napkins in a burnt orange linen for Kate's next birthday, and a dark green table cloth. The napkins would look like exotic flowers in the lush vegetation of the island. He smiled at his unwonted flight of fancy, and returned to the kitchen.

He took Harley's pizza out of the oven. It was packed with nutritious protein and vegetables, but he had spread it thickly with ribbons of Cheddar cheese to make it look as though he had bought it at the super-market instead of making it himself. The cheese had melted and formed a golden crust the way the boy liked it. Harley was still deeply suspicious of real food, although Andrew was hoping to educate him in its appreciation in due course. He looked critically at the table when he had finished: it wasn't exactly his trop-ical fantasy, but it would have to do.

He put his head round the door of the sitting room: 'Tea's ready!' He opened the back door and shouted, 'Tea's ready, Harley!' Then he called down the stairs to Kate: 'Coffee! Biscuits!'

As an afterthought, he placed the small parcel which had arrived that afternoon next to Kate's plate. He would give her the rest of the post after tea, otherwise she would bury herself in its contents and not say a word to any of them.

The back door flew open and Dave entered, panting, pulling Harley in after him.

'Door, Harley,' said Andrew automatically.

The door slammed.

Kate appeared from her workroom.

'Tea's in the dining room,' said Andrew.

'I'd better ring Aisling back,' she said, and disappeared into the sitting room. Andrew looked for a cosy for the coffee pot and failed to find one.

'Aisling? Kate here. Kate Ivory.'

'Right. Yes, Kate. I've only got a few minutes, so I'll be brief. Good news, Kate.'

'Yes?'

'Kate, we're really going to push ahead with selling this new book of yours, *Spring Scene*, isn't it?'

'Yes, that's it. That is good news. Why the change of tactics?'

'Well, you've got brand recognition now.'

'I have?' Kate wished that she had brought her cup of coffee in with her. If Aisling was going to talk jargon like this, the conversation would take more than a minute or two.

'Yes, Kate. So we've arranged a tour of book shops for you.'

Kate imagined herself seated beside a few hundred copies of her new hardback, signing the title pages with a warm smile and a gold-nibbed fountain pen. Harrods,

Hatchards, Waterstones, Dillons ... she swanned in and out of them all, bowing to her cheering fans.

'We won't be including London, of course,' Aisling was saying when Kate started listening again.

'Why "of course"?' asked Kate frostily, her dream melting abruptly.

'They get so blasé about authors in the capital. And in other cities like Oxford and Cambridge, York and Edinburgh, of course. We want to send you to places where you'll be appreciated. We wouldn't want to risk you sitting all alone in Hatchards with no one turning up. But there are plenty of other towns that never get a visit from a famous author.'

'Are you sure that these are places where people actually read books?' asked Kate.

Aisling laughed merrily. 'You're always so amusing, Kate! You'll go down really well, I know.'

'Where are you sending me?' asked Kate. 'Will I need my passport? And when, if it comes to that?'

'Oh, a whole list of book shops,' said Aisling airily. 'I'll send you a copy of the itinerary. And as to the when – well, Kate, how about next week?'

'*What?*'

'We just happen to have a tour already organised for you, you see.'

'You mean someone's dropped out at the last minute and you're frantically trying to find a replacement?'

'I wouldn't put it quite like that.' Aisling was a lousy liar. Kate could hear her blushing all the way down the phone line. 'We really believe this is your breakthrough book, Kate.'

Breakthrough to solvency, perhaps. 'Tell me who's dropped out. Who is it I'm replacing?' It would be nice to know in advance just how disappointed booksellers and fans would be when she turned up.

'Really, Kate, you mustn't worry about it. She was no one you've heard of, anyway. Practically a first-time author. Everyone will be delighted that you're there in her stead. And you won't be on your own. We have a companion for you. A lovely person called Devlin Hayle. Do you know him? No? Oh, he's such a charming man! Everybody loves him. You'll have a wonderful time, and sell hundreds of books, Kate dear. Are you still there? You sound a little odd.'

'I'm just overwhelmed by the thought of it all,' said Kate. 'Tell me more about this man Hayle.'

'Well, he's a historical novelist, like yourself. That is, not quite like yourself. He does write books that are a little less well-researched than yours, more at the popular end of the market.'

'Best-selling bodice-rippers?' queried Kate.

'Not quite best-selling. That section of the market is a little slow at the moment. And we have never encouraged people to use the term "bodice-ripper" – it sounds so vulgar. They call him "The Man Who Understands a Woman's Heart".'

'They do? Who are *they*?'

'They? Oh, everybody, of course! What a funny mood you're in. This tour will be as great a boost for your career as it will be for Devlin's, Kate.'

'And you say he's easy to get on with?'

There was a short pause at the other end of the line.
'I'm sure he is. And he comes from your part of the country, too.'

'Oxford? I should have met him, surely.'

'Not quite Oxford. A town nearby. His address is in Swindon.'

'*Swindon!* Famous for its university, its dreaming spires, its punts on the river, of course.'

'There's no need to be sarcastic. I believe that Swindon is famous for its railway station, and there's nothing wrong with that, is there? When I looked at the map, I saw that Oxford and Swindon are only a couple of inches or so apart.'

'Did you notice the scale of the map?'

'What? Oh, you're joking again. Ha ha. Well, I must be flying now, but I'll see that the details are in the post to you this evening. And I'll include Devlin's address and phone number so that you can liaise over where to meet and so on. It was lovely to talk to you. *Ciao!*'

If there was one thing Kate hated, it was people who used the word *ciao* instead of 'goodbye'.

'D'you want the last biscuit?' asked Harley.

'What?' Kate realised that she had been sitting silently watching her coffee grow cold since she returned from making her telephone call.

' "Would you like", not "do you want", said Andrew.

Kate scooped the skin off her coffee with her spoon

and then looked up to find three concerned male faces watching her.

'Everything all right?' asked Andrew.

'It wasn't bad news, was it?' asked Paul.

'I've left you one of the chocolate biscuits,' said Harley.

'Sorry,' said Kate. 'I was thinking.'

'That's the painful thing you do with your eyes shut, isn't it?' asked Harley innocently.

'Harley!' warned Andrew.

'So what does the woman want?' asked Harley.

'Aisling? Oh, she wants me to go off on a tour of book shops. Talking to the punters, signing the new hardback, that sort of thing.'

'Can't be bad,' said Paul.

'No. Of course it's a great opportunity for me.'

'You're not worried about talking to all those strangers, are you?' asked Andrew.

'No, I don't think so.'

'But?'

'But it starts next week, and it doesn't include London. I imagine that someone dropped out at the last minute and they thought I would be free since I have no responsibilities.' Even to herself she sounded childish and petulant.

'Come on, Kate,' said Paul. 'Even if you weren't their first choice, you've been given the chance now, so grab it with both hands. Go out there and amaze them all.'

'Wear some of my liveliest clothes, you mean? Read them some of my scorching prose?' Kate started to brighten at the thought of her shortest skirts and most outrageous ear-rings, not to mention reading aloud the rudest passages in her latest book.

'Something like that,' said Paul. 'No need to go over the top.'

'And she tells me that they have a companion for me,' said Kate. 'An absolutely charming man, apparently. Everyone loves him, or so she says.'

'Sounds a right prat,' said Paul.

'Who exactly is he?' asked Andrew.

' "The Man Who Understands a Woman's Heart". Devlin Hayle.'

'Wicked!' said Harley.

'I have a nasty feeling that he might well be,' said Kate, remembering the glint in Hayle's dark eyes and wondering whether it really was the result of a well-placed spotlight after all. That could make the tour more interesting, certainly.

'I agree with Paul,' said Andrew. 'I think you should grasp this opportunity and make the most of it. And when we've finished our tea, I think we should retire to the sitting room and start organising the practical side of your absence. Who is going to look after Dave while Harley is at school? And who is going to oversee Harley's homework, if it comes to that?'

'I'm sure that you and Paul can manage all that between you with great efficiency,' said Kate. 'And you'll make sure that Harley eats his greens and doesn't lose his football kit, too, I have no doubt.'

' 'Ere!' protested Harley. 'I don't need none of that. You just leave me alone.'

'Why don't you open your parcel, Kate?' said Paul. 'Then you can look at the rest of your post. Andrew and I will sort out the domestic details for while you're away. Though I do have to go away for a couple of days myself next week.'

'Where you going?' asked Harley.

'To London. On a course.'

'Really? What sort of course?' asked Andrew.

' "Dealing with difficult people". Though I'm not sure that two days is anything like long enough to cover the subject.'

Kate glared at him: it was not easy to tell when Paul was joking. Paul stared blandly back at her, so she picked up the small parcel next to her plate and turned it over.

'No return address. No legible postmark. And I don't recognise the handwriting.' She put it down again.

'I'd say it's on the small size for a bomb,' said Paul. 'And it's not the right shape. So it could be a small object of appreciation from one of your fans. I should risk opening it if I were you.'

Kate pulled at Sellotape and brown paper. A red cardboard box appeared. It was about two inches by one and a half, and an inch deep.

'What's that then?' asked Harley.

She removed the lid. Inside, on a bed of black velvet, sat a ring.

'It's made of real gold!' said Kate, removing it from the box. The others leaned forward to see better.

'Nine carat,' said Paul.

'Who on earth loves me that much?' wondered Kate.

'Is there a card or a note with it?' asked Paul.

Kate searched among the paper and Sellotape, lifted the black velvet base and peered underneath it.

'Nothing,' she said.

'Perhaps he's sent a letter separately,' said Paul.

'Maybe. But it's a bit odd, isn't it?' said Kate. 'I mean to say, who sends a ring to their favourite author?'

'It's more like four rings than one,' said Andrew.

'Twisted together to form a knot. It's one of those puzzle rings,' said Paul.

'Let's see,' said Harley, taking it from Kate before she could argue with him.

Seconds later the ring lay on the table, only now it was obvious that it was indeed made from four, irregularly shaped, linked hoops.

'It would have been nice to try it on,' said Kate, considering it regretfully. 'Does anyone know how to put it together again?'

They all looked at each other. Andrew and Harley shook their heads. Then Paul picked it up, fixed two of the hoops together, deftly twisted the third and fourth hoops around them and handed it back to Kate.

'There you go,' he said. 'It's easy when you know how.'

Chapter Three

Kate picked up the pile of mail and flicked through it.

'What yer got there then?' asked Harley.

'I don't know until I open them,' said Kate. 'But I doubt if there's anything very interesting.'

She looked at the first envelope. A charity gift catalogue. She lobbed it into the waste-paper basket. Next came a special offer leaflet from an office equipment supplier. It followed the catalogue.

Harley, Paul and Andrew were all in her sitting room. Paul was seated in an upright chair at her bureau, still examining the knot-ring and its packaging. Andrew was in the most comfortable armchair, methodically working through the clues in *The Times* crossword puzzle. Harley was stretched out on the floor, pretending to read a book about Saxon settlements in Oxfordshire. Dave was lying behind Harley, his muzzle resting on his master's shoulder. Kate herself was lounging on her favourite pink velvet sofa with Susannah, her marmalade cat, lying along the back. Susannah was purring; Dave was snoring. It's like basking in a pool of warm treacle, thought Kate. Comfortable, but perhaps not good for the character.

If she got used to it, would it take the edge off her writing?

'Someone might have sent you another fabulous gift,' said Harley. 'Or they might have written a letter with a brilliant offer. Like inviting you to Hollywood.'

'I don't think I like fabulous gifts when I don't know who they're from.'

'It must be from your secret admirer,' put in Andrew.

'I can't see the point of admiring someone in secret.' At this moment Kate noticed what she was sitting on. 'What's this?' she asked the room at large. She stood up so that she could see it better. The sofa was covered with a large square cotton throw, patterned with leaves and flowers. Pretty, she had to admit, but not *hers*.

'I brought it over. I didn't like the way the velvet was getting marked with Dave's muddy paws,' said Andrew. 'The cat's been scratching the seat, and hadn't you noticed they've both dropped hairs all over it?'

'I think that Susannah and Dave both blend in quite well with pink velvet,' said Kate. Whose house was this, anyway?

'They don't blend in so well with my dark suits,' said Andrew. 'I was shedding ginger dog and cat hair all over the Lower Reading Room yesterday. I was not popular with other staff members, I can tell you.'

'Is there anything interesting in your post?' asked Paul. 'Anything that might indicate who sent the ring?'

'Not yet,' said Kate. 'Perhaps it was a mistake. Perhaps it wasn't meant for me after all.'

'Unlikely,' said Paul. 'It's addressed to you person-ally, and to Agatha Street. It wasn't forwarded by Fergusson, so it must be someone who knows you.'

'Or someone who knows how to use a telephone directory. I believe that the dust jackets of my books mention that I live in Oxford.'

'Perhaps it's time you went ex-directory,' said Paul.

'Oh, that would be an awful bore!'

'Ain't you got nothing interesting?'

'Sorry, Harley,' she said. 'It's all the same old stuff here. Junk mail and special offers mostly. No invitations from movie producers, I'm afraid.'

She left the unopened envelopes on the sofa and went to close the curtains. As she looked out of the window she saw that as well as the fog, it was freezing out there now. Her car was covered with white frosting and the bare trees were grey against the dark blue evening. Her sitting room, in contrast, was warm and inviting. She picked up the remaining two letters. She opened the first one.

Dear Kate Ivory,

I have been reading your book, *Smoke Drifting over the Ocean*, and I would like to tell you that you have made some mistakes in it. First of all, on page 15, Bertrand describes Alina as 'looking like something the cat's brought in'. But that phrase wasn't used until 1920, and your book is set in 1860. How do you explain the dis-crepancy?

And then again, on page 22, Mrs Tarrant

advises Laetitia to 'feed the brute!' Didn't you know that this derives from a *Punch* cartoon of 1886, and so wouldn't have been used by a character in 1860?

I see that on page 29, Laetitia, Mrs Tarrant and Bertrand all set off for Eastbourne from the local railway station. This must be on the Tuesday morning. However, the Great Western Railway Company . . .

Kate leafed through the letter until she got to the end. The letter was from a J. M. Brent (Mrs). She didn't bother to read any further. There were three or four closely written pages, all doubtless pointing out her errors. What did the writer expect her to do – produce an amended second edition, incorporating her corrections? She crumpled it up and tossed it into the bin. Other, more conscientious authors, might reply to each point in turn, but she wasn't one of them. She opened the second envelope.

Dear Miss Ivory,
I have been very disappointed when reading your last two books.

What have I done wrong this time? And do I really wish to know? 'Bother!' she muttered.

'You got another crap letter?' asked Harley.

'I do believe I have,' said Kate.

'Must you use that word?' asked Andrew at the same time, looking up from his crossword puzzle.

Kate retrieved the first letter from the wastepaper basket, flattened it out and handed it over to Andrew. He skimmed through the first page or two, then handed it back to her.

'You're right, Harley,' he said. 'It's another crap letter. Bin it, Kate.'

'I'll have to send some sort of answer,' she said reluctantly, and left it lying on the coffee table. She continued to read the second letter.

Why isn't there a better photograph of you on the inside flap of the dust jacket? Fergusson has been using the same picture for three years now and it just isn't very good. I can hardly see what you look like under that hat, and with your hand obscuring your chin, you could be anybody. But then, you do have very pretty hands, and I like the big chunky ring you're wearing.

A nutter, thought Kate. Nothing but nutters and nit-pickers. Thank goodness he hasn't got my home address. The letter went on:

I have been imagining what you really look like, in spite of the photograph. I see you as tall, maybe five foot eight or nine, and wearing simple shoes with two-inch heels. You are willowy, with wavy blonde hair and very blue eyes.

I wish, thought Kate, trying to stretch out her five feet and five inches. And certainly her hair was sometimes blonde. On the other hand, sometimes it was red, and then again sometimes it was striped with many subtle colours. Once, though briefly, it had been a very pretty pale blue. And her eyes were definitely grey. She had tried to see shades of blue or green in them, but no, they were quite grey. Willowy? She tried swaying a little, like a fragile tree in a gentle breeze, while allowing her lids to droop and quiver provocatively.

'What's wrong?' asked Paul. 'Are you feeling all right?'

'Not feeling faint, are you?' enquired Andrew.

'Thought you was going to puke,' said Harley.

She had forgotten for the moment that they were there. 'I'm fine,' she said. 'I was just trying to live up to someone's idealised view of me.'

She read down to the end of the letter. More of the same compliments. It was signed J. Barnes. She looked down at her feet: they were encased in thick scarlet and yellow striped socks and running shoes too ancient to wear when she was actually running. Hardly the kid leather pumps that her admirer expected. He – or she? – would be deeply disappointed if they ever met.

She put the two letters together. She would reply to both of them with some variation on her usual, 'Thank you so much for writing, I appreciate your comments, I'm so glad you enjoy my books. *Spring Scene* is coming out this very month. I do hope you will enjoy it as much as the others.' After all, she couldn't afford to lose any readers, however irritating they were.

'Any more ideas about the sender of the four gold rings?' she asked Paul.

'No, I'm afraid not,' he said.

'Call yourself a detective!'

She looked at the ring, sitting on its black velvet bed. Four circles, linked together and twisted into a knot so that they made a single ring. She glanced round the room. Four people, linked and tied in a knot so that they formed one family. Wasn't there some classical story about a knot? The Gordian knot, that was it. No one could untie it until one of those heroes, Ulysses or Heracles or some such, came along with his sword and just cut straight through the whole thing with one stroke. Maybe that was what she needed: a Greek hero. Well now, Kate, if you're going to come up with images like that, she told herself severely, you'd do better to use them in one of your stories.

'I'll go down and deal with these now,' she said, taking the letters. 'Then I'll go for a short run.'

'Dinner's at eight,' said Andrew. 'And I've made a rather lovely soup.' He frowned at Harley who was pretending to throw up on the carpet at the thought of home-made soup.

'Are you sure you want to go out in this fog?' asked Paul.

'Yes, quite sure.'

'Would you like me to come with you?'

'No thanks. I'll be fine on my own. Oh, and does anybody know who cut the Gordian knot?'

'Alexander the Great,' said Andrew. 'Or so it is said, on very poor authority. Why do you want to know? Is it a crossword clue?'

'No, just a minor niggle.'

In London, somewhere off Pont Street, Aisling Furnavent-Lawne was meeting another of her authors. They were sitting in the bar of a quiet restaurant, popular with those who could entertain their guests on a generous expense account.

'Another whiskey?' she asked.

'Make it a treble,' he said. 'They serve mean measures here. And forget about the water.'

'A treble Bushmills for my friend,' she told the waiter. 'And I'll have freshly-squeezed orange juice.' She was not going to attempt to keep up with his drinking. She would be under the table long before they started to order their dinner if she tried to do so. She hoped that Kate Ivory had a good head for alcohol. Didn't she spend time in some wine bar with her friends?

She waited until the drinks came, then she said, 'I hope you're looking forward to your tour, Devlin.'

'Yes, I am. And I'm also wondering what this meeting is for. I thought that we had sorted out all the details long ago. Has something gone wrong?'

'Of course not!' Aisling spoke too quickly, and she blushed, as she always did when she told fibs.

Devlin went on looking at her until she added, 'Well, not *wrong* exactly. It's just that there's been a minor adjustment to the arrangements. I'm afraid that Rhea won't be able to make it, after all.'

'I was looking forward to ten days knee-to-knee with that little blonde bimbo,' said Devlin.

And it was exactly that attitude that had prompted Rhea to call off her part in the tour. But Aisling said, 'We've found another female author to go with you. She's so looking forward to meeting you. She's quite a fan of yours.' She would have to get hold of Kate and let her know that she was an admirer of Devlin Hayle's. 'And she's young and good-looking,' she said, hoping that Kate would not be wearing her Doc Martens or her worst scowl when she met Devlin.

'And who the hell is this paragon?' Devlin's eyes were becoming bloodshot. Aisling did hope that he wasn't one of those who got aggressive after a few drinks.

'Kate Ivory,' she said.

'Never heard of her,' said Devlin Hayle sweetly. 'Why do I have to get myself landed with this unknown?'

'She's hardly an unknown.' Aisling kept the bright smile on her face and beckoned the waiter over. 'Another Bushmills, please. In fact, make that two.' She was feeling in need of artificial stimulants herself. 'And is our table ready yet?'

She set about selling the idea of Kate Ivory as a travelling companion to Devlin Hayle. Tomorrow she would have to work just as hard at selling the idea of Devlin to Kate, and she wasn't looking forward to that, either.

*

'Good night, Harley,' said Kate firmly.

'Wha'?'

'Say good night to the dog, it's time to go home.'

'Oh, right then. Cheers. See ya, Kate.'

That was Harley dealt with. Now for the other two.

'Did you have a good run?' asked Paul.

'Invigorating,' replied Kate. 'Have you sorted out your sleeping arrangements?' she asked them.

'I'm off home,' said Paul. 'I have to be out at crack of dawn tomorrow.'

Kate tried to show no disappointment. 'What about you, Andrew?'

'I'm staying in the spare room,' he said. 'I've brought a clean shirt for tomorrow.'

'I'll be back tomorrow evening to sort out the arrangements for when you're away,' said Paul. 'Good night, Kate. Good night, Andrew.'

Kate helped herself to Andrew's discarded newspaper, put a CD on the stereo, and curled up on the sofa again.

There was a short pained silence from Andrew, then he said, 'What on earth is that noise you're listening to?'

'UB40,' said Kate. 'And it's music, not noise.'

'What? Never heard of it. And it's definitely more like noise than music. Whatever happened to that nice Monteverdi that your friend Liam gave you? Or one of the Mahler symphonies that we used to enjoy?'

'Never heard of them,' said Kate, and turned the volume up on 'Cherry Oh Baby'.

Chapter Four

Aisling was as good as her word. Next morning, when Kate's post thumped through the letter box there was a thick manilla envelope on top of the heap. She saw straight away that in the top left-hand corner it sported the Fergusson logo of an unidentifiable black beetle squatting on a capital 'F'.

Kate was alone in the house, apart from the animals, who had both found their favourite places and fallen asleep. She had closed the door on the dining room, folded up and removed the alien flowered throw from her sofa and retired to the kitchen, which was warm and snug and had quantities of comfort food within easy reach. She had scattered crumbs all over the table and ignored the cafetière and teapot in favour of instant coffee in a mug. She didn't care about setting anyone a good example, and no one was there to criticise. It felt wonderful. She helped herself to another chocolate biscuit from the packet and opened Aisling's missive.

She fetched a road map and spread it out on the table. Bloody hell! The route planned by Aisling zigzagged its way backwards and forwards across the country. Hundreds of miles every day. Was Fergusson about to provide her with a chauffeur-driven limousine so that she could arrive rested and glowing at each venue? No. Aisling's covering letter spoke vaguely about some mishap that had recently occurred to Devlin Hayle and his car which had put the latter out of action. So Aisling thought it would be a good idea if they took Kate's car, but perhaps Devlin would share the driving with her.

No way. Kate checked her insurance certificate: it had a special discount for women-only drivers, and she wasn't going to risk her no-claims bonus by letting some unknown man drive her car. Well, everyone knew about men drivers, didn't they? Aggressive, abusive, arrogant, careless, incapable of staying within a speed limit . . . It was a pity that her car was only a month away from its annual service, but she really didn't have time to take it down to the garage before setting off on the tour. She had more important things to look after, like her clothes and hair and updating the notes for her ten- and twenty-minute talks. She would try to take the elderly Peugeot through the car wash before next week. She had to admit that it was looking a little salt- and mud-spattered at the moment, which wouldn't make the best impression when they turned up at the first book shop.

She started to write a list.

Yellow jacket
Black skirt

Silk shirts
Doc Martens

And then another.

Arrange to feed cat
Buy extra cat food
Sort out ear-rings
Check who has key to house
Phone Devlin Hayle

She read them through. She could start at the end of the second list. Aisling's letter gave Devlin's phone number, so she went through to the sitting room and dialled.

'Hello?' It sounded like a very young child.

'Hello,' said Kate. 'Is Devlin Hayle there?'

'This is Iggy,' confided the infant voice.

'Jolly good,' said Kate. 'Could I speak to your Daddy?'

'No,' said Iggy, and giggled.

Perhaps it would be better to replace the receiver and try again later. But just then a voice in the background shouted, '*Iggy!*' and there were sound effects that Kate interpreted as the phone being dropped on the floor, Iggy squealing and running away, a shout of 'I told you not to touch the phone!' and, finally, adult footsteps approaching.

'Hello?' At least it was no longer the frightful Iggy.

'Could I speak to Devlin Hayle, please?'

'Who wants him?' The voice was female and youngish.

'My name is Kate Ivory.' She was not going to admit to wanting a man that she had not yet met.

'*Dan!*' The female voice didn't bother to remove the receiver far from her mouth before shouting. There was an indistinct response from the background to which she replied: 'I don't know. Some young female wants to talk to you. God only knows why.' More indistinct response in the background. 'Who did you say you were?' the woman asked Kate.

'Kate Ivory.' She enunciated very clearly. 'I am a writer. A historical novelist, to be precise.'

'She says she's called Kate Ivory,' said the woman as though she didn't believe a word of it. The response now came nearer to the phone at the other end and Kate caught the final words: '. . . you'll have to blame Aisling Furking-Lawne.'

Then, 'Devlin Hayle speaking.' A dark, gravelly voice. The sort of voice that is achieved by years spent in smoky pubs, drinking large quantities of whisky. Quite attractive, really.

'I thought I'd better get in touch, since we shall be spending a lot of time in each other's company,' said Kate. 'And we have arrangements to make, haven't we?'

'How delightful. Yes, of course. And I'd better give you directions on how to find my house, hadn't I, since you'll be picking me up here on Monday.' It was as though he had switched on a tap marked 'Charm', thought Kate. The prospect of spending time with the man was getting brighter by the minute.

*

Kate was still feeling cheerful when she went back into the kitchen after the phone call. She took another chocolate biscuit from the packet and opened the rest of her post. Most of it was the usual dull stuff, but there was an unfamiliar hand-written envelope, forwarded by Fergusson. A fan letter. She hoped that this one would be pitched at a level somewhere between the two that had arrived yesterday.

Dear Miss Ivory,
I don't usually read historical fiction, but one of yours was included by mistake by the library assistant among my library books last week, so I decided to read it anyway, as now that I have my leg, I find it very difficult to get out and about the way I used to and I rely on books to keep me occupied. I was about to give up on your book (I think it was called *The Smoking Ocean*) when I got to page 14 and came across something that really interested me.

At last! thought Kate. A convert! She read on.

Can you tell me whether the family's cook, Edna Burbage, is the same Edna Burbage that I knew at school in Clapham in 1917? She was a funny little thing then, and I don't remember that she was ever very interested in cooking, but I did hear that she went into service after she left school. I should be ever so glad to hear news of her if it is the same Edna that I knew all those years ago. I believe she joined the WRAF during the Second World War and got to be very senior, so it's unlikely that she's still earning her living as a cook and really I don't like the sound of the family you describe in *Smoking Oceans*, so I do hope she isn't.

Yours faithfully, L. J. Froster

Kate groaned and helped herself to another biscuit.

'Dear Mrs— ,' she started to write. Could she assume L. J. was a woman? Or that she, if a she, was married? Or if married she used Mrs? It was a minefield. She left it for the moment and continued with the rest of the letter.

How very kind of you to take the trouble to write to me after reading *Smoke over the Ocean*. I am so glad that you enjoyed the book and I hope that you will go on to read the others I have written . . .

She could write this sort of thank-you letter in her sleep, luckily. When she had finished, she went back to her lists. When she had decided which clothes to take with her she would have to make sure they were all clean and ironed and ready to impress the punters.

That evening, while she was enjoying something delicious prepared by Andrew, involving lemon grass and wild rice, Kate listened to the two men as they sorted out her domestic arrangements for her.

'So you'll come in on the Wednesday and Thursday when I'm away, to feed the animals and look after Harley,' Paul was saying.

'And you can manage my Tuesdays when I'm working late,' said Andrew. 'I'll be doing some cooking and freezing. I'll leave a list on the pin board to tell you what's there. Make sure that Harley defrosts a meal and eats it every day.'

'I'll try to get some green vegetables into the boy and see that he takes a reasonable amount of exercise.'

Ho hum, thought Kate. Is this what living in a family is like?

'The plants need watering about twice a week at this time of year,' she put in. She might as well pretend to be as interested as they were in her arrangements. 'And the ones on the kitchen windowsill should be sprayed gently with water once a day.' This was probably true, but Kate rarely remembered to do it herself. 'And could someone record *ER* for me on Wednesday evening?'

'I believe that they have television sets in most hotels these days,' said Andrew.

'Who said I'd be staying in hotels?'

'Where else is there?' asked Andrew, baffled.

'B and Bs,' said Paul. Then, as Andrew still looked blank. 'Bed and breakfast places. Private houses that let rooms to passing strangers.'

'How peculiar. Still, it takes all sorts, I suppose.'

'I expect Fergusson noticed they cost less than half

as much as a decent hotel. I'll leave you a list of where I'm staying on which nights,' said Kate. 'Just in case you need to get in touch with me.' Not that it sounded as though they needed anything at all from her except the use of her kitchen.

'You will remember to note down how to pick up your phone messages from a different phone, won't you?' said Paul. 'I've got your mobile phone number so that I can get in touch with you in an emergency.'

'I don't often switch it on,' said Kate. 'And it would be dreadful if it went off in the middle of one of my talks. Or even one of Devlin's.'

'So make sure you can pick up your messages from the answer phone,' repeated Paul. 'I can always leave you a message then, if I need to.'

'It's quite easy,' said Kate. 'I just dial my own number, then dial another number – four, I think, or perhaps it's two – and then punch in another couple of numbers so that the phone knows that it's me and not some nosy stranger, and then it plays over everything on the tape.'

'Fine,' said Paul. 'Just make sure you know what all those different numbers are before you leave. It might even be a good idea to write them down so that you don't forget what they are. And by the way, that new machine doesn't use tape.'

'You two do fuss so. I ran my own life before you turned up, and I can do it again without a couple of minders.'

*

45

It was amazing how many clothes you needed for a ten-day tour of England, thought Kate on Monday morning. Paul tried to tell her that the towns she was visiting might well run to launderettes and dry-cleaning shops so it was only necessary to take two or three smart outfits and a couple of pairs of jeans and sweatshirts. After all, as Andrew pointed out, different people would be seeing her each day, so she didn't need to worry about wearing the same thing all the time.

'And what about Devlin Hayle?' she asked.

'What about him?' said Andrew.

'Why should you worry what he thinks?' said Paul.

'And as Kate found it too difficult to answer their questions, she treated them as rhetorical and kept a dignified silence.

But the boot was filling up with suitcases, overnight bags and plastic carrier bags.

'I'd better put in my walking boots,' said Kate. 'And a waterproof top.'

'Nonsense,' said Andrew. 'You won't have time for hiking.'

'And what about leaving room for Devlin's gear?' said Paul.

'Oh, men travel light,' said Kate.

'Let's hope so. This car of yours won't make it down Agatha Street, let alone five times round the country, with all this weight on board.'

'And it's time you left,' said Andrew, looking at his watch.

'Speaking of which, why aren't the two of you at work?'

They both looked sheepish. 'I rearranged things so that I could see you off,' said Andrew.

'So did I,' said Paul.

Kate banged the door shut, placed her road atlas on the passenger seat and her mobile phone in the pocket on the driver's door. Then she kissed Paul and Andrew goodbye, gave them each a hug, and got into the car.

'Look after Harley for me!' she called.

'Drive safely!' and 'Good luck!' they called back.

The last she saw of them was their miniature figures in her driving mirror as she drove down the street, before she turned the corner and took the road for Swindon and Devlin Hayle. Paul was looking as solemn as ever, but Andrew was smiling and waving. She was glad, later, to have that memory of them.

Chapter Five

February is probably not the best month to visit Swindon, Kate admitted, as she entered the town and started to watch for the landmarks that Devlin had given her. Uninspiring streets. Grey skies, light drizzle. Garage on left. Pub on right. Take next left. She was stuck behind a container lorry which was trying to overtake a bus. Eventually the traffic moved on again. Look out for Tandoori restaurant. Turn right. OK so far. Mark Pattison Road. This was it. Kate drove slowly down the street. She was still at the low numbers, and she was looking for number 104. The houses were big but running to seed, and they had tiny front gardens filled with bicycle frames and dustbins, and windows speckled with the black mould that grows in damp buildings.

Which are you, Devlin Hayle? A newcomer who has yet to make a decent living, or a has-been whose income is falling year by year? Or are you perhaps a literary author with high principles who prefers to write well and live badly? But remembering the jacket of Harley's book, she doubted that Devlin was excessively high-minded.

She found the house and parked her car between an overflowing rubbish skip and an elderly Ford. Then she approached the door.

There was a lot of noise coming from number 104. It reminded her of her neighbours, the Toadface family, in the old days before Trevor moved out. Shouts, bumps, cries, the thud of music all garnished with a layer of daytime television. She rang the bell.

The door opened a few inches.

'Yes?' enquired a sharp female voice. Kate thought it was the same as the one that had taken over the phone from young Iggy.

'Devlin Hayle?' she asked.

The door opened a little wider. 'And which of his totties are you?' asked the woman. Kate could see that she was of medium height, rather thin and had a lot of red hair. The hair was tangled and needed washing.

'My name is Kate Ivory.' Well, was that dignified enough for you? Andrew would have been proud of her.

'And you're looking for *Devlin* Hayle?' The woman had a cigarette in her mouth, and now she took it out and blew out a long stream of smoke.

'Is that a problem?' asked Kate.

'Well, Dan was good enough for his parents and good enough for me when we met. There was none of this Devlin crap then. But that's the literary world for you.'

She stared at Kate for a while longer, then shouted over her shoulder: '*Dan!*'

A rumbling noise that sounded like 'Whatdyer-want?' came from inside the house.

'Someone here looking for Devlin Hayle,' she shouted back. 'I suppose she means you. Though it says Daniel on your tax demand.'

'I'll sodding call myself what I like, and it's none of your business.' The rumbling voice was a lot closer now. The woman abruptly disappeared and her place was taken by a tall, broad man with a mop of dark hair, a face largely hidden by beard, and a wicked pair of eyes. He threw the door wide, looked intensely at Kate for a moment and then treated her to a huge dose of Charm. Well, I've passed some sort of test, she thought, as his face broke into a well-prepared smile. She wished that she had worn something more eye-catching than her jeans and a green fleece top.

'You must be Kate Ivory! It's marvellous to meet you. Can I invite you in for a coffee? No? You're right, we should probably be getting on. I'll just fetch my bags. Is that your car out there? Yes, very nice.' And still talking, he retired down the passage and into some back room, leaving Kate on the doorstep. 'Some pid-dling little E-reg,' she heard him say in reply to a question from the redhead. Every now and then children of different sizes darted back and forth in various stages of undress. They all possessed a mop of dark curls, and any of them could have been Iggy.

'Right, here we are then.' Devlin had reappeared, a zip-topped bag in each hand, a coat over his arm. He was followed by the redhead, who carried a battered leather briefcase.

Kate opened the boot, saw that she had crammed in more luggage than she thought, and closed it again quickly.

'Well, I think the back seat is the best place for your things, don't you?' she said gaily. There were one or two of her own possessions on the seat, but she was sure she could make enough room for Devlin's.

The redhead handed over the briefcase and Kate wedged it in beside the other bags.

'I do believe we're ready to leave,' she said brightly. She could feel a certain tension between the other two and she couldn't wait to get away from it.

'Goodbye then, Jacko,' said Devlin, placing a kiss about an inch away from her cheek.

'Housekeeping money,' she snapped.

'But I'm going to be away for ten days. You don't need to feed me while I'm away.'

'There are five kids in that house, and they're all yours,' said Jacko. 'I don't give a fuck what you do for the next ten days, but they still need to eat.'

While the women watched, Devlin dipped into his hip pocket and brought out a roll of notes. 'Twenty do you?' he asked.

'No.'

'Forty?' he asked, peeling off another.

'Make it fifty,' she said, and held out her hand. Devlin pulled a face as though explaining to Kate that this was a mean and grasping woman, and handed over the extra ten pounds.

'Goodbye, darling,' said Devlin, not attempting a kiss this time. 'Don't go giving that money away to the first hard-luck merchant who comes along, will you? Remember it's for the housekeeping.' Jacko just turned on her heel and went back up the crumbling steps and into the house. She slammed the door behind her. She did it with a fair amount of éclat, considering she was still wearing her dressing-gown and a ratty pair of slippers.

'Could you take over the map-reading?' Kate asked when they were settled in their seats and Devlin had untangled himself from his seatbelt.

'Sure,' he said. 'Just leave it to me. Map-reading is just one of my talents.'

'It's quite straightforward once we're out of Swindon on the A419, but I'd appreciate some help getting out of the town.'

'No problem,' he said. 'Which road did you say?'

'The A419.'

'Hmm, yes, I see it now,' he said, turning the map upside down and peering at it sideways. 'Are you sure that's the best route? I'm sure it would be quicker to take the B4006 and then go out through Purton Stoke.'

'You're the one with local knowledge. I leave it up to you.' A shiny blue car, out of place in this seedy neighbourhood, pulled into the kerb behind the rusting Ford. In her mirror, Kate saw two large men in matching black track suits and very white trainers get out of it and mount the steps to Devlin's door.

'Friends of yours?' she asked.

'What?' Devlin turned round and looked through the back windscreen. 'Fucking hell!' He leant across Kate and pushed the lock down on her door. Jacko appeared at the door of Devlin's house and pointed at Kate's car.

Kate switched on the ignition and checked her wing mirrors before signalling that she was about to pull out. The two men were coming down the steps and approaching fast. No necks, she thought. How odd. I suppose it's all the muscle in their shoulders that does it.

A large face appeared at her window and mouthed obscenities. She was glad that Devlin had locked the door. A fist thumped on the lid of her boot. The face at the window wore a steel ring through his bottom lip. And he had shaved off his eyebrows.

'Drive!' shouted Devlin, and when she didn't respond quickly enough, he yanked the steering wheel over towards him. 'Hand brake off, clutch out and give it lots of gas!' he yelled.

'Oh, for goodness' sake!' grumbled Kate as she pulled away, narrowly missing the rubbish skip and leaving a streak of black rubber on the roadway.

'Perhaps they only wanted to talk to you,' she said.

'Perhaps the Pope prays facing Mecca,' said Devlin.

'Do I gather they're not exactly friends of yours?' she asked. Both figures, tiny now in the mirror, were waving fists at them. Then they turned and climbed back into their own car.

'What now?' asked Kate.

'Turn left at the top here,' said Devlin. 'Then take the next right, and then left again.' He glanced back through the rear windscreen. 'Now take a right, and we'll be back on the main road. You can put your foot

down, no one takes any notice of the forty-mile limit.'
Kate followed his instructions and after this he seemed
to relax a little.

'Sorry about that,' said Devlin. 'No, you're right.
They weren't friends. Rather nasty types, actually.' He
had slipped back into one of his suave characters.
'There's been a bit of a misunderstanding, but I haven't
got time to sort it out now. It can wait till I get back next
week.'

'As long as they don't bother your wife.'

'Jacko? She can handle them, don't you worry.'

'Had a lot of practice, has she?'

'Let's just say she knows how to look after herself.'

They were driving along a featureless road and
Kate had lost track of what direction they were travel-
ling in when, as they approached a small crossroads,
Devlin suddenly shouted, 'Hang a U-ey!'

'What?'

'A U-turn. Quick, make a U-turn!'

Luckily the only car on the road behind them was
still some distance away, and Kate made a tight turn so
that they ended up travelling in the opposite direction.
To her surprise she hadn't even grazed another vehicle.
Her driving skills must be improving at last.

'Do you think you could give me a little more
notice next time?' she said mildly.

'Yes. I thought I saw those two blokes, but I must
have been mistaken.'

'Which way now?'

'I'll have to check the map.'

It was when they finally reached the A419 that Kate

wondered whether they hadn't taken a strangely roundabout route. She wasn't much good at map-reading herself, but it hadn't looked that complicated when she checked it out earlier.

'Do you mind if I smoke?' asked Devlin, fetching a packet of cigarettes from his jacket pocket.

'I do, rather.'

'Bugger.'

Which was the sum of their conversation for the next few miles.

'Don't you think it's getting a bit chilly in here?' said Devlin, breaking a long silence.

'The heater's a bit unreliable,' she said. She thumped the grey dashboard. 'You have to encourage it from time to time.'

'A blast of hot air has just hit my knees,' said Devlin. 'So I imagine that you've persuaded it to work. Is there anything else I should know about this car of yours?'

'It's a very good car, even if it is an E-reg,' said Kate. 'Reliable. Fast, if it isn't overloaded and it's in the right mood.'

'I thought it could do with a clean,' said Devlin.

'Well, look out for a car wash,' said Kate, wishing that she had done so herself before setting out for Swindon.

'Can we have some music?'

'You mean you'd like me to sing?'

'Haven't you got a radio or a cassette player?'

'I have, but they're removable.'

'And?'

'I removed them. And then left them at home on the kitchen table.'

Devlin sighed. Kate felt that she was lacking as a conversationalist, and now she had failed to provide any other entertainment for her passenger.

'How far along this road before I need to turn right?'

They drove through small, rolling hills, sometimes passing through patches of dense mist, until finally, as the car laboured up one last incline, they came to the Cotswold market town where their first signing was to be held.

'This is all very picturesque,' said Kate, looking around at old grey stone buildings and the clock tower at one end of the square.

'Bloody turnip land,' said Devlin.

'So you're not a country-lover?'

'Hate the place. Hate fields and hate trees and hate all this cold, clean air. Hate the bloody turnips. Let's find out from the book shop where we're staying tonight, and I can slope off to catch up on my smoking. I need an old-fashioned pub with a proper beer and nicotine atmosphere. I've been getting withdrawal symptoms after the hours with you in your stuffy little car.'

'Thank you so much for doing the map-reading,' said Kate pointedly. Really, it was just like dealing with Harley. Only Harley didn't swing from charming to repulsive in such a short time. It would be interesting to see which of his personalities Devlin produced for the book-shop owner.

Kate followed Devlin's tall figure into the shop. He needs a black cape and a broad-brimmed hat, she thought. Maybe a cigar, too. Then he could take over the sherry commercials where Orson Welles left off. He was certainly in his larger-than-life persona. He raised his arms, knocking over a display of cookery books as he did so, and called out, 'Aisling! Darling! How wonderful to see you!'

With a name like Aisling Furnavent-Lawne, she should have been stunning. Kate had thought up to now that publicity persons were only taken on if they were stunning-looking and had been to a posh private school.

'Oh, Devlin!' gushed Aisling, scarlet to her hairline. She had a wonderfully well-modulated voice. She was tall, with wide shoulders and a long, bony face dominated by large features. She continued to blush unbecomingly as Devlin enfolded her in a bearhug.

'Where are my books?' asked Devlin, releasing her and looking around the shop. 'You have got my new hardback, haven't you?' he accused a young salesgirl.

'Of course,' she said. 'They're over there.' And she gestured behind her.

'Too far back,' said Devlin. 'Take those cookery books away and put mine here, in the front. And one of each title in the window, please. Put one of the showcards in the window display, too. Now, show me where the drinks are, and where I'll be sitting for the signing.'

As Devlin moved further into the shop, Kate approached Aisling.

'Hello, I'm Kate Ivory,' she said. It seemed a terrible anti-climax after Devlin Hayle, she had to admit.

'Who?' Aisling appeared dazed after her run-in with Devlin.

'Kate Ivory. I write historical novels. I'm published by Fergusson. Remember me? I'm your other author on the tour.'

Aisling squinted at Kate, then fished in her tiny patent leather handbag for a pair of glasses. They may have been the latest in fashion accessories, but they did nothing for her. 'But of course! Kate! How lovely to meet you at last! Do come in and make yourself at home.'

'Do you think they have a few copies of my books, too?' asked Kate. 'Will there be room for them in the shop when Devlin's finished taking it over?'

Kate looked over to where Devlin was charming the owner of the shop into displaying his books, his photograph and the showcards that the publicity department had sent, prominently all over the shop. Charisma surrounded him like a cloud of cigar smoke.

'Now, come back into the office,' said Aisling. 'I've got your showcards there, and lots of copies of *Spring Scene*. We're very pleased with the cover, I do hope you are too.'

They walked through the shop, ignored by the entire staff, who were now hanging on Devlin's every word when they weren't scurrying back and forth to carry out his orders. In spite of the fact that it was mid-afternoon, he had acquired a tumbler of what looked like whisky.

'Here we are. Don't you look lovely?' said Aisling, producing Kate's showcards.

Kate had to agree that the showcards were very good. Half a dozen dust jackets from *Spring Scene* were fanned out across the middle. Above it a photo of Kate smiling at the public. It was her own face that she saw, but younger, brighter, smarter than her everyday self.

'When did you have that photograph taken?' asked Aisling.

She must have noticed that it no longer looked much like her. 'Only two or three years ago,' said Kate. 'Maybe five.'

'He's done some very neat airbrush work on it, hasn't he?'

'Perhaps it's time I had a new one done.'

Aisling looked at her critically. 'I should stick with this one for another year or two if I were you.'

'Now, show me where we'll be sitting for the signing. Then I'd like to go and wash and change and get ready.'

They walked back to where Devlin was holding court.

'I'm sitting here,' he said to Kate. 'Where are they going to put you?'

'We had thought that you could both sit at the same table,' said the book-shop owner. Devlin stared blandly at her until she added, 'But of course we can find another small table to put at right angles to it for Kate. Emily, go and get the small table from the office.'

'Don't worry about me,' said Kate. 'I can fit in anywhere.' And she smiled brilliantly at the shop staff. If this was going to be a charm competition, she was about to start competing. 'And I'll give you a hand to move my books to the front of the shop,' she added, ignoring the expression of panic on the owner's face.

'What's this new title of yours?' asked Devlin, picking up a copy and looking at it critically. '*Spring Scene?*' He laughed. 'I think I'll just call it *Bruce* since we're going to be such close friends. Or *Brucest*, even.'

Kate looked blank for a moment, then put the two together. 'Shit!' she said. It was obviously too late to change the title now, so she'd just have to hope that Devlin was the only person to notice.

'Now, I'll take you both to where you're staying,' said Aisling eventually. 'We want you back here in plenty of time. There's been great interest in the tour, you know. As well as the people who have let the book shop know they are coming, we've had several phone calls to the office asking about the itinerary and where you can be found on which days.'

'Were these enquiries for both of us or just for me?' asked Devlin.

'As a matter of fact we did have several asking about you, Devlin. But there was – were – some for Kate, too.'

'Did they give their names?' asked Devlin, looking behind him.

'Why? Are you being pursued by amorous women?' asked Kate. 'Or is it another simple misunderstanding?'

He scowled at her. 'As long as you didn't give out my address,' he said to Aisling.

'Oh, I wouldn't do that! It's against company policy. I just gave them the list of dates and venues so that they could come to one of your signings.'

'Terrific,' said Devlin, walking with long strides and trailing whisky fumes in the air behind him.

'Well, here we are!' said Aisling, stopping next to a BMW with the current year's registration letter.

'Why not take Devlin in your car, and I can follow you in mine,' said Kate. 'It's faster than mine in an emergency,' she said to Devlin.

'What a good idea,' said Aisling. 'Where are you parked?'

Once they had established that they were parked a matter of yards from one another, it took only a minute or two to sort themselves out into two carloads.

'And before I forget, Kate dear, I've brought you some more mail. You've very popular at the moment. Letters are raining in from the public for you. I do hope that they're all friendly.'

'Positively admiring,' said Kate, taking a couple of envelopes from her. At least that was two more than she had brought for Devlin, and she smiled at him and waved the envelopes to make quite sure that he had seen. 'They all think that my books are absolutely wonderful,' she said. 'I'm looking forward to reading these.'

Chapter Six

'No,' said Devlin, 'No, it just won't do. Let's have a look at yours, Kate. I bet they've given you the best room.'

'You're worse than Harley,' said Kate.

'Who?'

'A thirteen-year-old friend of mine. You're nearer in emotional age to young Iggy, I should say.'

'Shall we look at the other room?' suggested the landlady, Mrs Woods. 'I think you'll find they are very similar.'

'Fair enough,' said Kate, shrugging. In the absence of Aisling, who had retired to some private part of the house and closed the door, it was up to her to present Fergusson authors as quiet and reasonable lodgers.

The house where they were staying was solidly built of grey stone, the central heating was efficient and the rooms were spotlessly clean. They even had *en suite* bathrooms. As far as Kate could see, there were no discos or pubs nearby likely to keep them awake. Mrs Woods had already offered them tea and biscuits and had enquired as to their preferences for a morning newspaper. What else could you want in a B & B? Devlin was just being difficult. Devlin and Kate followed her down the corridor and she opened the door to another room.

'Yes,' he said. 'This will do me fine. You can have the other one, Kate.'

'What precisely is the difference?' asked Kate.

'This one points east-west; the other is north-south.'

'And that's important?'

'If you understood the creative soul you would know what I was talking about.'

'Well, since I can't see any difference in the rooms, you're welcome to take this one,' she said. Perhaps it would keep the man happy for an hour or two. And what did he mean about a creative soul? She wrote books too, didn't she?

They moved their luggage upstairs and Kate finally sat on the bed and breathed a sigh of relief. She looked around her at the pleasant room, attractively furnished if you liked wall-to-wall Laura Ashley. Then she went to the window and looked out at the view of brown muddy fields and grey stone walls. The same view as from the window in the other room, she realised. Which meant that whether this was east-west or north-south, then so was the other. The stupid bugger must be playing power games.

After she had hung up the clothes she would be wearing later, she turned to the two letters that Aisling had brought for her. Here was a morale-booster, anyway. Two more than Devlin. She opened the first.

Dear Miss Ivory,

I do not usually read works of historical fiction,

but while I have been convalescing from an attack of pneumonia, I have found myself unable to concentrate on my usual choice of books. One of your novels (I forget the title of it now) was included in a selection which my niece brought to my house and so I read it, lacking anything better.

And thank you very much, thought Kate. Why are you bothering to write if you can't think of something nice to say?

I am writing to you because you describe in your book a small enamel box, made around 1830, in the form of the Radcliffe Camera, Oxford. It happens that I have a great interest in enamel boxes, although most of them were made before that date, of course, but I have never come across one such as you describe. I wonder whether you could give me further details and let me know where this box may be seen, as I feel it must be a great rarity and I should like to study it in greater detail.

Incidentally, I see from a notice that appeared this morning in my local book shop that you will be appearing in person to sign your books and give a short talk. Perhaps we could talk then about the enamel boxes in which you would seem to share my interest.

Yours sincerely,
Jane Bell (Mrs)

Give me strength, thought Kate. Doesn't the woman understand what *fiction* means? I made it all up, Mrs Bell, because that's what novelists do, I fear. On the other hand, it was nice to know that at least one of her fans would be turning up to cheer at her talk. She picked up the second letter.

Dear Kate Ivory,
I am so looking forward to meeting you at my local book shop.

Now this was more like it. This was what an author liked to read in a fan letter. And Aisling must have been doing her stuff to get her fans to her signings.

I have always wanted to meet you, ever since I saw your photograph on the dust jacket of *Flames in the East*.
Did you get my little present? I do hope you like it. It is, of course, a symbol, and you with your great insight into matters of the heart, will understand what it means.
Yours devotedly, J. Barnes

Perhaps, after all, it was not quite the letter she was hoping for. She assumed that the little present J. Barnes was referring to was her four-part ring, since she had received no other gifts from admiring readers. If she had realised that the giver would be at one of her talks, she would have brought it with her, instead of leaving it behind on the table in her sitting room. Not clever, Kate. Which was J. Barnes' local book shop? There was no address at the top of the letter. She looked for the postmark: it was the usual illegible splodge. How should she play it when J. turned up? It was a somewhat spooky letter, after all. She wondered whether to knock on Devlin's door and ask him what to do. The Man Who Understood a Woman's Heart ought to be able to suss it out, or failing him, The Man with the Creative Soul might take a guess.

She went along to Devlin's room and paused outside the door. There were voices coming from behind it. Bellowing, muttering. Had he got company? Should she retire without interrupting him? The voices did not sound as though their owners were engaged in any intimate activities. She knocked.

'Bugger it!' came the reply.

'Devlin?'

'Come in, for God's sake! Stop lurking about outside the door.'

She entered.

Devlin was standing in aubergine velvet trousers and a pewter grey silk shirt. A silver grey scarf lay on his bed.

'I can't get this to go sodding right,' he said.

'What are you trying to do?'

'Tie this scarf,' he said. 'What the hell does it look like?'

'Right over left, left over right,' said Kate, trying to be helpful.

'Take the working end through the second loop,'

said Devlin, ignoring her, 'then pass it behind the standing end and – '

Kate looked round the room. It was festooned and draped with Devlin's belongings, but she couldn't see anyone else.

'Where's your friend gone?' she asked.

'What?' Devlin held up one end of the now-crumpled scarf and glared at it. 'What friend?'

'Nothing. My mistake.' She realised that the voices had both been Devlin's, as he wrestled with recalcitrant clothing. The blue shirt draped over the bedside lamp looked as though it had been flung away with some force. Black trousers cowered in a heap by the wardrobe door. 'Can't you use a granny knot? I do, usually, and I let the ends just hang down.'

'You would,' said Devlin rudely. 'I like a square knot, so that it sits just right and the ends hang down vertically instead of sticking out sideways.' He twisted one end round the other and grunted with satisfaction. 'What was it you wanted?'

'I was wondering, do you get many fan letters?'

'One or two. A few, sometimes. Ah! Got it!' The scarf, defeated, had formed itself into a beautifully neat knot. Devlin passed the loop over his head and admired his handiwork in the mirror. 'What do you think?'

'Very clever,' said Kate. 'Absolutely right. Suits you wonderfully well.'

Devlin smiled. 'What were you saying just now?'

'It's about fan letters. Could you look at this one and tell me whether you think . . .' What? That J. was a

67

nutter? She stopped speaking and simply handed the letter to Devlin and watched as he read it through.

'Man's a nutter,' he said, handing it back.

'So you think it's a man?'

'Could be a woman, I suppose. You can't tell from the handwriting, or from the notepaper.'

'I thought it might be a woman because of the over-heated devotion.'

'You feel that's a purely feminine trait?'

'I associate it with frustrated middle-aged women, I suppose, but that makes me both sexist and ageist.'

'And surely such a woman would write to Tom Jones or Barry Manilow rather than Kate Ivory.'

'Women *do* write to me. Probably because they're the ones who read my books.'

'There's a logical deduction!'

'No need to be snide. What about the present he sent me?'

'The symbol? What was it?'

'I imagine it was the gold knot-ring that arrived just before I left Oxford. No note. No indication of who had sent it.'

'One of those puzzle things that falls apart when you look at it?'

'That's it.'

'How odd. Well, if he says it's a symbol, I suppose it's symbolic of a mystery. An enigma, even. You'll just have to wait and see what happens.'

'Not just a puzzle, but a ring. A gold ring. What does he mean by that?'

'Well now, that has many connotations, hasn't it? From the sexual to the spiritual. Very interesting.'

'It's just struck me: if he knew my address to send the ring, then why did he send the letter via Fergusson?'

'Perhaps it isn't the same person after all.' Devlin returned to the mirror and ran his hands through his hair until it looked artistically windswept.

'Does it need a little gel, do you think?'

'Not really. But what should I do about it?'

'Hmm?' Devlin had lifted his upper lip and was examining the space between his two front teeth.

'The letter. What should I do?'

'Write him a polite but non-committal reply when you get back to Oxford. Ignore it for the present. You can't do much else, can you?' Devlin had completed the examination of his teeth and was adjusting the collar of his shirt. He had lost interest in her letter and Kate knew she should leave his room. But she still needed reassurance.

'He says he's coming to one of the talks.'

'He's probably harmless.'

'What if he isn't?'

'You'll be safe enough in a crowd, I should think. Just don't get yourself pinned in a corner with any madmen.'

'How can you tell who's mad?'

'Staring eyes. Wild hair. Straw in ears. The usual.'

'Thanks a lot, Devlin!' But she laughed, never-theless.

'I'll see you downstairs,' he said, opening the door

and waiting for her to leave. 'And don't worry about it. Haven't they brought in some new law to protect attractive women from the attentions of wicked stalkers? You've got nothing to be nervous about, believe me.'

'But you think he could be a stalker?' The thought was quite flattering.

'I thought it was usually television personalities and actresses who got stalked. I've never heard of anything exciting happening to a lady novelist, I'm afraid.'

Kate returned to her room, feeling more cheerful. She tucked the letters into a folder, to answer when she returned to Oxford. She had nothing to worry about really. Devlin was large and solid enough to inspire confidence. She would be safe while he was around.

Chapter Seven

Kate and Devlin had arranged to meet Aisling downstairs in the hall at five forty-five. When she saw Aisling, Kate was glad that she had not worn anything subtler than her very short black skirt and canary yellow jacket. Aisling was in scarlet, with a black and silver chiffon scarf and large red ear-rings.

'I do like your ear-rings,' said Kate, who was a connoisseur of such things.

'Thank you. They're not quite as big as yours, though, are they?' Which Kate took as a compliment.

When Devlin appeared five minutes later, she saw that there was an aubergine velvet jacket to go with the trousers, and the silk scarf was just right with it. The bagginess of his trousers and the cigarette burn on the pocket of his jacket detracted only slightly from his arty elegance, but presumably he had reckoned that no one would see him below the waist when he was sitting down at the table.

'I like your skirt,' said Devlin appreciatively, staring at Kate's legs in their patterned black tights. He had apparently decided to stick with Charming mode for the evening. As they went out to Aisling's car, and Kate

71

felt Devlin's hot breath on her neck and his hand squeezing her shoulder, she wondered for a moment whether tonight he wasn't moving from Charming to Lecherous.

'Well, why don't we go and find out what the customers think?' said Kate.

'Not bad,' said Kate, as they entered the shop. 'Loads of punters. Let's hope they're all in the mood for buying books.'

'Well done, Annette darling,' said Devlin. 'You've made a lovely display of my new hardback.'

'*Ravage the Moon*,' Kate read from the dust jacket. 'That's a subtle title.'

'It beats the "trailing clouds of glory" style of yours.'

'No fisticuffs just yet, please. Can I get you both a drink?' asked Aisling.

'Whisky,' said Devlin.

'Apple juice would be fine,' said Kate, who didn't want to acquire a shiny red face and slurred speech quite so early in the evening.

'Apple juice coming up. I'm not sure they've got whisky in stock, Devlin. How about wine?'

'Just make sure that every future book shop has a bottle of single malt – Bushmills, preferably – waiting for me when we arrive.'

Aisling fluttered her chiffon scarf and reappeared with their drinks. They were both sitting down, smiling and looking welcoming, and hoping that someone would soon approach with a request for a book to be signed.

'Would you mind signing these?' asked Annette, placing a pile of a dozen or so beside Kate. 'They're for our stock and for customers who rang to reserve a copy.'

'Of course.' Thank goodness for that, thought Kate, as she turned the first copy to the title page and signed it in her best handwriting.

'What about me?' demanded Devlin.

'You wouldn't want me to destroy that marvellous display, would you?' said Annette, and went to pour herself a tumbler full of white wine. 'It's apple juice,' she said to her assistants, who knew better but didn't comment.

Devlin did seem particularly jumpy, thought Kate. She didn't expect him to be the shy kind, or one of those who got nervous in the company of strangers. As he became more tense, so she made an effort to appear more serene.

She signed copies of her books for Win, for Jack, with best wishes, for Jim, for Bobbi, for Janet, and she smiled and said how glad she was that they enjoyed her books, and how pleased she was to see them here, while Devlin sat fuming by her side. She didn't much like the way his arm was draped over the back of her chair, or the way he smiled at *her* readers, as though he had been responsible for producing the books that she was signing.

Annette, happier now that she had downed half a pint of wine, came and joined them.

'Time for your talk now, don't you think? Just four or five minutes each and a brief reading from your latest work. I'll introduce you in turn.' She turned to the dense crowd of people, all busy swilling the book shop's wine and stuffing in the miniature saúsage rolls.

'Quiet everybody! Our distinguished authors are now going to talk to you. First, Kate Ivory' – a growl from Devlin at her side at this – 'who will tell you briefly about herself and then read from her new work, *Spring Scene.*'

Kate smiled, and stood up, and spoke. I work at set times. I have to be disciplined. I do enjoy the research. It's easier for me because I live alone. She heard the well-rehearsed phrases and the polite laughter. Then she read a couple of paragraphs from *Spring Scene*, leaving them, she judged, wanting to know more. She sat down to general applause and spent the next ten minutes signing more copies of her book.

Devlin stood and started to talk. He did have a very good voice, thought Kate. Full and deep and sonorous. He told amusing anecdotes and read short excerpts from his books, but she reckoned that he gave very little away about himself. His public face was a mask that protected him from strangers.

While he was speaking she had a chance to look around the shop. There were the usual well-dressed, middle-aged customers. Women mostly, some of whom had brought their husbands and teenage children with them. She could hear the till ringing repeatedly, so the shop must be doing reasonable business. She hoped that it was her books that they were buying rather than someone else's. But then she saw, standing one on either side of the door, two figures who were quite unlike the others: young men in black track suits with muscles bulging from their arms, and heads that appeared to grow out of their shoulders. Hair as short as Harley's, and she did believe that one of them wore a steel ring through his lower lip. They looked more like bouncers from a night club than customers in a book shop, though they were certainly taking notice of Devlin. Perhaps this was what his fans looked like. She hoped that one of them was not J. Barnes.

'Do you know who they are?' she whispered to Aisling.

'No idea,' Aisling whispered back.

Devlin was drawing to a close. He was holding up the new hardback and telling the customers how very much he hoped that they would enjoy it. Kate expected him to tell them that he was, after all, the Man Who Understood a Woman's Heart, but fortunately he didn't.

Devlin put down the book, smiled around at the gently applauding customers, and then went rigid. Kate looked up at his face. He was staring at the two bouncers. At this point, Kate noticed that one of them was missing out on eyebrows.

'Who the hell let those two in?' hissed Devlin.

'Aren't they fans of yours?' said Kate innocently.

'Don't be bloody stupid! I've got to get out of here.'

'You'll be lucky. It's solid between here and the door, and I don't think those people will move until they've finished the last of the wine.'

'Aisling, find another way out.'

'What on earth do you mean?'

'Don't be feeble. There must be a door for deliveries. At the back. On the other side of the office, maybe. Stop looking moronic and go and look.'

If Aisling was unused to being spoken to in this manner by her authors, she didn't show it, but stumbled away towards the back of the shop.

'Pick up your bag, your notes and any other of your belongings that you wish to take with you,' said Devlin. 'When Aisling finds us a way out, we're moving. OK?'

'If you say so,' said Kate. 'By the way, your two friends have started to make their way towards us.'

'They've got some way to go, and they're not making much headway. They've got to negotiate the crowd by the cash desk before they can get to this end of the shop.'

It was true that they hadn't got far, but there were odd cries of pain, as the regular customers were shoved aside by the two heavies.

'Who are they?' asked Kate.

But at this moment Aisling returned.

'Yes, there's an exit through the office,' she said. 'I've unbolted the door, and Annette says she will bolt it again behind us.'

The three of them, still smiling, started to move away towards the back of the shop. They were stopped by a middle-aged couple dressed in grey tweed.

'We've caught you!' cried the woman.

'Looks as though you're trying to escape,' said the man, nudging Devlin. 'That won't do, will it?'

'We're such fans of yours!' cried the woman.

'We're Mr and Mrs Brent,' said the woman.

'William and Joy,' said the man. 'It's my wife who's the reader, not me. And you can call me Bill.'

'And we're hoping you'll join our little group at O Sole Mio, as our guests, of course,' said Joy.

'God preserve us!' said Devlin under his breath.

'O Sole Mio?' queried Kate.

'A really nice Italian restaurant,' said Joy. 'It's very popular with people like us.'

'People like *who*?' muttered Devlin, looking back across the room at Eyebrows.

Another couple joined their group. They were nearly indistinguishable from the Brents, but dressed in green tweed rather than grey.

'Let me introduce my friend Jessie Russell,' began Joy.

'We have to go,' Devlin hissed into Kate's ear. 'Get rid of these people!'

'There could be safety in numbers,' Kate whispered back. 'They're giving us protection, not to mention camouflage.'

'And a free meal,' said Devlin.

'Let's all stick together, like Kate says,' added Aisling.

'What are you three whispering about?' asked Joy. 'Is it a conspiracy?'

'Just a little shop talk,' said Aisling. 'You know what these literary types are like, always arguing the merits of the historic present.'

The heavies were getting near, but Devlin and Kate stayed close to the Brents and their friends, the

Russells. Eyebrows looked undecided about confronting such a large group of people.

'Why don't we leave now?' asked Devlin, edging towards the door.

'Yes, I'm simply starving,' added Kate.

'I'm sure it's quicker through the back way,' said Aisling, who had also noticed the two men in track suits and didn't want to make the front page of the local paper: Fergusson Authors in Bookshop Brawl. It was not the kind of headline that her boss would approve of.

'Where's this restaurant?' asked Kate, hooking her handbag firmly over her shoulder and wishing that she, too, was dressed in track suit and running shoes.

'Out on the Cheltenham Road. About two and a half miles along on the left-hand side. You can't miss it.'

Devlin was pushing through a group of dedicated wine-drinkers by now, Kate on his heels. Aisling followed, apologising for them as they went.

'We'll see you at the restaurant,' she called over her shoulder to Joy Brent. Perhaps Aisling was used to unconventional behaviour by her authors, after all. She certainly knew how to drive the BMW at high speed, Kate noticed, when they had sprinted for the car and bundled inside it. The Brents and the Russells were not far behind them, filling the street with birdlike squeaks of excitement.

'Don't you think you should tell us what that was all about?' said Kate, grabbing for the panic handle as they rocketed round a corner and on to the main road.

'I've no idea,' said Devlin.

'Weren't they the two who tried to stop us from leaving Swindon?' The car was eating up the miles along the dark road.

'I suppose they might have been.'

'How many people do you know with pierced lips and shaved eyebrows?'

'All right, I admit it, they were the same two.'

'And so what did they want?'

'Money?' said Devlin. 'Revenge? Sex? Who knows? What does anyone want?'

'What's that place on the left?' broke in Aisling, taking her foot off the accelerator and allowing the car to slow down to sixty or so.

'O Sole Mio,' said Kate, reading the neon sign. 'High Class Italian Cooking. Pizzas, Pasta. I think we've found our restaurant. Let's get inside quick, before Eyebrows and his friend catch up with us.'

Chapter Eight

Back in Oxford, Andrew was opening a tin of cat food.

'Turkey and giblet flavour, you lucky feline,' he said. Susannah wound herself round his legs with delight, leaving thick deposits of ginger fur over his charcoal grey trousers. Dave sat underneath the kitchen table watching them, his tongue lolling out.

'Your turn next,' said Andrew, spooning out chestnut brown worms and orange jelly on to the cat's dish. He sniffed. 'It smells disgusting, but I suppose you'll love it.'

He put the bowl down on the floor by the back door and went through into the sitting room.

'Harley, what's that you're watching?'

'*Neighbours*. It's brilliant.' Harley's voice had acquired an Ozzie accent and now rose enquiringly at the end of each phrase

'I'm sure it isn't good for you,' said Andrew.

'Kate lets me watch it,' said Harley, as though that clinched the argument.

'And have you done your homework?'

'Yeah.' It sounded more like Yih.

'Well, after I've fed him, you'd better walk the dog.'

'Right on yer, mate,' said Harley.

Andrew gave up and went back into the kitchen. When he had fed the animals, he would get on with chopping up vegetables for the healthy stir-fry that he was going to serve Harley and himself. Pom pom tiddly pom te pom pom pom, he sang, possibly from *Rigoletto*.

The phone rang. Bugger! thought Andrew, retreating from the fridge. But before he could reach it to reply, the ringing stopped and Kate's own voice said, 'Please leave a message after the bleep.' Well, Kate, that was a bit curt, thought Andrew, while a voice quacked a message into the machine. The voice stopped, the machine beeped three times and a green light winked at him. It occurred to Andrew that if Kate should wish to telephone and speak to him, she would find herself speaking to her own machine, instead. He stared at the array of buttons. There were also two lights, the winking green one and a steady red.

'Harley?'

'Yih?' He was still deep in *Neighbours*, apparently.

'Do you understand this device?'

'Yih. Wha'yer want it to do?'

'I want to switch the answering bit off, so that I can speak to Kate if she calls.'

'You can do that anyway. Pick up the phone when she starts talking, like, and the machine will switch off. Easy.' He turned his full attention back to the screen.

'Yes. Well. I'm sure it is, Harley. Thank you.' Andrew looked at the machine a moment longer and returned to the kitchen. He didn't mind technology when it had to do with food.

A short time later, Harley appeared at his shoulder, picked up a slice of red pepper and lobbed it into his mouth.

'I'm off with me mates,' he announced.

'You'll return in thirty minutes for the rest of the food?'

'Yih. And, Andrew?'

'Yih? I mean, yes?'

'If Kate rings, like, you'll ask her how she's doing, won't you?'

'Yes, I'll do that. And is there a message for her from you?'

'Nah. Just, like, I hope she's, like, doing good.'

'I'll pass it on.'

'And how she's, like, doing with Devlin Hayle.'

'I'll ask her that, too.'

'Cheers.'

The door slammed behind him.

O Sole Mio looked as though it had once, in the Age of Formica perhaps, been a brash roadhouse. Now someone had bought a few acres of red checked cotton and turned it into an aggressively Italian restaurant. The walls were decorated with highly-coloured views of the Italian coast, there were swags of fishing nets, there were green glass floats, there was a tape of Neapolitan music playing a little too loudly.

However, the place was full, and the food smelled pretty good. It was as well that someone had booked a table for them.

'I didn't believe this sort of place still existed,' said Devlin to Kate.

'Is that really a plastic lobster?'

'And a plastic crab. And that looks like plastic bougainvillaea over there. Let's hope the wine list is reasonable.'

They were seated at a long table by the window. Red checked curtains were decorated with green bobble fringes. Candles burned in empty Chianti bottles and the tablecloth was, predictably, checked red cotton.

'Bring us a couple of bottles of Barolo,' Devlin ordered the waiter who handed them their menus. 'We'll drink it while we're considering what to order.' The wine appeared within seconds and was poured into their glasses.

'That's better,' said Devlin.

Kate drank some of hers and agreed with him.

Now that they were seated at the table and there were apparently no thugs wishing to dismember them, she could take a proper look at the fans who had invited them to join their meal.

The Brents, Joy and William – 'call me Bill' – were probably in their late fifties. Joy had greying hair and bright blue eyes. She looked like one of those women who, after a lifetime of taking a back seat and doing what her husband wanted, was about to burst upon the world as one of its great organisers. Bill was a little less grey, but was going bald. Joy doubtless already ran several local charities. Bill looked ready for a retirement spent in carpet slippers or the potting shed, but

Joy could well be about to launch herself into a new entrepreneurial career. In a year or two she might have thrown out all the grey tweed and decked herself in powerful blue pinstripe. Bill looked destined for beige cardigans and yellow golfing sweaters. Joy leant forward, eyes reflecting red light from the candle, nose jutting, and fixed Kate with the look of a predatory bird.

'I wrote you a letter, actually,' she said.

'Ah, really? What would it have been about?' Was this at last the sender of the gold ring?

'I just pointed out a few little flaws in one of your books. I do hope you didn't mind, but I thought you'd want to know.'

Wrong, Joy, wrong. Kate tried to remember her recent letters. Perhaps the one that featured five closely typed pages of errors was signed J. Brent (Mrs). Had she answered it before chucking it into the bin? She hoped so.

'How kind of you,' said Kate, trying hard to smile as she said it.

'I hate it when bloody readers do that,' put in Devlin, who had finished his first glass of wine and was halfway down his second. 'Bloody interfering wankers, I call them.'

'No you don't,' said Aisling, who had caught this last remark. 'You are always delighted that any reader of yours has taken the trouble to put pen to paper, Devlin.'

'No,' said Devlin, who was reaching the truculent stage rather faster than expected. 'They're a bloody pain. You have to read through their bloody boring letters, and then you have to waste more time writing back to say thank you and pretend you're grateful. Well, I'm not. I'm bloody pissed off with them.' He looked belligerently round the table. 'Bloody wankers!'

'We'll remember that in future,' said Jessie Russell. 'I can see that it might be irritating to have someone arguing with all your hard work. Your books give us so much pleasure, it seems a shame to quibble over details.'

'Bloody right,' said Devlin.

'And do be careful of your sleeve on that candle flame,' added Jessie, as the smell of singed velvet joined the aromas of their first course.

'What?'

Jessie poured a glass of water over Devlin's arm. 'Better?' she enquired, dabbing it dry with her table napkin.

Devlin glowered at her, said, 'Thank you,' in response to a look from Aisling, and downed the rest of his wine. Had Jessie done that on purpose? wondered Kate. She wasn't sure that she trusted that open, innocent smile of hers.

'My goodness! Don't you authors lead exciting lives!' It was the man sitting on the other side of Jessie. He caught Kate's eye and said, 'I haven't been introduced yet, but I'm Jim.' He was attached to Jessie and came from a generation where it was safe enough to assume that he was Mr Russell. He was less green tweed than corduroy, she thought, looking him over. And he wore one of those green and cream checked shirts that were sold only in provincial outfitters, or in Oxfam. Knotted tie. Lots of thick, wiry, greying hair.

Mud-coloured eyes behind bi-focals. A solicitor, probably. Maybe an accountant. He looked a lot jollier than Bill, at any rate, and twinkled at her when he realised that she was looking at him. The arrival of their waiter ended her scrutiny.

'Ah, food!' Devlin didn't wait for everyone to be served, but threw a slice of Parma ham into his mouth as though he had starved for days. He chewed noisily. He picked up a plump asparagus stalk, dipped it in melted butter and raised it to his lips, then he looked across at Kate over the dripping green tip and leered at her. In case she hadn't received the message, he waggled his eyebrows. She sighed and dipped her spoon into ripe melon.

'I'll tell you for free one mistake you make in your books, Katie.'

'What would that be?' She put down her spoon and drank some more wine.

'Not enough sex. You want to spice it up a bit. It's what the punters want, you know, and you ought to give it to them. Your characters are a load of uptight bloody wankers. That's what's wrong with the women you write about. They'd all be a bloody sight happier if they just had a bloody good— '

'Not everyone wants to read that sort of thing, Devlin,' said Aisling.

'I think your jacket's on fire again,' said Kate, and watched as Devlin slapped at his sleeves, a look of alarm on his face. Jessie threatened to pour more water over him, but Devlin managed to let her know that he had already dealt with the problem.

The waiter was pouring wine and Aisling used the diversion to lean across to cover the top of Devlin's glass. The waiter paused. 'Not just for the moment,' she said. Brave woman, thought Kate. When Devlin notices, he'll probably kill her.

'I'm not sure that I agree with you, Devlin, about the sex, I mean. I think many of us like Kate's novels just the way they are.' It was Jessie Russell again. Kate looked at her with new interest. Jessie obviously had great intelligence and judgement. She was rounder and softer than Joy, and her eyes were brown rather than blue; and perhaps she was even steelier underneath the Pringle twinset. It was obvious that she had once been very good-looking, and she was still pretty in a slightly faded way. She was probably a woman who was frequently underrated. Kate smiled at her.

'Bloody turnips,' said Devlin. 'Not a pint of red blood between the lot of them.' But luckily this comment was drowned by the clatter of plates as the first course was cleared and the main course was brought. Kate peered into other plates, just to make sure that she had made the right, the best, the biggest choice. Into the gap in the conversation, Bill Brent said, 'Of course, I don't read books.'

Devlin's mouth opened, doubtless to deliver a rude and stinging reply, but Kate managed to get in first.

'I'm sure you have much more important things to do with your time.'

Jim Russell's quiet voice joined in. 'I do think you're missing a lot, Bill. There is so much to be gained from reading modern fiction. The insights into people's behaviour, the colourful worlds of other times, other places. I believe you can learn more from a good novel than from any volume of psychology.'

'I don't know about that,' said Bill. 'I don't have time for any of that fancy stuff.' His face was growing red and there was a film of sweat on his skin. Oh dear, thought Kate. Another man who is about to get aggressive on his wine.

'I'm the one who's the reader in the family,' said Joy. 'All the time I was bringing up the children I used to escape into a world of books. They were my lifeline to a wider world.' She looked nervously at her husband, as though she was expecting a loud outburst at any moment. Were these the delights of married life? wondered Kate. The Russells, on the other hand, looked as though they had said everything they had to say and could ignore one another for the rest of their joint lives.

'I'd have thought that bringing up our children would be enough for any woman. What you women want with careers and books and all that nonsense, I don't know.' Hadn't she had a letter from a reader who held similar views? wondered Kate.

Devlin leant across the table and speared a particularly succulent wild mushroom in white wine and garlic sauce from Kate's plate. 'Mm, what a delicious little morsel,' he said, looking meaningfully at her.

'I thought so myself,' she said. 'Which is why I ordered it.' She looked across at his plate to see if there was anything she could purloin in return, but didn't fancy the messy sauce splashed all over the place.

'Help yourself,' said Devlin. 'You can wrap that pointed tongue around anything you see on this side of the table, Katie dear, any time you like.'

'How kind of you, Devlin dear.' Kate drank some more wine. Devlin seemed a lot wittier when she wasn't completely sober.

'I don't like dirty talk in front of the ladies,' said Bill truculently.

'Dirty talk?' asked Devlin innocently. 'What dirty talk?'

'And what ladies, if it comes to that?' Kate murmured to Aisling.

'I think he's referring to his wife and to Jessie Russell rather than to us,' replied Aisling.

'Smut,' said Bill. 'I don't like it.'

'Really? What a pity. It can be such enormous fun, you know. With the right partner, of course.' Devlin twinkled rather bloodshot eyes at him. Bill subsided again, and concentrated on his food. You have a mean little mouth, thought Kate, and narrow eyes. Say what you like about Devlin, at least he isn't petty-minded like you, Bill Brent. And your hair's dropping flakes of dandruff over the shoulders of your jacket. Perhaps Joy will leave you now that the children are grown. She might have wished many worse things on the unfortunate Bill, but noticed that Devlin was looking restive. The spotlight had been away from him for two minutes too long. She had learned that a restive Devlin was likely to cause havoc.

But before she could think of something to say, Joy

Brent said: 'Do tell us, Devlin, where do you get your ideas from?'

Wrong question again, Joy, thought Kate.

'Yes, Mr Hayle, do tell us. Do you use incidents from your own life?' asked Jim Russell. 'Earlier this evening, at the book shop, I thought it was all so *very* exciting. Were you rehearsing a scene for your next adventure story?'

'Call me Devlin.' Devlin's dark brown voice would have done justice to Ishmael. 'Well, I might be able to use that little fracas in one of my works, but unfortunately I write *historical* fiction, you see. And my ideas come out of my imagination – out of here,' and he tapped his forehead with his large fingers, unfortunately transferring a glob of pesto sauce in the process. 'And I find that my creativity is greatly helped by the ingestion of a certain reasonable quantity of alcohol.' Here he glared at Aisling. 'It helps the juices to flow, if you know what I mean,' and he leered again at Kate. 'It produces the sort of full-blooded, swashbuckling fiction for which I am justly famous.'

'Fill the man's glass,' said Kate. 'It's his liver that's at stake, not ours.'

'Now,' said Devlin expansively, 'what else would you lovely people like to know about us and our art, eh?'

'We wouldn't want to intrude on your mystique,' said Joy. Was she being serious? Kate wasn't sure.

'He who pays the piper, as they say,' said Devlin.

'I'd like to know more about that scene in the book shop,' said Jim. 'Those two great thugs, especially the one without any eyebrows; the way we all escaped through the back door and then the speed at which Aisling drove away from the car park. You really must tell us what it was all about.'

'Oh yes,' said Jessie. 'I felt as though I was in the middle of one of your adventures.'

'I thought it was a piece of bloody play-acting,' said Bill, 'put on for our benefit.' He looked up at Devlin as though challenging him to a duel. Devlin sat back in his chair with his eyes half-closed and an enigmatic smile playing about his lips. He spoiled the impression only slightly by nearly overbalancing in his chair.

'Would you like to choose a dessert?' asked the waiter, interrupting and handing out menus.

'Mm, sticky toffee pudding,' said Joy.

'Tiramisú,' drooled Jessie.

Devlin enquired about the varieties of ice cream. Bill and Jim went for something with chocolate and whipped cream.

'Coffees?' asked the waiter. Which took another minute or two to sort out.

'And brandy,' said Devlin. There was already an unusually large number of empty wine bottles on the table. Devlin must have ordered them when they weren't looking.

'You'll have a brandy, Bill, won't you? And you, Jim?' It was obvious from his tone that only wimps refused brandy. 'Girls?'

'Not for us, we've had sufficient,' said Joy, whose disapproving look in Bill's direction was having no effect. Jessie sat looking mildly amused, though perhaps she was just legless. Kate shrugged her shoulders at Aisling and they emptied the last of the seventh bottle of Barolo into their glasses.

'I always say,' said Aisling, 'if you can't beat 'em, you might as well join 'em.' True enough, but Kate hoped she remembered who was driving them back to their digs.

'Time for your story,' Kate said to Devlin. He had had plenty of time to think up something good.

'Ah well, it goes back a very long time.' Devlin's sonorous voice was only slightly slurred. He tapped the side of his nose. Oh no! Not that old chestnut, thought Kate. 'It's all a bit hush-hush, so I'll have to swear you to secrecy.' Murmurs of appreciation all round, except from Kate and Bill Brent. 'I'm sure you know about my years in the Service.'

'Which Service would that be?' asked Aisling unkindly.

Devlin swirled his brandy round in his glass and sniffed it appreciatively.

'I'm sure I don't have to spell it out to *you*, Aisling.' Kate suppressed a giggle. 'Well, there I was, in a certain Central American state, working undercover for my country.'

'What was it you were doing out there?' asked Bill.

'I was supplying arms to the side that we were supporting,' said Devlin. Bill opened his mouth to ask another question, but Devlin silenced him by blowing a stream of Gauloise smoke in his direction. 'The Resistance. The Popular Front. A brave band of guerrillas fighting for democracy and freedom. You can imagine,

I got myself involved with some pretty desperate characters.'

'The sort that shave their eyebrows?' asked Kate.

Devlin ignored her. 'The Resistance fighters were hiding out in the mountains. The government troops were getting close, led by a renegade Freedom Fighter, and they were running out of stores and ammunition. They were relying on my small convoy to pull their chestnuts out of the fire.'

'Talking of chestnuts . . .' murmured Kate.

'I was driving the lead truck,' continued Devlin.

'How did you know the way?' asked Aisling.

'I had Miguel sitting beside me. He had lost an arm in battle, and his nerves were shot to pieces, but he knew that country like the back of his hand.'

'I hope for your sake it wasn't the hand he'd lost in battle,' said Kate.

'Do you want me to tell you this story or not?' demanded Devlin.

'Yes! Yes!' they all chorused.

'We'll behave, we promise,' said Kate.

'Well, there I am, driving this truckload of automatic rifles and grenades through the steaming heat of the jungle. Every few hours one of the trucks breaks down and we improvise a repair. We push them through swamps and pull them through torrents. The leeches fasten on our feet and legs and we have to pull them out, their jaws still locked into our flesh.'

'Who's for the sticky toffee pudding?' asked the waiter. 'Tiramisú?' It took a minute or two to sort out who had ordered what.

'Do you think you could move your story along a bit?' said Aisling. 'I'm not sure I want to hear about leeches and suchlike while I'm eating my pudding.'

'It's no use being squeamish,' said Devlin. 'We still have to hack our way through the giant stinging ants and the poisonous snakes.'

'Couldn't we get to the drug barons and the helicopter fitted with a machine gun that strafed you as you lowered the truck down a cliff, killing the faithful Miguel?' asked Kate.

'How did you know about them?' asked Devlin suspiciously.

'Just a wild guess,' she replied.

Devlin took a large spoonful of strawberry ice cream. 'Very well,' he said. 'I will move my story forward, leaving out much of the fascinating detail as I do so.'

'Did you make it to the mountain hideout?' asked Jessie. 'Did you still have all the arms and ammunition with you?'

'I did,' said Devlin. 'After Miguel was killed, we had to rely on a sketch map to get us there, but we made it in time. I and the other drivers of my convoy fought shoulder to shoulder with the Freedom Fighters, and we defeated the Generals' troops.'

'How splendid!' said Jim.

'What did you say the name of this country was?' asked Bill, through a mouthful of chocolate gateau.

'I didn't. I still have to protect my friends by my silence.'

'But if you were a hero, why are you being hunted now?' asked Joy.

'When the Generals learned of my involvement, you can imagine that they put me at the top of their hit list.'

'And you're telling us that those two men in track suits came from South America?' asked Jim.

'Not exactly,' said Devlin, who had not noticed the slight shift in geography. 'But these people have influence everywhere. A phone call, a fax, an e-mail message, and wheels are put in motion.'

'So these two were what you would call agents?' insisted Jim. 'And you think they're trying to – what's the word? – exterminate you? Rub you out?'

'It all sounds most exciting,' said Jessie. 'Are you sure they didn't follow you here to the restaurant? I wouldn't like to meet up with Central American gangsters in a dark car park in the Cotswolds.'

They all looked towards the door, but there was nothing more threatening to be seen than a waiter delivering a chocolate fudge sundae.

'I have to be on my guard at all times,' said Devlin.

'I'm sure you do,' said Joy. 'How nerve-racking it must be for you.'

'And perhaps it's time we got back to our digs, before they do catch up with you and string you up by your thumbs,' said Aisling.

Bill was still muttering about the unreliability of arty types, but they eventually sorted out the bill, and then their coats, and went out into the cold February night. Devlin was filling the air with his Gauloise fumes as he shambled across to the BMW. The others, after calling good nights and thank yous, disappeared into dark corners of the car park.

'Home, James!' shouted Devlin.

'Maybe he'll sleep in the car on the way back,' murmured Aisling at Kate. 'That story-telling session must have taken it out of the poor man.'

Maybe this evening will soon be over, thought Kate.

Back at their digs, Kate looked at her watch. Was it too late to ring Andrew? She felt it was necessary to touch base after that oddity of an evening out. Andrew had never been an early-to-bed person, so probably it would be all right. And then again, would he still be at her place? She hoped so. She liked to think of her little house full of people while she was away, the cat asleep on her duvet, the dog under the kitchen table. Paul, Andrew, Harley. Though Paul was probably in his own flat, Harley would be at home with Tracey and Jace by now, and if she didn't get a move on, Andrew, too, would have left. If only she could be sure that she wanted all these people around her while she was actually at home. She dialled her own number.

'Please leave a message after the bleep.'

Bother, it was her own voice talking to her. 'Hello? Andrew, are you there? Could you lift up the phone?' But if no one was in, she would pick up her messages. She opened the notebook where she had written down the numbers she needed.

'Hello?' There was a click as the machine switched off. Ah good, someone was in, after all.

'Andrew? It's me, Kate.'

'Ah, Kate. So Harley was right. The phone does work if you intercept.'

'Good for Harley. How is everything?'

'Everything's going beautifully here. How is the tour doing?'

'It's been fascinating so far.'

'And how are you getting on with that man Hayle?'

'He's a pig, but I quite like him.'

'I shall never understand women.'

'Look, Andrew, are there any messages for me?'

'I can't see any.'

'I was thinking of telephone messages. Is the light flashing?'

'Yes. Is that what it means?'

'I believe so. Could you play them to me, do you think?'

'Now you mention it, I did hear the machine talking away to itself earlier this evening. I'll try to relay it to you.' A pause. 'I'm reading all these funny little buttons. This looks like it. Right.'

There was a long, extended beep and then a silence.

'Do you think that was the right one?' asked Andrew.

'I think, actually, that you may have erased the message,' said Kate.

'Oh dear. I am sorry.'

'I don't suppose it matters. If it was anything

important, they'll ring back. You didn't notice who it was?'

'It sounded like a small duck quacking, I'm afraid. And there's no interesting post for you today. Just circulars and a couple of bills.'

'They'll wait till I get back. How is the family? Are they all behaving?'

'The animals have eaten their evening meals, and earlier I introduced Harley to the concept of the stir-fry. He, meanwhile, has been practising his Australian accent, probably in order to irritate you when you return.'

'Give him my love. Hug the animals for me. And take a kiss for yourself.'

'Oh, very well. Thank you. Goodnight, Kate.'

'Goodnight, Andrew. I'll ring again tomorrow.' Why had she called them her family? Was it just a slip of the tongue or was she going soft?

As Kate hung up, she smelled stale Gauloises behind her. Devlin said: 'Is that the man in your life?'

'Have you been standing there long?'

'Long enough. Why don't you want to tell me who he is?'

'His name is Andrew. He works at the Bodleian Library. He is looking after my animals and plants while I'm away. All right?'

'A bit terse, and you still haven't answered my original question.'

'Andrew is an old friend of mine. That's all.'

'I'm glad to hear it.'

'I don't see why. It's really no business of yours.'

But Devlin only laughed, planted a boozy wet kiss on her cheek, and carried on up the stairs to his room.

Chapter Nine

Earlier in the day the landlady had shown them a sitting room they could use, and Kate decided to take advantage of it for a short time before going to bed. She needed to relax, away from people, before she could sleep. She found a log fire, comfortable sofas, some subdued lighting, and Aisling Furnavent-Lawne.

'How did you enjoy your dinner?' asked Kate, sitting down on a venerable green sofa. 'I thought it was an amazingly good meal for somewhere out in the sticks like this.'

'I must say I'm surprised every time I get a passable meal outside London.' She lifted a bottle from the table. 'This is on Fergusson, by the way, and I think we've earned it. If Devlin is going to expect a bottle of single malt whiskey every day, I think they can stand us a decent bottle of wine. Or even two.'

'How did you hide it from the man?'

'I bribed him with Bushmills. He's taken the bottle to bed with him.'

'Aren't you worried about alcoholic poisoning?'

'I'm not worried about anything except surviving

the next ten days, preferably with my sanity in one piece. Here, have a glass.'

'Good idea,' said Kate, passing over one of the goblets that stood ready on the sideboard. 'This is a very civilised boarding house, I must say.'

'Tell that to Devlin,' said Aisling. 'He hasn't stopped grumbling since we got here.'

'It's a way of life with him,' said Kate. 'And speaking of Devlin, what did you think of that story he told us?'

'Not bad for an improvisation. If we'd given him more time he'd have checked the geography and politics of the area and not made so many obvious mistakes. But you have to score him ten for delivery, don't you?'

'I think the Russells and the Brents were taken in some of the time. So you think it was all moonshine?'

'Don't you? You can't tell me you believed any of that fairy story,' said Aisling.

'Well, he's certainly being followed by two thugs in black track suits and white trainers.'

'I can think of a dozen likelier explanations than the one he gave us.'

'The whole episode seems unlikely when I look back on it,' said Kate, swallowing her wine.

'Would you like another glass?' asked Aisling. 'Fergusson can afford it.'

'Thanks. It's really very good.' Much better than the usual plonk she bought in the supermarket at home, anyway. 'I mean to say, there we were, enveloped in red gingham and surrounded by plastic crustaceans, drinking ourselves silly and gorging on sticky toffee pudding, and Devlin tries to convince us that we're in the middle of a James Bond movie.'

'We were so involved in swashbuckling stories that we had to write ourselves into one. Perhaps those two thugs at the book shop really were just customers, and all the rest is a figment of Devlin's imagination,' said Aisling. 'And why was Devlin so sure that he was the one they were chasing? They didn't follow us to the restaurant, did they?'

'Unless they'd had a helicopter handy they'd have had trouble keeping up with you,' said Kate.

'Well, from my point of view, all that happened is that we went to a book shop for a signing, and then joined four fans for a pleasant meal in an Italian restaurant. Devlin got drunk and amused the company with a ridiculous story about gun-running in Central America which no one was supposed to take seriously.'

'It's good to meet the fans, isn't it?' said Kate. 'In the flesh instead of through their ratty letters. It's good to know that there are real people out there who buy my books and read them.'

'Well, it's what this book-shop tour is all about. Anything else is just in Devlin's overheated imagination.'

'Except that when we left Swindon, these two characters turned up, leapt out of their car and tried to get into ours. They weren't trying to sell us bibles, either.'

'Was it the same two?'

'I'm sure of it. Well, I'm sure of one of them, at least. He jammed his face against my side window, so I got a good look at it. Pierced lip and shaved eyebrows. Can there be more than one like that?'

'It's probably all the rage in turnip land. The countryside may be dotted with young men who have shaved off their eyebrows and pierced their bodies in all sorts of places. There are certainly plenty of nose studs around.'

Kate remembered Harley. 'That's true.'

'And you're probably adding on the threatening impression after what happened at the book shop. It's a well-known fact that we change our memories of the past to fit in with our experience of the present.'

'I've never heard that before. And you didn't see the flattened face squashed against the glass and hear his fist thumping on my bodywork.'

'There's always another explanation. Suppose they wanted to clean your windscreen? These cowboys can be very aggressive, you know.'

'And then there was the way that Devlin made me take off at top speed, leaving a large proportion of my tyre tread behind on the road. And when there was a car following behind us, I had to make a quick U-turn, and then take some unlikely back roads to get to the Cotswolds.'

'Maybe he's just a lousy map-reader.'

'Well, I think he is, too. But there was more to it than that.'

'Perhaps he was doing research for his new book.'

'I can't see how it would fit into a swashbuckling story of the eighteenth century.'

'Oh, you know how authors work. They're always doing odd things. More wine?'

'Thanks.' This was so relaxing that she would be asleep herself any moment. She took her shoes off and stretched out on the sofa.

'They could have been policemen. The thing about policemen nowadays is that they're indistinguishable from criminals.'

'I wouldn't say that,' said Kate, thinking of her friend Paul Taylor, who could never be mistaken for anything other than an upright citizen and upholder of the law.

'Not all of them, maybe. But some.' Aisling, too, had removed her shoes and put her feet up on the arm of her sofa. 'They could have been two simple policemen trying to collect parking fines.'

As Kate finished her third glass of wine and poured herself out a fourth, she almost believed what Aisling was saying.

'Or perhaps it was some jealous husband complaining about Devlin's affair with his wife.'

'That sounds more in character.'

'Two jealous husbands,' said Aisling, who was reaching the burbling stage of inebriation. 'Or one husband and a friend. Or— '

'Or someone standing up for Devlin's wife.'

'Another possibility! Jacko's loyal, tough brothers, coming to get the man what did their sister wrong.'

'Only I did meet his wife,' said Kate.

'Jacko,' said Aisling. 'Jacqueline really. Only Devlin calls her Jacko.'

'Yes, Jacko. And she was medium-sized, with red hair and thin features. She didn't look remotely like those two gorillas.'

'I don't look much like my brothers. That doesn't prove anything.'

'Do your brothers look like gorillas?'

'No, they look like accountants. Little weedy things with hollow chests. So sad.'

'I'm sorry about that.' Was Aisling moving into the tearful stage?

'It's not your fault.' Aisling dabbed at her eyes with a tissue. 'Have some more wine.'

'Thanks. Well, if it's to do with a woman, let's hope they don't find out where he's staying. They might decide to check on whether he's spending the night alone or not.'

'Yes,' said Aisling. 'And they might tear the house apart in the process.'

'I think it's time we went to bed and got some sleep in before that happens.'

'I think we should finish the wine first.'

'Good idea.'

Chapter Ten

Kate awoke at about three o'clock and sat bolt upright.

That was the trouble with drinking so much wine in the evening: you fell asleep immediately, but then woke up again a couple of hours later. On the other hand, something could have woken her. A floorboard creaked in the corridor. There was, of course, another well-known and inevitable result of heavy drinking, which resulted in creeping around the house in the middle of the night. If that was what she could in fact hear. If she hadn't imagined it. Anyone's imagination might work overtime after a day like yesterday. But she wouldn't be able to get back to sleep until she had found out one way or the other.

It was pitch dark, and she couldn't remember where the light switch was, so she sat listening a little longer. She thought she heard the click of a door closing in the distance. Had she? There was a nasty thumping noise inside her head and she couldn't hear anything very clearly. Thinking was tricky, too. Perhaps Devlin had persuaded Mrs Woods to share his bottle of whiskey and whatever else was on offer, and she was now returning to her own room. Perhaps he had persuaded

Aisling . . . but no, she couldn't bring herself to imagine such a thing.

Then she sniffed. She thought, bloody Devlin, he's been smoking.

Then it occurred to her that she wasn't smelling cigarette smoke.

She fumbled for the bedside light, still failed to find it, flung herself out of bed and stumbled towards the door and the main light switch. Forgetting her fear of invading thugs, she opened the door.

The smell of smoke was stronger here. Didn't the house have a smoke alarm?

At this moment there was a piercing screech, repeated over and over. Yes, the smoke alarm was working after all.

The landlady appeared, and behind her, Aisling in pink satin pyjamas.

'Where's Devlin?' said Kate, and ran towards his door.

She rattled the knob. Bloody door wouldn't open. Stupid man must have locked it. She fiddled with the key and at last burst into the room.

'Devlin!'

'Yerwha'?' came from the bed.

At least he was still alive. The smoke was thick in here and he would be passing out from smoke inhalation if she didn't make him get out fast.

'Wake up!'

'What's wrong?'

Devlin's head appeared from under the duvet, and a little more of Devlin followed it, slowly.

'Your room's on fire.'

The wastepaper basket was a mass of flames, the carpet in that corner of the room was smouldering, and the curtains would catch light at any moment.

'Oh?' Devlin still seemed confused. But then, he might well be if he'd drunk all the Bushmills that was missing from the bottle on his bedside table, on top of the wine and brandy at the restaurant.

'Get up! Get out of bed!' There was no way she could manhandle a comatose Devlin out of the room on her own. Where the hell was Mrs Woods? And Aisling?

'Ah.'

Devlin crawled out from under the duvet and rolled out of bed. He landed on all fours on the carpet.

'Have you got a dressing-gown?'

'What?'

'Never mind. But it's cold out there and you're not wearing any clothes.'

'It's cold. What am I doing out of bed?'

'Escaping from a fire. Stand up!' She started to cough herself. Bloody man! Why couldn't he just do as he was told?

'What's all the smoke doing?'

'Killing you. Killing us both. Just get out of here, will you?'

At this moment Mrs Woods arrived with a fire blanket and an extinguisher and proceeded to deal with the fire in an efficient way.

Devlin by now was coughing, spluttering and swearing. Kate coughed and spluttered too, but managed to keep her swearing under control. She wrapped the duvet round him. He was a very hairy man, she noticed, and quite muscular. She'd never liked the first attribute, but she rather fancied the second. She bundled him out of the room and into the hallway.

'Is he all right?' asked Aisling, handing out glasses of water. The pink satin was still immaculate.

'I think so. He can still talk and move, anyway.'

'How about you?'

Kate looked down at herself: she was covered in black smuts and grey streaks of ash. 'Dirty but unharmed.'

'Should we call a doctor?'

'I am here,' said Devlin. 'You could try asking me what I want.'

'Do you need a doctor?' asked Aisling patiently.

'No bloody doctors. They're no good for anything except syringing out ear wax.'

'Well, that's settled then. No doctor.'

'Get the bottle of Bushmills,' he ordered Kate when he was sitting on the floor. 'And there's a packet of cigs in the bedside drawer. And matches.'

' "Thank you so much for saving my life, Kate," ' she muttered, as she went back into his room to do his bidding. Perhaps it was because he took their obedience for granted that all the women around him ran to do what he asked. They should take a look at Jacko and that raft of kids: that was how you could wind up if you did it too often.

It stank of smoke and of the chemical extinguisher

in Devlin's room, but she found her way to his bedside table and rescued the whiskey. She thought twice about fetching his cigarettes, but what the hell! He was unlikely to set fire to the house twice in one night, surely. On her way back she looked again at Devlin's door. She hadn't made a mistake about it: the key was on the outside.

She handed him the bottle and the packet of cigarettes. He drank without bothering to wait for a glass.

'That's better,' he said, coughing again.

'He's drunk,' said Aisling, who seemed unaffected by the quantity of wine she had put away during the evening.

'That's how I like to be. Drunk,' said Devlin.

'Fine. I'm glad you're recovering,' said Kate.

'I'm sure that whiskey is the wrong treatment for smoke inhalation,' said Aisling.

'Bloody good stuff,' growled Devlin. 'Cures anything. Everybody knows that.'

'Good. Well, perhaps now you could explain to me how it is that you managed to lock yourself in your room and leave the key on the outside of the door?'

'What?' He looked at her in surprise, she was sure of it.

'First you're chased by a couple of hit men, then someone locks you in your room while you set fire to yourself. I think it warrants an explanation, don't you?'

'You've got it wrong,' said Devlin. 'It can't have happened like that.' He lit a cigarette and drew in a lungful of smoke to join the other substances that were churning about in there. 'And they weren't hit men.'

'How do you know?'

'Oh, shut up! My head hurts.' He coughed again, spectacularly.

Mrs Woods appeared at his side and removed the cigarette from his mouth.

'I don't trust you with these things, and they're not doing you any good,' she said. 'Come along, I've got another room ready for you, but I must insist that this time you do not smoke in bed.'

'All right. Just lead me to the room,' said Devlin meekly. 'And, Katie, you can come with me.'

'No thanks, Devlin.'

'Spoilsport. You don't know what you're missing.'

'I can take a reasonable guess, and the answer's still no.'

'The fire wasn't as bad as it looked,' Mrs Woods told the other two. 'It was lucky that we got to it as soon as we did.'

'Should we call the fire brigade?' asked Aisling.

'It's not necessary. The room's quite safe now. And those men make such an awful mess.'

'We'll get back to bed, then,' said Kate.

'Did you get any sense out of him?' asked Aisling.

'Devlin? No, less than ever.'

'Didn't he have any explanation of what happened?'

'No. He was asleep when I went in. It looked as though the wastepaper bin caught light somehow and then it started to spread to the rest of the room.'

'He must have been drunk.'

'Quite likely,' said Kate, who forebore to mention their own state when they stumbled their way upstairs.

'Let's get some sleep and try and pin him down to an explanation in the morning,' said Aisling.

Back in her room, Kate had a quick shower and changed her T-shirt. Then she put a coat on and found her boots. She was feeling as jumpy as a flea on Ecstasy. It was useless trying to get back to sleep straight away, she would have to take a look around to make sure that everything was safe for the rest of the night. She appeared to be the only one who was at all worried about the presence in the neighbourhood of an arsonist and would-be murderer. The others could go to bed and return to their blameless sleep, but she needed to know that she wouldn't be attacked in her bed as soon as she closed her eyes. She waited until the house was quiet and she assumed that everyone was back in their correct bed, and then she slipped out of her door and, boots in hand, made her way downstairs. She hoped that Mrs Woods didn't have a burglar alarm as effective as her smoke detector.

Which was the best way out? The front door looked bolted and locked so that it would make too much noise if she tried to open it. She went through the dining room and into the kitchen. The back door was more promising. She closed the door into the dining room and quietly slid the bolts back, then turned the large but simple key. The door opened and there was no screeching alarm. She just hoped that it wasn't one of those silent affairs that rang in the local nick.

She slipped her bare feet into the boots and laced

them up, then she went out. Outside it was very cold, slightly misty and completely dark. You forgot how dark it got in the country. The moon and stars were hidden and the only light came from the small wall light that she had switched on in the kitchen. She left the door ajar in case she needed to return in a hurry and moved round the side of the house towards the front.

Nothing. The cars, Aisling's, hers, and what was presumably Mrs Woods's own vehicle, were parked on gravel in front of the house. She listened again. Nothing. What a boring place! Who on earth would want to live in turnip land? What the hell was she doing here?

If someone had come into the house and set fire to Devlin's room, they would be long away, she told herself. Why should they hang around? *To make sure the fire was effective.* As she stood in the chilly gloom, she started to become used to the silence and the darkness and she could make out the shapes of trees and other houses. In the distance she heard a car start up and drive away. She saw its headlights moving along the invisible road in the direction of the town, then it turned right and the lights disappeared. Whoever was in the car was driving fast, she noticed, and they didn't care whether they disturbed their sleeping neighbours.

She turned and went back into the house. What have you found out? What have you proved? Nothing. Zilch. Except that if someone was here, they could have walked away from the house, reached their car – which they had parked out of sight round the corner –

and then driven back to wherever they came from at high speed.

She imagined telling this to Paul and shook her head. He would not be impressed.

She switched off the light, removed her boots and tip-toed barefoot back to her room.

But as she lay in bed, wishing that she could get back to sleep, she couldn't help thinking about the locked door with the key on the outside. She tried to think of innocuous explanations, but the only thing that made sense was that someone had locked Devlin in, having first set fire to his room. After all, she knew from her own experience that anyone could have walked into Devlin's room, shouted at him, thrown a few plates around and then let off a small bomb without much danger of waking him. Setting fire to his room would have been no problem. But Paul would tell her that the most likely way that the fire had started was that Devlin had been drinking and smoking and had dropped off to sleep with a lighted cigarette in his hand. Or, since the wastepaper bin was on fire, that he had tossed a match into it, not realising that it was still alight.

But then, the packet of cigarettes she had fetched for Devlin had been unopened. And she hadn't noticed an ashtray full of cigarette ends next to his bed. Mrs Woods had mentioned that guests were expected not to smoke in their bedrooms, and perhaps Devlin had obeyed, as he had when she had asked him not to smoke in her car. But in that case, how had the fire started? She came back to the intruder who had waited to see the outcome, then driven off into the night.

The thoughts were chasing themselves around in her head, making less and less sense. But just as she was falling asleep at last, she remembered that Devlin's room was originally planned to be hers. And so who had the fire-raiser imagined he was locking inside when he turned that key?

Chapter Eleven

They were all late down to breakfast. Looking at the other two, Kate hoped that she didn't have dark circles round her eyes like Aisling, or bags underneath them like Devlin.

'Eggs and bacon for everyone?' asked Mrs Woods.

'Coffee and toast, please,' said Kate.

'And the same for me,' said Aisling.

'Eggs, bacon, sausage, tomato, mushrooms, fried bread, and a slice of fried black pudding if you have it, please, Mrs Woods,' said Devlin, giving her the full benefit of his sultry brown eyes.

Mrs Woods looked a little frosty this morning, in spite of Devlin's full-frontal charm assault, but she cheered up when Aisling – speaking of course for Fergusson – offered to pay for all the damage to Devlin's room. She brought in a folded invoice which Aisling read through, raised her eyebrows at, and then paid in full with a cheque on an exclusive bank.

After that, fresh coffee appeared at regular intervals throughout breakfast, and Devlin's plate was piled high with the largest cooked breakfast that Kate had ever seen. For herself, she was glad that she was sticking to plain toast and black coffee.

'Now, I have to return to London today,' said Aisling.

'Why do you have to?' asked Devlin, chewing on sausage.

'Because we're throwing a launch party for Joslyn Emmett this evening.'

'She's the one who was given a million advance for her last book, isn't she?' asked Kate, nibbling at dry toast.

'For the world rights, yes.'

'Pounds sterling rather than dollars, too. I can see why you have to be there,' said Devlin, forking in three mushrooms. 'But what about us?'

'It's all organised. Rick and Roland have often worked with us before, so they know just what to expect.'

'Who are Rick and Roland?'

'They sound like children's party entertainers,' said Devlin.

'And no one who hasn't met Devlin could possibly know what to expect,' said Kate.

'But you're not going to set fire to anything today, are you, Devlin?' said Aisling, glancing again at the receipted invoice for last night's damage.

'Or get pursued by hit men,' said Kate, accepting another cup of black coffee and spooning in the sugar.

'I don't know what you're talking about,' said Devlin, looking mulish. 'I am the easiest of people to get on with, and book-shop owners all over the country look forward to my visits.'

'If you say so,' said Kate, helping herself to more toast.

'Any chance of another egg, Mrs Woods? Scrambled, this time, if you can manage it,' said Devlin.

'Yes, of course, Mr Hayle.'

'Then perhaps you'd make it two eggs, Mrs Woods.'

'You know where to go, Kate?' asked Aisling.

'Yes, I have the address,' said Kate. 'Though it does seem to be quite a drive from here.'

'Don't worry,' said Devlin. 'I'll do the map-reading for you.'

'Then we'll be lucky to make it by nightfall.'

'You might be less sarcastic if you ate a decent breakfast.'

'This is a perfectly decent breakfast. What you've eaten is positively obscene.'

'Don't squabble, you two. You've got another nine days of one another's company, remember, so keep it friendly.'

Kate and Devlin glared at one another. Devlin scrunched on fried bread. Kate looked away.

Aisling went on: 'Rick and Roland are the owners of the book shop. It is the biggest and best book shop in the area, and I hope that you will maintain the excellent relationship that we have with them.'

'Yes, Miss,' said Kate.

'Certainly, Miss,' said Devlin, and spoiled it by giggling.

'Rick and Roland— '

'Are they inseparable? Joined at the hip?' asked Devlin.

'They sell a lot of your books,' said Aisling baldly. 'So don't set fire to anything. And be nice to them.'

'We will, we will,' promised Kate, kicking Devlin's shins under the table. He nodded in agreement, his mouth full of scrambled egg. They both knew that selling books was important.

'And Rick and Roland will have the details of the place where you'll be staying tonight and tomorrow. You realise that you'll be two nights in the same place?'

'Yes. By some oversight, you managed to arrange two consecutive signings within thirty miles of one another,' said Devlin.

'I've done my best. It wasn't always easy,' said Aisling.

'You're wonderful,' soothed Kate.

'Tomorrow's signing is at Dillon's. One of their smaller shops, but they're well used to putting on events like this so you'll have no problems. I'll see you both again the day after tomorrow in – er, where is it now? – Devonshire.'

'*Devonshire!*'

'That's hundreds of miles away!'

Kate and Devlin were united in their indignation.

'Don't exaggerate. It's only a couple of hours by car,' said Aisling.

'Two hours in your car, perhaps. But have you seen the heap that Kate's driving?'

'Oh, very nice. And where's your car, I should like to know? Which lamp post did you wrap it around? Or

119

was it scrunched up like a tin can inside that rubbish skip?'

'I think I'll be leaving now,' said Aisling. 'Do have a lovely time, won't you? This trip is supposed to be enjoyable for all concerned, you know.'

As she left, Devlin was saying, 'And don't hog the limelight this time. My fans would like a chance to meet me, but they can't get past that phoney smile and clutching hand of yours.'

'Coming from you, that's rich,' Kate replied.

Aisling grabbed her overnight bag and fled.

Rick and Roland were indeed the owners of a very nice book shop. It was spacious, with high ceilings, good lighting and plenty of room to wander round the shelves.

'You found us all right?' asked Rick.

'We did, in spite of Devlin mixing his left with his right, and getting the map the wrong way up,' said Kate.

'I hope you had a pleasant journey,' said Roland.

'Apart from being frozen when the heater wouldn't work,' said Devlin. 'And then when the windscreen wipers stuck, I did wonder whether Kate would drive into one of those pretty little dry stone walls.'

'This is my sort of book shop,' said Kate diplomatically. 'May we look around?'

There were comfortable chairs where people could sit, and the two owners were obviously very knowledgeable about their stock.

'You should serve coffee at the table over there,' said Devlin.

'We do,' said Rick.

'And we have your bottle of Bushmills,' said Roland. 'But we thought you'd like to wait to open it until after you've delivered your talk.'

Roland was taller than Devlin, and if not quite as wide, he did look fitter. Kate was interested to see whether Devlin would punch him on the nose and grab the bottle of whiskey, and more interested to see what Roland would do if he did. But Devlin must have remembered about his local book sales and thought better of it, for he walked meekly behind Rick to where they were going to sit for the signing.

'Perhaps you'd better put the showcards a little further away from our chairs,' said Kate. 'The contrast between our fit and smiling photographs and our bleary real selves is a little sharp today.'

Roland looked at Kate and Devlin, compared what he saw with their images on the showcards, and repositioned the latter.

Rick said, 'You have a table each, and there will be a couple of dozen copies of your latest titles there for you to sign if things are going slowly.'

'Excellent,' said Kate.

Devlin was looking carefully round the shop.

'Where's your office?' he asked.

'It's round the corner, at the back there,' said Rick. 'Why do you want to know?'

'No reason, just interested.'

'He probably wants to know whether there's a back way out, and where he can hire a minder,' said Kate.

'The back door is through there, though it will be locked in the evening.'

'I'm nervous of fire,' improvised Devlin. 'I always like to know where the exits are.'

'I don't see how a minder would help,' said Rick.

'That was just one of Kate's little jokes.'

'Shall we get back to this evening's arrangements?' said Rick.

Devlin reluctantly stopped taking an inventory of exits and brought his attention back to the day's work. 'How long a talk do you want from me?' he asked.

'Four or five minutes. And a brief reading. Leave them wanting more, I always think. Is that all right by you?'

'Fine,' they both said.

'I'll show you the way to your digs,' said Rick. 'You've got an hour and a half before you need to be back here.'

Devlin glanced back over his shoulder to where, presumably, he imagined the Bushmills was stashed, but Rick, looking amused, took them out to the car and gave them directions to the house where they were staying.

'You don't think they want me to stay at their place, do you?' muttered Devlin.

'I doubt very much that you're their type,' said Kate. 'You're quite safe, Devlin. Just stick close to me and I'll protect you.'

Devlin looked at her to see if she was joking or not, decided she was, and laughed unconvincingly.

Back in Oxford, Kate's phone was ringing in the empty house.

'Please leave a message after the bleep.'

'Hello, Kate. It's me again. You don't give your name or number, but I recognise your voice. I'd recognise it anywhere. Can you recognise mine? I doubt it. There's nothing remarkable about it, is there? Well, I know you're not at home, but I like to talk to you anyway. I think of you picking up your messages later today and hearing my voice. Listening to me tonight, in the dark, on your own. What happened yesterday? Didn't you get my message? You should have done. You really should. I can't talk any more for the present, but I'll call again tomorrow. Goodbye now.'

Kate and Devlin met, with half an hour to spare before they needed to be at the book shop, in their landlady's kitchen. The digs were very different from last night's, not so smart, but warm and cosy. The kitchen was the place where everyone would naturally congregate in this house.

'May we join you, Mrs Knapper?' asked Devlin.

'Call me Kim,' she said. 'Come in and sit down. Would you both like a nice cup of tea?'

'Yes please.'

'And I expect you'd like a bite to eat. There are

chocolate biscuits in the tin here, and I've made some scones.'

'Scones sound delicious,' said Devlin, while Kate helped herself to her favourite chocolate biscuits.

'This jam's home-made. Strawberry.'

'You're spoiling us, Kim,' said Devlin.

'Oh, Fergusson are good payers,' she said. 'They make it worth my while.'

While she was boiling water and making the tea, Kate spoke to Devlin in a low voice.

'I think it's time you warned me what else might happen on this tour. How many other people are after you? What is it that they want? And what are you mixed up in?' She had tried to ask him during the long car journey, but between bouts of map-reading he had feigned a profound sleep.

'Had you thought of becoming an investigative journalist?'

'Don't avoid the question.'

'You'd do well on one of those late-night current affairs programmes where they grill politicians.'

'I'm serious, Devlin. And I hope you don't expect me to believe the story you told us over dinner last night.'

'Why not?'

'It was a mixture of *Romancing the Stone* and *Le Salaire de la Peur*, with some James Bond thrown in. I don't believe real life is ever that interesting.'

'Well, maybe I did make some of it up. But why should you be bothered? You make your living by telling attractive fibs too, don't you?'

'I try to keep mine to the written word. And I'd like to know what to expect so that I can be prepared for the rest of this trip.'

'What a plucky little thing you are!'

With difficulty, Kate stopped herself from kicking him, hard. She had twenty minutes now before they left for the book shop, and she was determined to find out what was happening.

'Come on! Give me a few clues.'

'I just seem to have this gift for getting into trouble all the time.' Devlin spoke in the same tone he might have used if he had been telling her that he had a gift for painting the Sistine Chapel ceiling. 'The last major inconvenience was when I got involved with Affrica.'

'Is this a variation on the Central American theme?'

'Not Africa. Affrica.' He spelled it for her. 'A very beautiful woman.'

'Who probably started life as Blodwen. Or Joan.'

'Affrica is a model.'

'Oh yeah?'

'The kind of model you see on the cover of a glossy magazine or swaying down a classy catwalk with ten thousand quids' worth of clothes on her back.'

'And how did you get involved with her?'

'Don't look so incredulous. The world is full of women who find me irresistibly attractive.'

'OK, for the purposes of this story, I'll believe you.'

'We met at the Groucho. She was waiting for her agent, and I was waiting for mine. We passed a little time together until they turned up, and then we met up again, by arrangement, at the Bootlace, where we had a few drinks and got to know each other.'

'So what was the problem?'

'Unfortunately, her previous bloke had been this Arab prince – a member of one of those Gulf States royal families. He was very rich. Unbelievably rich, actually. Also very macho and very jealous.'

At this moment Kim came over with the teapot.

'How do you like your tea?' she asked.

'As it comes,' said Kate.

'Hot and strong,' said Devlin, treating Kim to one of his smouldering looks.

'Sugar?'

'Yes please.'

'Do you have any skimmed milk, Kim?' asked Kate.

'I'll go and get you some.' And Kim disappeared into the pantry, as Kate had hoped she would.

'And you think he's sent a couple of his heavies to teach you a lesson?'

'I think it's all too likely.'

'They didn't look much like Arabs. And I'm sure that was basic Anglo-Saxon they were speaking back in Swindon.'

'He could afford to hire a couple of locals,' said Devlin.

'Where's Affrica now?' asked Kate as Kim put a jug of skimmed milk on the table.

'I hope it's where it's always been!' said Kim. 'But I expect you're talking about that writing of yours, aren't you?'

'That's right,' said Devlin. 'And yes, Affrica is where

she was before, draped all over her princeling's Mayfair penthouse.'

'So, why— ' Kate started to say.

'More tea before you have to leave for the book shop?' asked Kim.

'Yes please,' said Devlin, and entered into an animated conversation with her about the merits of leaf tea as opposed to teabags.

Kate sat wondering why, if Affrica had returned to him, her Arab prince was bothering to chase Devlin all over England. But then, she had to admit, she knew very little of the ways of Arab princes, or of supermodels either, if it came to that.

Chapter Twelve

'I have to confess that there are one or two other little problem areas in my life,' said Devlin, as they drove back to the book shop.

'Really?' said Kate, wishing that the distance between their digs and the shop was greater. 'We have another eight days of our tour, so I look forward to hearing all about them.' They had another three continents to get through, for starters.

'I don't mean to get involved with other women, but I just can't resist it when I'm given a direct invitation.' He paused for a couple of seconds as though waiting for Kate to make her own approach.

'What about your wife?' she asked baldly.

'Jacko? That's one of my confessions,' he said. 'Jacko and I never actually made it official.'

'What about all those children?'

'Bastards, the lot of them,' he said. 'I'm sure we'll get round to it one day, when it feels like the right moment. It has led to one or two— '

'Save it for later,' she said, 'the book shop is just round this corner. But we could go and look for a place to eat when we've finished amusing the punters, and you could tell me about it then. Though this town doesn't look as though it has many good restaurants.'

'You think we can avoid our delightful fans tonight and spend an evening alone?'

'I think we're getting plenty of practice in escaping from people.'

'I saw a likely looking pub on our way in,' said Devlin.

'We'll give it a try, then.'

'Did I tell you how good you're looking in that blue thing?'

That 'blue thing' had set Kate back a very large sum in Oxford's poshest dress shop.

'Thanks. You're looking all right yourself.' Devlin was wearing plum corduroy with a cobalt blue collarless shirt. It smelled a bit smoky, but it looked fine. He had combed his hair and trimmed his beard.

'Yes,' he said. 'Sort of like the Queen of the Night, with all those sparkly bits on it.'

'We're here,' she said, grateful that they had arrived before Devlin could reach any further poetic heights of description.

It was as well that she had managed to park right outside the shop, for Kate was wearing high-heeled dark blue suede shoes, and she just managed to teeter across the pavement and in through the door without falling over.

'Come on,' she said. 'What are you waiting for?'

'Just checking,' said Devlin, staring hard at the cars parked in the road near theirs.

'I don't know what you hope to see in the dark,' said Kate.

'Bloody turnips. Why can't they light their streets properly?'

'Time to go in,' said Kate.

'All right,' said Devlin, turning away reluctantly from his inspection. 'There's nothing here that I remember seeing before, anyway.'

'I hope you haven't got another sprint planned for this evening,' said Kate. 'I don't think I'd do very well in these heels.'

'It's going to be a successful and problem-free evening,' said Devlin. 'I feel it in my bones.'

Looking around at the crowds of customers supping up their Australian Chardonnay and digging into the cheese and olive twists, Kate thought how similar they all were to last night's crowd. The same middle-aged women, the same bored-looking husbands and the same sulky teenagers. Actually, the same Australian Chardonnay.

'Loosen up,' said Devlin. 'Allow yourself to drink a glass of wine.'

It seemed a good idea, so she did.

They signed what seemed like dozens of books. For Debbie, for May with best wishes, for Nicki, for Jan. They smiled and hoped that Debbie and May, Nicki and Jan would all enjoy their books very much. And how kind it was of them to turn out on a cold February evening like this.

'Well done,' said Rick on his way past with a fresh pile of books.

'You're doing really well,' said Roland, bringing Kate another glass of wine and Devlin a very small whisky.

This time Devlin gave the first talk.

He was well into his third anecdote, the one about the time when he was running a workshop in a women's prison, when the phone rang.

The phone had rung once or twice before, but Rick or Roland had answered it promptly, and it hadn't bothered them. But this time Roland put the phone down on the counter and came over to Kate and Devlin.

'It's for you,' he hissed at Devlin. 'She says it's very urgent.'

Devlin looked put out, but smiled at the audience, said, 'Well, I'm very sorry about this, but it must be a real emergency. I'll leave you in Kate's capable hands,' and went to take his phone call.

The counter was not far from their signing table, and every word was audible.

Kate doggedly told the audience about how she planned her books, how she researched them, how she organised her time. She told them how she had sold her first book. But she could see that none of them was listening. What was going on in the background was so very much more interesting.

'No, I did not!' shouted Devlin into the phone. There was a yelping noise from the earpiece, then Devlin said, 'I don't care what she says, it just isn't true!' Pause for more yelping.

'Well, if you're going to get personal, how about the way you leave your knickers to dry on the kitchen towel rail.' High-pitched burble from the phone.

'Don't be disgusting! I certainly do take my socks off!'

By this time Kate had given up trying to speak to the audience, and just sat praying that Devlin would soon finish his telephone call.

'If you think you can find someone else to take on your extravagant habits and that gang of miniature criminals, you'd just better get on with it!' He slammed the receiver back into its rest. Roland sighed loudly. Rick drummed his fingers on the counter.

Devlin returned to his seat to find a totally silent audience, their collective eyes upon him.

'So sorry about that, ladies and gentlemen. My wife is expecting our first child, and you know how emotional women can get in this situation.'

Kate took a tissue out of her bag and buried her face in it.

'Have you finished your talk, Kate?'

She nodded, still speechless.

'Then I'll continue with mine. As I was saying, there I was, standing in front of this group of desperate female criminals . . .'

The phone rang.

Rick came up behind her. 'It's for you, Kate. He says it's urgent.' Kate crept away from the table. 'Try to keep the volume down, will you?' said Rick. 'And make it as brief as you can.'

Kate nodded and picked up the receiver. 'Hello?' she whispered.

'Kate? Is that you? I can hardly hear you.'

'Hello, Andrew,' she whispered. 'Just tell me why you've rung. There's a room full of people here, hanging on your every word.'

'What?'

'Speak, Andrew!'

'I got your phone number from the list you left with us,' said Andrew, sounding huffy. 'I imagined it would be acceptable to contact you.' Kate said nothing, so he went on. 'I have a couple of queries for you. First of all, I don't think your Christmas cactus is looking very happy. Do you think I should water it, or do you think you've already overdone it?'

'Water it!' hissed Kate, not caring. She could buy another sodding cactus if it died.

'Then there's the problem with your answer phone. I just can't make the thing work. I come in and its beady little eye is flashing away at me, but when I try to persuade it to disgorge its messages it just beeps at me. It's most disconcerting.'

'Don't worry,' whispered Kate. 'Whoever it is will probably write a letter if it's urgent.' Or send a carrier pigeon.

'Well, I don't think you're being very nice. I've tended your plants, I've fed your animals and your friend Harley, and I've filled your freezer with all sorts of delicious little goodies. You might at least sound grateful.'

Devlin was in full flow now and no one seemed

interested in her phone conversation. It was, after all, a lot less dramatic than Devlin's had been. Kate raised her voice a notch.

'Dearest Andrew,' she cooed, 'of course I appreciate what you're doing. I don't know what I'd do without you. I love you dearly, really I do. Now, go and hug Susannah and Dave, tell Harley to get on with his homework, and accept a big wet kiss for yourself from me.'

'Well, Kate. There's no need to overdo it.' Andrew sounded pleased but embarrassed.

'Good night, Andrew.'

'Good night, Kate.'

She made kissing noises into the receiver, and then hung up.

As she crept back to her place, Devlin was just winding up his talk.

'Glad you could join us again, Kate,' he said jovially. 'Ironed out your little difficulties at home, have you?'

The audience tittered and Kate hissed, 'Better than you did, anyway!'

Devlin went smoothly back into his peroration and stood looking smug while the audience applauded enthusiastically.

'That's how it's done, Kate,' he said. 'I could give you a few pointers over dinner, if you like.'

'Sod off!' she replied, unfortunately into a sudden hush in the room.

'Now,' said Roland. 'Are there any questions for our authors?'

'I'd like to know,' said a woman in the front row,

'how you manage to fit your writing in with your family commitments.'

Devlin rose to answer, while Kate suffered another coughing attack.

Chapter Thirteen

'This is the place,' said Devlin, pointing to a long, low, stone building. 'The White Hart. Car Park at Rear.'

'Good Pub Food Available At All Times,' said Kate.

She swung the car past the creaking sign, into the narrow entrance, and parked by a trough of crocuses.

'Do you want to check out the other cars? Make sure there are none you recognise?' To her own amazement she found that she was speaking seriously, not in jest.

They both prowled round the car park, peering into the two or three cars there.

'Are these all local registration numbers?' asked Kate.

'Certainly nothing from London,' said Devlin.

'Nothing more suspicious than a box of Kleenex in this one.'

'A pair of green crochet cushions and a pine air freshener over here.'

'It's starting to rain. I don't want to get my shoes wet,' said Kate. 'Can we go inside now?'

'I'm just checking on this last car.'

Kate was startled by the sound of high-pitched hysterical barking.

'Bloody turnips have left their bloody dog in the back of this one,' said Devlin. 'I suppose it's their idea of the latest in car alarms.'

'Let's go inside and sample the Good Pub Food.'

'I could do with a drink,' said Devlin.

Three whiskeys later, Devlin was starting to relax.

'Have I told you how much that dark blue suits you?' he said.

'Only a couple of times so far,' said Kate. 'And I believe I've already told you how plum-coloured corduroy matches your eyes. Shall we order some food? I'm starving.'

'You have no soul,' said Devlin mournfully. 'You are a very hard and unfeeling woman. There is no romance in you at all.'

'I put it all into my novels,' said Kate. 'It earns more money that way.'

'That's what I mean about you.' Devlin caught the barman's eye and another whiskey appeared by his elbow. 'Don't you know there's more to life than money and success?'

'There is? Like what?'

'Music, love, romance. Gazing into someone's eyes and seeing your own feelings reflected there.'

Devlin fixed her with his famous smouldering gaze, but spoiled it by failing to keep his eyes in focus.

'You're squinting. You should leave the booze alone for a while.' As Devlin started to look quarrelsome, she picked up a menu and handed it to him. 'I think you need some food inside you. The beef and ale pie looks OK to me,' said Kate. 'What are you going to have?'

Devlin ignored her. 'And all you've had to drink is one glass of nasty mineral water. It's not good for you, you know. It's full of sodium and all sorts of unhealthy things.'

'Perhaps, but I'm driving. Why don't you try the lamb chops with rosemary?'

'Oh, very well.'

They ordered the food, and Kate drank an orange juice while they waited for it to arrive.

'Let me ask the man to put some vodka in that for you.'

'But I don't like vodka.'

'You're no fun to go out with. Do you know that?'

Kate drank some of her orange juice. 'I'd like to hear more about your life, Devlin.' Few men could resist this approach, she had found.

'Shall I start with my childhood, or would you like me to begin earlier than that?'

'Can we fast forward to the part where you started making enemies?'

'You don't have a very good opinion of me, do you?'

'I'm only going by my brief but exciting experience of your career over the last couple of days. Come on! Tell me all about it.'

They had left the bar and were sitting at a table in one corner of the room, well out of earshot of the other customers.

'Well, there's old Edmund. He might have a bit of a grudge against me.'

'And what did you do to him?'

But at this moment the waitress appeared with their food order.

'Which one's the lamb chop?'

'That's for my friend here. And I'm the beef pie.'

In Oxford, the phone was ringing.

'Please leave a message after the bleep.'

'Hello, Kate. It's me again. Your faithful friend and admirer. Did you hear the message I left for you yesterday? I do hope so. We may meet again quite soon, but I doubt whether you will— '

There was a click as the receiver was lifted at Kate's end.

'Hello. Who is this, please?'

Silence. Then the burr of the dialling tone as the caller replaced the distant receiver. Paul Taylor played the message back, frowning. He dialled 1471 to find out the caller's number, but the featureless voice told him that the number had been withheld. It probably wasn't important, but Kate did seem to get herself involved with some very odd people: first someone sending her a ring, now this anonymous fan leaving messages on her machine. Unless it wasn't a fan, but someone she had met on her travels and formed a friendship with. Or some more intimate relationship. But now he was just being ridiculous. He returned to the kitchen to clear up the animals' bowls. It was time he returned to his own flat.

At the White Hart, Kate and Devlin had finished their main course, had eaten their way through home-made ice creams, and were now ordering coffee.

'And a brandy with mine,' said Devlin.

'You were going to tell me about Edmund,' said Kate, feeling happily full of good food.

'Ah, dear old Edmund. He and I were collaborators, you know.'

'What did you collaborate on?'

'A book, of course.'

'What was the subject? Or was it fiction?'

'No, it was a solid work of fact. We even had a publisher interested, and he was about to cough up a hefty advance.'

'So what went wrong? I'm assuming, of course, that something did go wrong.'

'Something always goes wrong, don't you find?' Devlin was reaching the maudlin stage, Kate suspected. She headed him off.

'Did you manage to write the book?'

'We did. But then we had a bit of an argument and decided not to collaborate any more. We'd been working over at his place, on his computer, and I picked up the stuff that I'd been working on and went home.'

'What did you argue about?'

'It was nothing. He said something about me not

pulling my weight. But that was ridiculous. He had no original ideas, and he couldn't put a sentence together that wouldn't bore the pants off you. So I left. I wasn't staying to be insulted like that.'

'And he didn't forgive you?' It all sounded a bit mild to her to produce homicidal tendencies in his ex-partner.

'It was only one lousy little floppy,' said Devlin.

'What was?'

'I just took one lousy little floppy disk home with me.'

'What was on it?'

'Nothing much.'

Kate rephrased her request. 'What did Edmund say was on it?'

'He said all his research was on it. And that I'd stolen it.'

'Not very nice. But if he'd done the research, he could get on with the book, even if he was a crap writer.'

'But he didn't have his research results any more, he said. It was all on the disk.'

'Surely he had a back-up.'

'He had a copy on his hard disk, but somehow that had got itself erased.'

'How did that happen?'

'How should I know?' said Devlin sulkily. 'Why are you being so horrible to me? You're starting to sound just like Edmund.'

'We can't have *that*,' said Kate. 'Why don't I get you another whisky?'

'Make it a brandy.'

She went to the bar to get Devlin his drink and herself another orange juice, though to tell the truth she was heartily sick of the stuff. She was looking forward to pouring herself a glass of something pleasanter, and containing alcohol, when she got back to their digs.

'Mind you,' said Devlin, 'I didn't do it on purpose.'

'Do what?'

'Erase his files from his hard disk. It's just that I'm not very good with computers. It was a mistake. A genuine mistake.'

'But Edmund didn't see it that way?'

' 'Fraid not. Especially when I went ahead with the book and got the hefty advance all for myself. They weren't very interested in Edmund's contribution, you see. He really was a crap writer.'

'Why was he involved in the project in the first place if he was so hopeless?'

'Well, it was sort of his idea, really.'

'Let me get this straight. Edmund has an idea for a book, does the research for it, gets a publisher interested, and then asks you to join him to help out with the writing. You nick the idea and the floppy disk with all his info on, and go on to write the book and earn the money.'

'Hey! I had ideas too, you know. I did some work on the background!'

'But you did take his research results from that floppy? It does sound as though he was the one who had done most of the work up till then.'

Devlin looked at her, his expression hurt. 'He had a

very good data base. It would have been criminal not to use it. In fact, there was some quite useful stuff in there for my last historical garbage, too.'

'You are quite impossible! No wonder the man has it in for you!'

'I was hoping you'd understand my point of view.'

'I understand it, all right. I just don't approve of it. What's Edmund doing now?'

'He had a bit of a breakdown, I believe. Suffered from severe depression. Pity, really. But it's all a question of moral fibre, don't you think?'

'Only wimps have breakdowns, you mean?'

'Well, it stands to reason, doesn't it?'

Devlin had got to the stage of inebriation where it was really pointless arguing with him, so Kate didn't bother to try.

'I gave it back to him,' said Devlin.

'What?'

'The floppy disk. I did give it back to him. I don't know what he's beefing about all this time afterwards.'

'People can be quite unreasonable when their work is stolen, can't they?' said Kate. 'What did you say the registration number of his car was?' And she planned to check under her bed before she went to sleep, too. She could imagine that anyone, even a wimp lacking in moral fibre, would come gunning for Devlin after that little episode.

'Did I tell you about Melanie?'

'No.' Kate was starting to get tired of Devlin's peccadilloes.

'Her husband was a great brute of a man!'

'Don't you think it's time we went back to our digs?'

'Oh, all right. There is a bottle of Bushmills there, isn't there?'

'I'm sure Fergusson won't let us down.' She was hoping there'd be a bottle of claret there for her own use, too.

'And I don't know what Joe's making such a fuss about, either.'

'Is this another wronged husband?'

'No. *Joe*. He knows he'll get his money eventually. It's just a question of time. My luck will turn, won't it?'

'I'm sure it will.' Time to leave, she thought.

They split the bill between them and made their way back to the car, Devlin staggering just a little as they went.

'Yes,' he said. 'He was a great brute of a man. Poor little Melanie was only looking for a bit of love and understanding. What could a man do? I couldn't let her down, could I?'

'I'm sure you did your best.'

'No. It's just not fair.'

'What isn't fair?'

'The way he blames me for what happened.'

'What *did* happen?'

'What?' Devlin had evidently lost the thread of their conversation. 'And Rodge. He's not a reasonable man, either. After all, it's Jacko's idea as much as mine not to get married. He can't blame me for it.'

'Who's Rodge?'

'Jacko's brother.'

'What's that got to do with Melanie?'

'Nothing. Why don't you pay attention?'

Kate gave up trying to make sense of what he was saying. 'Oh damn! I've left my jacket behind in the pub.'

It had stopped raining and the air was mild for February. 'You take the car keys and let yourself in. You have to open the driver's door, not the passenger one. I'll be back in a moment.'

She walked as fast as her high heels would let her back into the pub. As she went through the door, she thought she heard the hysterical dog yapping inside its car again. She went to find her jacket.

When she came out into the car park, she was surprised to see that Devlin was not sitting in the passenger seat of her car. What had the stupid bugger done now? She walked round to the other side and saw a dark heap lying on the ground. Devlin!

She bent down. She heard heavy breathing. Once she realised he was still alive she stopped feeling worried and just felt angry with the man again. He had probably passed out from all the whiskey and brandy he'd drunk.

'Devlin! Wake up!' She stretched out a hand to help him to his feet. Even in the dim lighting she could see that something had happened to him.

'What's happened to you? What's wrong with your face?'

'Bloody great brute,' he mumbled. 'Poor little Melanie, I only wanted to cheer her up.'

Kate couldn't make out whether someone really had beaten him up or if he had simply stumbled while trying to open the car door. She couldn't hope to get any sense out of the man in that state.

'Should we take you to Casualty, do you think?' she said.

'Bloody waste of time. We'll sit there all night waiting for some bloody doctor to tell me there's nothing wrong with me.'

Well, he was conscious enough to come out with a long sentence, anyway. There couldn't be too much wrong with him.

'Just get into the car, Devlin, will you? I'll get you back to Kim's place.'

'Has anyone ever told you what a bossy cow you are?'

'I believe they have. Just once or twice.'

When they got back to their digs, she let Kim deal with Devlin. She appeared to be quite used to large men who drank too much. She sponged his face, revealing a black eye and a swollen jaw, and then got him upstairs and into his room with very little trouble.

Kate was glad to sit for half an hour with her feet up, enjoying a glass of good wine, with the compliments of Fergusson, and pondering the various rambling stories that Devlin had told her that evening. It seemed to her that England must be crammed with men – and occasionally women – who had it in for Devlin. The man had probably made even more enemies without even noticing it. It could well have been Melanie's brute of a husband or some other poor bastard that Devlin had ruined in his casual way who had thumped him in the car park. Or Rodge, though she hadn't quite got the gist of that story. Or Devlin could have fallen over and hit his eye on the bumper and his jaw on the tarmac. Kate tried to visualise how he might have fallen, but gave up. For the moment, she was past caring.

She checked her room thoroughly and locked the door before going to bed.

When she went down to breakfast the next morning, she found that the night had been quite uneventful. Kim's house was still in one piece. Devlin's swollen jaw had subsided and he was wearing dark glasses to hide his black eye. As a matter of fact, they made him look more interesting than ever.

When he had drunk his first cup of coffee and was well into his cooked breakfast, she attempted conversation with him.

'How are you feeling this morning, Devlin?'

'I'm fine. How are you, Kate?'

'I just wondered whether you'd have a bit of a headache.'

'Is this a subtle way of disapproving of my drinking last night?'

'It was more a way of asking about your swollen jaw and black eye.'

Devlin lifted his dark glasses so that she could see his shiner better.

'I was hoping that you could tell me how this happened,' he said. 'Did you thump me with your handbag, or did you use your fist?'

'You're telling me you don't remember what happened?'

'Not a thing. But I thought it might have something to do with you. Perhaps one of your admirers suffered an attack of jealousy and duffed me up.'

'When we came out of the pub last night, I left you to unlock the car while I went back inside to collect my jacket. When I got back, you were lying on the ground, breathing heavily and groaning.'

'Did you see who did it? What car were they driving?'

'I'm afraid to say that my first thoughts were for your safety. I didn't notice anyone else in the car park, and I didn't see anyone drive away. But that doesn't mean that they weren't and they didn't. I was too concerned at the time to get you upright and into the car.'

Devlin looked disbelieving.

'You must have seen something.'

'Sorry, Devlin. I thought you had probably stumbled and fallen while walking to the car. It didn't occur to me at first that someone had attacked you. Are you sure that nothing's come back to you about what happened?'

'Not a thing. You could even be right. Though how I stumbled and gave myself a black eye, while simultaneously thumping my jaw on the tarmac, I can't imagine.'

Devlin turned his attention back to his newspaper, while eating his sausage and bacon, and Kate drank another cup of coffee.

'I see old Pettit's popped his clogs,' said Devlin.

'The author?'

'The author of a fifty-one-volume series about the Hundred Years War, to be precise.'

'Was he a close friend of yours?'

'I knew him, but he wasn't a friend, exactly. More like a competitor, you could say.'

'So you're not too upset at his passing.'

'I'm delighted. They're more likely to buy our books now he's gone, aren't they?'

'I hadn't thought of it like that before.'

Kim came in with a fresh jug of coffee and more toast.

'You were in a fair old state last night, weren't you?' she said to Devlin.

'I was mugged in the pub car park,' said Devlin with dignity.

'Drunk, more like,' said Kim, laughing. 'Though they all make up stories to cover it,' she said to Kate.

'I do believe something nasty could have happened to him,' said Kate.

'Probably picked a fight with one of the Cottam lads while your back was turned,' said Kim. 'They're great ones for getting drunk and fighting, too.'

Well, maybe Kim was right. But if she was, it had been a remarkably short and quiet brawl.

Chapter Fourteen

It was a relief not to have to drive a couple of hundred miles with a truculent Hayle in the passenger seat, and Kate looked forward to exploring some of the local countryside. She might have left her hiking boots at home, but she had got her Doc Martens with her. Before leaving the house, she decided to check what was happening at home. She was sure that everyone was fine without her, but who knows, there could have been an urgent message for her.

She dug out the notebook where she had written the instructions, and went to make the telephone call. At least if the house was empty she needn't worry about Andrew erasing her messages before she could get to them. She dialled and listened.

'Hello, Kate. It's me again. Your faithful friend and admirer . . .'

Who on earth was that? It was such a neutral voice, with no distinguishing features, that she couldn't recognise it. And then, in mid-phrase, it was cut off. Probably someone had realised that they were leaving a message on the wrong answerphone. There were plenty of people around called Kate, and she didn't give her name or number on her message. There were no other messages for her and she resolved to put the whole thing out of her mind by taking some strenuous exercise.

She certainly felt fresh and relaxed when she left the digs for that evening's signing. Devlin was moody and mysterious in his pewter velvet and shades, with a dark blue shirt and a pale grey tie.

'A touch of the thirties gangster this evening,' she remarked, as they set off.

'A certain devil-may-care *je ne sais quoi* is what I was aiming for,' he replied. 'And I like that silky thing you're wearing. All those sultry smoky colours with just a touch of burnt orange. Very fetching.'

They went through their usual routine before entering the shop, checking on cars parked in the street nearby.

'He or they might have used the car park,' said Kate.

'No, they'd want to get away in a hurry, don't you think? And what about this blue Rover? Have we seen it before?'

'I've seen a blue Rover before but I can't be sure it's the same one. There are lots of them around.'

Devlin peered through the windows of the book shop. 'I can't see any black track suits tonight.' Kate didn't mention the fact that they might well have changed their clothes by now. Devlin's paranoia was difficult enough to deal with as it was, without encouraging him to get any worse.

'The punters look harmless enough. I think we can cope with them. Come on, Devlin, let's go and greet our public.'

Devlin held the door open for her and they went in.

Some time later, as they sat signing books and smiling and talking to the customers, Kate said, 'Why is that man over there staring at us?'

'What man? Where?'

'Grey trousers, blue anorak, stocky build, carroty hair. In the Sports section. He looks vaguely familiar. Have we seen him before?'

'Oh my God!'

Kate signed another book. 'I do hope you enjoy reading it,' she said. Then she turned back to Devlin. 'Who is he?'

'Rodge.'

'Remind me which of your victims that is. I rather lost track last night of what you'd done to them all.'

'Rodge is Jacko's brother.'

'Red hair, like Jacko,' said Kate. 'I see it now. He's the one who thinks you should have married his sister by now.'

'It's not my fault,' said Devlin.

'It never is.'

'He won't like seeing us together like this.'

'We're working, not socialising. Can't he see that?' replied Kate.

'I doubt it. He's a very jealous man on his sister's behalf. He's always had it in for me. He turns her against me.'

'From some of the stories you were telling last night, I'd say he had good reason.'

'What shall we do?'

'The store has one or two security people floating round, so he's unlikely to attack you here. When we've finished our stint, we'd better leg it.'

'He's pretty fit, he could well catch up with us.'

'So, if one of us creates a diversion the other can run for it. And, by the way, you'll notice that I'm wearing more sensible shoes today. If we make it to the car, we should be able to lose him on our way out of the town.'

'There are rather a lot of ifs in your plan.'

'So come up with a better one.'

'Suppose he makes a scene?'

'Just calm down and keep smiling. I'll get you out of here, don't worry.'

And how was it that she had become responsible for Devlin's safety? The man seemed able to get his own way without even trying.

The store's promotions officer came over.

'How are you two bearing up?'

'Just fine,' said Kate.

'It's going very well. We've sold a lot of books.'

'Which is what it's all about,' said Devlin.

'Not all yours, of course,' said the promotions officer. 'We've had quite a run on gardening books, for some reason.'

'So glad to be of use,' said Devlin. And as the young man moved away, he said to Kate, 'Bloody turnip land! I ask you! Gardening books!'

'Makes you weep,' said Kate. Forgetting about Rodge, they both laughed.

'Right, that's it!' said a voice behind them.

'Hello, Rodge,' said Devlin. If he had been a dog he would have rolled on his back and waved his legs in the air, thought Kate. 'What brings you here?'

'I happened to be in the area and I just thought I'd check to see whether you really were working or not, the way you told it to Jacko.'

'Well, as you can see, I am.'

'And who's *she*?'

'My name is Kate Ivory, and I, too, am a historical novelist engaged in promoting my latest book,' said Kate, surreptitiously doing up a couple of buttons on the front of her dress.

'How did you swing this?' asked Rodge.

'I didn't. Miss Ivory agreed to join me when my original partner dropped out. We had never met until this Monday.'

'True,' said Kate.

'You looked pretty friendly to me,' said Rodge.

'All an illusion, old boy,' said Devlin. 'We hate each other's guts, don't we, Kate?'

'Deeply and irrevocably,' said Kate.

Rodge was still breathing through his teeth, and his face was a nasty colour.

'Miss Ivory?' It was a timid voice, and the person behind it was small and thin and dressed in forget-me-not blue wool. A furry hat sat on her white hair like a friendly kitten. 'My name is Jane Bell. I wrote to you.'

Jane Bell? Which one was she?

'We share an interest in enamel boxes, I believe,' said Miss Bell.

'Of course!' Kate turned away from Devlin and Rodge. 'You must sit down, Miss Bell. Let me get you a chair.' Kate found somewhere for her to sit, and then placed herself beside her. No one could attack them, or even make a scene, while they were in the company of such a dear, fragile little old lady, could they?

'Thank you so much, my dear. You know, since I inadvertently read one of your books, I've become quite a fan. They slip down quite easily, don't they, rather like a gin and tonic.'

'The similarity hadn't struck me before, but I'm glad you enjoy them.'

'I've bought your new one, and I hope you'll sign it for me.'

Kate brandished her fountain pen. 'Of course!'

'If you could write some kind message here for me, it would give me great joy.' She reached out an arthritic hand and placed it on Kate's arm. Her knobbly fingers were covered in gold rings of all kinds.

Kate wrote her floweriest dedication and signed her name with a couple of extra loops and a squiggly line underneath for good measure.

'Now, tell me all about your boxes,' said Kate, and spent the next five minutes in conversation with Miss Bell. When they had finished, and Miss Bell had moved away, she saw that Rodge had returned to a normal colour and his voice had dropped a few decibels.

'There now, have you got yourselves sorted out?' she asked.

'Rodge and I are the greatest of friends,' said Devlin.

'Well, just watch it!' said Rodge, but he sounded much less belligerent.

'We will, don't worry.'

'That was simple enough,' said Kate as Rodge moved away from them and back towards Sports. 'My little diversion worked admirably, I think.'

'I hope you're right. The sport he's interested in is body-building, and if he decided to thump us he'd make a better job of it than the man in the car park last night.'

'Do you think you could tell me what Edmund looks like?'

'What on earth made you think of him?'

'I thought it would be useful if I could give the police a description when they find your murdered corpse.'

'I don't know where you get these gruesome ideas from.'

'It's something to do with the days I've spent in your company, Devlin.'

They both worked silently for a while, until the crowd in the shop started to thin out.

'I think we can get going soon,' said Devlin.

'Good. We should make our escape while we're still winning.'

'Wha' you doing?'

Andrew Grove was standing in Kate's Oxford sitting room, staring into his reflection in the gilt-framed mirror above the fireplace.

'Just checking my contact lenses, Harley. You can't see them, can you?'

'Just the edge, like, if you get it in the light.'

'Much more flattering than spectacles, don't you think?'

'They're all right, I suppose.' Harley obviously didn't think that some old git like Andrew should still be concerned about his looks.

'And what are you doing, Harley?'

'I've finished me homework,' said Harley defensively.

'I'm glad to hear it. But that doesn't answer the question.'

Harley looked shamefaced. 'I wanted to find out how it works.'

'How what works?'

'This.'

He held up Kate's knot-ring. It was once more in four pieces.

'Oh dear.'

'Well, it's easy enough to get it apart. It's putting it back together that's hard,' said Harley.

'I can see that. Well, I have no gift for that sort of thing myself. You'll have to go on trying, or else wait for Paul's return. I'm sure he'll show you how to do it.'

Harley returned to his twisting and looping, with little success.

'I hope Kate won't be too upset about it.'

'I don't think she was that bothered,' said Harley.

'I think it's about time you went home now, Harley,' said Andrew when he had stopped admiring his image in the glass. 'It's nice having your company, but it must be nearly your bedtime.'

'Right,' said Harley, who was anyway growing tired of playing with the ring. 'I'll just say goodnight to Dave.'

When he had left, Andrew bolted the back door and returned to his work in the kitchen. He was filling Kate's freezer up for her while she was away with all sorts of nutritious little delicacies. And he wanted to prepare a casserole for Harley's tea next day, as he would be working late and wouldn't have time to make anything much when he got home. Funny how he thought of this place as home now.

Pom pom pom pom pom te pom, he sang, remembering a hymn from his childhood days.

Some time later, as he was finishing the washing-up, the doorbell rang.

On his way to the front door, he realised that one of his lenses must have fallen out again. His sight on one side was blurred, and when he opened the door he couldn't recognise the figure – or perhaps there were two of them – who stood there.

'Is this Kate Ivory's house?'

'Yes it is, but she isn't in, I'm afraid.' He pushed his head forward, trying to focus on the wavering outlines. 'Here! What do you think you are doing?'

'Coming inside.'

Kate and Devlin were up early the next morning after their comparatively abstemious evening and met in the kitchen over breakfast. Devlin as usual tucked into a vast platter of fried food, while Kate stayed with the cereal and fruit. It was after breakfast, while she was studying the map to find the best route to Devon, that the telephone rang. Kim answered it.

'It's for you, Kate,' she said. 'What have you been getting up to? It sounds like the police.'

Chapter Fifteen

It was Harley who found the body and called the police.

He was still sitting on the stairs when they arrived. They entered through the open back door. His face was white and he looked as though he might be sick at any moment.

One of the policemen took him next door to his own house, sat him down in the kitchen and made a cup of tea. All the rest of the Venn family had left for work, school or playgroup. Someone went to fetch Tracey so that they could question Harley. Ten minutes later they returned, Tracey already talking loudly as she came into the kitchen.

'Why are you always picking on my lad?'

'We're not picking on him. We just want to ask him some questions.'

'I know my rights! You can't bully a child like this!'

It took another five minutes to calm her down and persuade her to sit quietly in one corner while they found out what Harley knew.

'Now, tell me what you were doing in that house, lad,' said the policeman.

'It's me dog. They look after it for me, like. And I went round first thing to let him out for a pee, and take him for a walk.'

'You do that every morning?'

'Yeah.'

'How did you get in?'

'I've got me own key while Kate's away.'

'Kate?'

'It's her house, innit?'

'Do you know where she is now?'

'She's off signing her books.'

This information defeated the policeman, who was unused to the habits of authors. Harley explained. 'She writes books, see. And she's off round the book shops, signing them and talking.'

Behind them, Tracey made a disparaging noise that sounded like 'Caw!'

'Can you give me her full name?' asked the policeman, registering the fact that Tracey disapproved of literary types.

'Kate Ivory.'

'Do you know when she gets back?'

'End of next week.'

'And do you know where we can get hold of her?'

'There's a list of places she's going next to the phone.'

'How long after finding the body did you ring the police?'

'Straight away. And I didn't touch nothing, neither.'

'Did you recognise the man lying on the floor?'

'I dunno. I didn't look too close.'

'Who do you think it was?'

'I dunno. It was . . . messy.'

'Yes, all right, I understand.' He hadn't enjoyed looking at the body himself, and he was supposed to be accustomed to such things.

'Who else lived in the house besides Kate Ivory?'

'No one lived here, like, but she had these friends what was always hanging round.'

'Can you give me their names?'

'Well, there's Paul. Paul Taylor. He's the one what helps me with me maths. He's her bloke, like.'

'Do you know where he lives?'

'Nah. It's up Headington somewhere. But I ain't got the address.'

'Do you know where he works?'

'Nah.' This was, strictly, true. He wasn't going to let on that he knew Paul was a policeman.

'And who else is there?'

'Then there's Andrew. He does the cooking, mostly. He was here yesterday evening. He give me me tea, I finished me homework, and then I went home.'

'What's wrong with the tea I give you?' Tracey put in suddenly.

'Nothing.' He didn't point out that she rarely did give him his tea, but handed him a few quid and told him to go and fetch his own from the takeaway.

The policeman frowned. This sounded a most unconventional household. No wonder someone had been battered to death.

'Do you know this man Andrew's surname?'

'Nah.'

'His address?'

'Nah. North Oxford somewhere.'

The policeman sighed. North Oxford was a large area. 'Do you know where he worked or anything else about him?'

'He's just some git who works at the big library. He's a friend of hers.'

'Is that the Central Library in Oxford?'

'No, the other one. The big old place opposite the White Horse.'

'Anyone else?'

'Nah. That's it. Paul, me and Andrew.'

'Might either of these men have stayed overnight?'

'I shouldn't think so. Paul's away on some course at the moment, and Andrew usually pushed off home after he'd finished cooking.'

The policeman made another note. 'Now, you opened the front door with your key. Did you go through into the kitchen and open the back door, as well?'

'No, I didn't get that far. I see him as soon as I get inside. I don't think about nothing else after that.'

'Was the back door usually left open?'

'No. Andrew would have locked and bolted it before going home.'

'Did you touch the body?'

'No! He was dead, wasn't he? I wasn't going near that.'

'How did you know he was dead if you didn't approach the body?'

'There was all this blood. And stuff.'

'Fair enough.'

'Why don't you leave him alone?' shouted Tracey. 'You said you wasn't going to bully him.'

'Drink some of the tea, Harley. I've put plenty of sugar in it. You'll feel better in a minute. Right?'

'Right.'

'And what did you do then?'

'I just went to the phone and rang 999.'

'You did the right thing. Now, stay here, Harley,' he said. 'I'm going to give the boss the information you've given me. You've been very helpful.'

Harley did not seem pleased that the police found him helpful. 'What about Dave?' he asked.

'Who's Dave?'

'He's me dog. And he's still shut in the kitchen. He really needs to go out now. Poor little bugger will be sat there with his legs crossed. You can't expect him to wait no longer. And then I have to get off to school.'

'I should have thought you'd be keen to miss a morning's school.'

'I've done me homework,' said Harley proudly. 'Now, can I go and get Dave?'

'I have to go straight back to Oxford,' said Kate.

'You can't do that. What about me?' Devlin was incorrigible.

'You want me to drive to Oxford via Devon?'

'What's the rush? Why do you have to go home? Can't it wait?'

'No. That was the police on the phone just now. They've found a dead body in my hallway.'

'Well, if he's dead there's no point in hurrying, is there? There's obviously nothing you can do to help.' Devlin spoke as if finding dead bodies in one's house was an everyday occurrence. And given Devlin's life-style and propensity for making enemies, maybe it was, at that. Kate started to leave the room. She had to pack. She had to get away.

'Wait a minute! Kim will make you some more coffee. You can't go off like that. You're in a dreadful state.'

He was right. If she drove while she was feeling like this, she would wrap her car round the nearest telegraph pole. She came back and sat down at the kitchen table. Kim, reading the situation, brought more coffee.

'Have some sugar in it,' she said.

'All right.' Kate spooned it in.

'Now, all I'm suggesting is that you should ring Aisling and tell her what has happened. Then we can make arrangements. Really, rushing off to Oxford isn't the best thing at all at the moment.'

There was something in what Devlin said. Kate sipped at the coffee. The caffeine might be doing her nerves no good, but the sugar was helping to calm her down.

'You sit here and relax,' said Devlin. 'I'll speak to Aisling.'

He was being far too kind. Kate didn't trust him one little bit. On the other hand, she was grateful that just for the moment someone else was taking over, making decisions and telling her what to do. At least it gave her a chance to sort out in her own mind what had happened. She ran over the telephone conversation with the policeman. He had told her his name and rank but she had been in no state to remember them. Then what had he said?

Harley Venn had discovered a dead body in her hallway when he came in to fetch Dave that morning. No, they had no official identification of the body yet. Harley hadn't brought himself to look closely at the body, but had given them plenty of information about the set-up in the house. They would be happy if she returned as soon as possible and told them whether she recognised the deceased.

'Is it a man or a woman?' she had asked.

'A man.'

'Well, what else? What does he look like?'

A pause. 'I'm afraid I can't tell you anything more about him at the moment.'

'Why not?'

'I have no further information on the subject.'

'Can you tell me how he died? Was it a heart attack or what?'

'A doctor has been called. We'll know the answer to that question when he has made his report.'

Brick walls were easier to talk to. 'Is Harley all right?' she asked.

'Yes. The lad was keen to get to school, so we let him go. He's been very helpful so far.'

'I'm glad to hear it. He's a good kid.'

'Yes, he is. And unusually articulate for a boy that age.'

So Kate and Andrew's training was bearing fruit. She felt as proud as if Harley had been her own son.

'When can we expect you back in Oxford?'

'Now,' she answered. 'Straight away. I'll be there as soon as I can.'

Devlin returned to the kitchen.

'I've spoken to Aisling,' he said. 'We've consulted the map, and we've decided where we can all meet. Then you can continue to Oxford, and Aisling can drive me to Barnstaple.'

'Barnstaple?' It made no sense to Kate.

'Barnstaple in Devon. The next venue on our scheduled tour, remember?'

'Oh yes.'

'Don't worry. We've worked it all out.'

'Good. Can I go now?'

'Kate. Listen to me.' Devlin spoke very slowly and clearly. This was good, thought Kate. She might be able to understand what he was saying if he spoke slowly enough. At the moment all his words were hidden behind the monstrous thought that there was a dead body in her hallway at home. Was it a stranger? Or was it someone she knew? She didn't dare consider the possibilities.

'Kate,' Devlin was saying. 'We – you and I – are now going to drive to Cheltenham. Aisling is setting out for the same destination. It will take her about two hours to get there. It is only twenty-five miles or so from here, so it will take us less than an hour. We have time to pack.'

'Cheltenham?' asked Kate at last. 'I've been there. Whereabouts in Cheltenham?'

'The Moathouse. You don't have to drive into the town, it's on the outskirts.'

'That's good.' Things were nearly making sense to her at last.

'Then you can drive to Oxford. It should take you about an hour.'

'An hour,' she repeated.

'If you're up to it.'

'And if I'm not?'

'I expect we can find you a train.'

'I'll be all right by then. I'll make an effort.'

'Good.'

'And what are you going to do?'

'Aisling will drive me to Barnstaple. At the speed she goes, it will barely take a couple of hours. Here are our phone numbers. The first one is the number for the book shop. The second is the number of our digs. And here, I've written down the addresses for you. When you find out what's happening back in Oxford, give us a ring, and we can make arrangements to meet up again.'

'You want me to carry on with the tour?'

'Of course. Isn't that what you want?'

'I hadn't considered it.'

'You won't want to stick around the place, will you? There'll be policemen swarming all over the house.'

Policemen. Paul Taylor. What if he was the one lying dead on the floor?

'*Kate!*'

'Sorry. What were you saying?'

'Wall-to-wall blue uniforms. Fuzz. Your house will be full of men in white overalls, dusting grey powder over everything. How did the bugger die, by the way?'

'I don't know. They wouldn't tell me.'

'If there was much blood, you'll have to get the carpet cleaned.'

'Don't be disgusting.'

'I'm being realistic. I'm telling you that once you've told the police what you know – which can't be very much since you were here at the book shop and in the local pub all yesterday evening – it would be much better for you to be away from the place while it gets examined and cleaned up.'

'I suppose that makes sense.'

'Of course it does. Trust your Uncle Devlin. And if you're going to be away from Oxford, you might as well be on your book tour.'

'Smiling and talking and shaking hands with complete strangers.'

'It will be good for you. An hour or two's heavy smiling, and you won't be able to think of anything at all.'

She laughed.

'That's better. Seriously, though, getting back to work is the best thing you could do. What would you be doing otherwise? Sitting and brooding, or staring at the spot on the carpet where he breathed his last.'

'Who can it be?'

'We won't know that until you've taken a look at him. If indeed you do know him, of course. Though it seems unlikely that a complete stranger would let himself into your house just so that he could die on your best Axminster.'

'Yes, that's what I'm afraid of.' It was easier to think that he might be a stranger.

'Where are we supposed to be going after Barnstaple?' she asked.

'Somewhere down near the South Coast. Sussex, I think.'

'I could get there quite easily, couldn't I?'

'Of course you could.'

'You and Aisling are being very good to me.'

'All part of the service. Like I say, give us a bell when you know what's been happening. I'd prefer it if you didn't make it in the middle of my best anecdote, though.'

Kate raised a faint smile, then finished her coffee and went upstairs to pack.

She got half way through ramming clothes into her suitcase when it occurred to her that she could get hold of Paul by telephoning him. If she asked him to, surely he would drop everything and rush to her side. If there was one person you needed at a time like this, it was a policeman. She hadn't got his London number but his own office would have it. She ran downstairs and dialled his Oxford office number.

'Yes, that's right, my name is Kate Ivory. I'm an old friend of his. A close friend. No, I haven't got his

London number because I didn't ask him for it. He's only away for a couple of days or so and I didn't think it was important. Yes, well, now it is. Very important indeed.' *Why don't you just give me his sodding phone number!* 'You have heard of me? You can? That's very kind of you. Yes, I've got a pencil and paper. Thank you. Goodbye.'

She dialled again.

'Denton Management Training.'

'Hello. Can I speak to Paul Taylor, please.'

'Who?'

'He's on a course. The Oxford police station gave me your number to contact him.'

'On a course. Yes. Well, I'm afraid that all the participants on our training course are out at the present time taking part in the practical component of their course, so I am unable to call Mr Taylor to the telephone.'

'When will he be back?'

'I really can't answer that.'

'Can you take a message for him?'

'I will try to see that he gets it.' The voice at the end of the phone inspired no confidence in Kate.

'My name is Kate Ivory. I am returning in a couple of hours to my house in Oxford. Will he please ring me there as soon as possible. It's urgent.'

'I'm sure it is,' said the voice soothingly. 'Goodbye, Ms Ivory.' Click.

If he didn't ring her back soon after she arrived in Oxford, she would phone Smug Management Training and insist on speaking to him until someone got off their bum and found him for her. At least they hadn't said that they'd never heard of him, or that he hadn't turned up this morning. Really, it wasn't likely that the body in her house was Paul. Really.

She dialled again.

'Hello. Bodleian Library?'

'Could you find Andrew Grove for me, please?'

'I'll try, madam.' He didn't sound keen.

'Please do. It's important.' Her voice came out high and breathy.

She waited. At least no one was playing canned Vivaldi in her ear. She waited for a long time. Had she been cut off?

'I'm sorry, madam, but I am unable to locate Mr Grove. It is possible that he is on his coffee break. Would you like to try again later?'

'Yes. Thank you.' She wanted to tell him to scour all the reading rooms and the staff common room, but she thought he might find the request unreasonable. The Bodleian was a big place. Andrew was bound to be there somewhere.

'Now, there's no problem about getting there in time,' said Devlin, when they had stowed their bags in Kate's car. 'It isn't far to Cheltenham, and we know where the Moathouse is. So you can take it really steady.'

Kate did up her seat belt and switched on the ignition. Her hands were shaking.

'I think you'd better pull into this lay-by,' said Devlin, after they had driven a couple of hundred yards. 'I'm not normally a nervous passenger, but I don't think you're in any fit state to drive.'

'What do you suggest we do?' asked Kate when they had drawn to a halt.

'We'll swap places. I'll drive. You can navigate.'

'But what about insurance?'

'It's legal to drive on mine, and what can happen in twenty-five miles?'

They changed places and Devlin switched on the engine again. 'Oh dear,' he said. 'I didn't realise that reverse was over there. What a funny place to put it.'

They emerged from the lay-by in a series of bounds. 'Just getting used to the gears,' said Devlin.

As they joined the traffic on the main road, car horns blared at them.

'Where did you say the indicators are?' asked Devlin.

Kate decided that she would be happier with her eyes closed.

There was a nasty crunching sound as Devlin changed gear. 'And it's no good closing your eyes. You have to look out for the signs for the M5. It's your turn to navigate, if you remember.'

Kate opened her eyes and looked out for signposts. 'Next turning to the left,' she said. Indicators blinked on each side of the car in turn and there was another unpleasant gear change.

'Don't worry,' said Devlin. 'I'm getting the hang of it.'

He stalled the engine while waiting to get on to the roundabout, changed lanes so often that Kate got used to the sound of horns and the sight of fists waving at them. It all helped to keep her mind off what was waiting for her in Oxford.

'Now, Kate, are you sure you're safe to drive?'

Aisling was wearing electric blue today, and the colour made Kate's head hurt.

'Oh yes.' Her driving had to be better than Devlin's, and somehow he had got them here. She wasn't sure that her car would ever be the same again, but perhaps a nice quiet drive to Oxford would soothe its ruffled feelings.

'I'll explain what's happened to Deborah Merch when I see her. I'm sure she'll understand why you can't make it this evening and forgive you.'

'Why should she have to forgive me?'

'You don't want to get a reputation for not turning up to engagements. You soon find that you no longer get the invitations. People like to know where they are.'

'And that's another reason to get back on the tour as soon as possible, I suppose.'

'Only if you feel you can, Kate. If you feel you can.'

'I have the telephone numbers. I'll be in touch as soon as possible.'

'Good. Well, Devlin and I will be on our way. Drive safely, Kate.'

She was feeling better by the minute. She did like her own company in the car, anyway, and had been growing tired of the constant companionship of Devlin Hayle.

'Goodbye, Aisling. Goodbye, Devlin.' More kissing in the air and they were off.

Chapter Sixteen

It was just after two o'clock in the afternoon when Kate got back to Fridesley. She drove cautiously down Agatha Street looking for somewhere to park. There was nowhere, and she had to leave her car round the corner in Fridesley Lane.

There was a police constable standing in front of her door, and yellow tape preventing anyone from getting closer than the front gate. Next door, little Toad-face – sorry, Tyler – had his nose squashed flat against the window pane, watching everything that was happening. It wasn't yet time for Harley to be back from school, but she found she was looking forward to seeing him.

'You can't come in, Miss,' said the policeman.

'I live here,' said Kate. 'I believe one of your officers wants to see me about what's happened.'

When she took in the policeman and the tape, and even little Toadface glued to the window, she realised that her last hope of it being a question of a natural death had fled. The police thought it was a crime, that was obvious.

She ducked under the tape, the policeman stood to one side, and she went into her house.

But it no longer seemed like her house. There was a chalked outline on the hall carpet and a dark stain that looked like blood. Devlin was right, she thought, the carpet will have to be cleaned.

'The inspector would like a word,' the policeman called after her.

'Fine,' she said.

'You can wait in the front room,' he said.

'Thank you.' Thank you for allowing me to wait in my own sitting room.

If the hallway had seemed an alien place, the sitting room in contrast seemed all too normal. There were the left-over birthday cards on top of her bureau. Someone had forgotten a nearly empty wine glass on the bookshelf. The knot-ring lay where she had left it on the coffee table. A discarded page of Harley's homework had drifted to the floor. If she looked carefully at the pink velvet sofa she would doubtless find dog and cat fur. Susannah, the ginger cat, was there, curled up on a cushion. She sat down beside her and stroked the top of her head. Susannah started to purr. Damn. Kate found she had stuffed her knuckles into her mouth to stop herself from crying, like a child. Though whether she was crying for the death of the unknown man, or for the despoiling of her house, she did not know.

She forced herself to walk over to the phone and check the messages. There were none. So Paul hadn't phoned her back yet. No need to get worried: the stuffed shirt at the management training place had probably failed to pass on the message. She listened. There were people in the dining room, but no one had come to see her yet. She checked the number and dialled.

'Denton Management Training.'

'I wonder if I could speak to Paul Taylor. He's on one of your courses.'

'Just one moment.'

She listened to canned baroque music through the earpiece for a couple of minutes.

'I'm sorry, madam, we don't appear to have anyone of that name here at present.'

'What do you mean? This is the number I was given by his office. Aren't you running a course on dealing with difficult people.'

'I'm afraid not, madam. Someone has been having a joke with you, I would say.'

'No! Please check again. It's very important. Have you got the name right? Taylor. Paul.'

'Very well, madam. Please wait another few moments.'

This wasn't a man, it was a robot, she fumed as she listened to more of the Muzak.

'I have double-checked, madam, and we have no one of that name with us at present. And we do not offer a course such as the one you mentioned.'

'Thank you,' she said, and replaced the receiver. Her stomach was churning. Why did Paul lie to her? Why didn't he telephone? Could he possibly be the one who had died in her hall?

The door opened and the inspector came in.

'I'm Detective Inspector Cartwright. Eva Cart-wright.' Kate had been expecting a man, she realised.

'And you want to ask me some questions. Why don't you sit down in the green armchair?' Kate had decided to keep the initiative in her own house instead of allowing herself to be bossed around. Susannah moved on to her knee and she stroked the cat absentmindedly as she gave her answers.

'Who was it?' asked Kate.

'I'm sorry?'

'Do you know yet who died in my hall?'

'No, we don't. Not for certain. We're hoping that you can help us with a positive identification. If you could just fill me in on a few details first, we could go down to the mortuary and you could view the body.'

'Very well. Let's get it over.' She had to know if it was Paul, or anyone else that she knew.

'If we could start with your full name, date of birth and occupation, please.'

Kate gave them.

'Marital status?'

'Single.'

'You've never been married?'

'No. What possible relevance has this got?'

'Please be patient and bear with me. It's a question of formalities. Now, you've lived here for how long?'

'About five years.'

'On your own all that time?'

'Yes.'

'Several people seem to have keys to your front door. Why is that?'

'I don't see that it's your business.'

'I'm afraid that everything is our business in an enquiry like this.'

'Oh, all right then.' She could hear her voice rising towards hysteria. She took several slow, deep breaths and forced herself to control it. 'First there's Harley. He's the thirteen-year-old from next door. I look after his dog for him when he's at school because his mother's new boyfriend doesn't like dogs. And he stays on in the evenings to do his homework, because it's quieter here – usually it's quieter – and there's someone on hand to help him when he gets stuck.'

'Harley Venn,' said Eva Cartwright. 'We've met him already. Who's next?'

'Next comes Andrew Grove. He's an old friend of mine who has recently split up with his girlfriend. He comes round here for the company, and because he has taken up cooking and uses us as tasters for his new recipes. He's one of those who help Harley with his homework.'

'Do you know anything else about him?'

'He's in his forties, I suppose. He works at the Bodleian, in their Theology Department. I think he's been there for years. Probably grew up and went to school in the place by the look of him.'

'Thank you. Is there anyone else who has a key? Any other neighbours?'

'Harley's the only neighbour I know, really, and I've already told you about him.'

'So there are no other keys?'

'There's another friend of mine. A man called Taylor.'

'Does he have a first name, or is that it?'

'Paul Taylor. He's a good friend.'

'Have you his address?'

Kate hesitated for a moment, and then gave it. 'He's away at the moment. On a course.'

Eva Cartwright asked no more about Paul Taylor.

'Did any of your friends ever stay here overnight?'

'Andrew usually went home to his own flat. He only stayed if he'd had too much to drink to drive home. Then he used the spare room.'

'I see.'

Kate kept quiet about Paul staying. You never knew about policemen: Paul might want to keep his relationship with her a secret, for all she knew. It was a common enough name and perhaps she didn't recognise it as a fellow police officer's. God! She wished he was here with her. Where the hell was he and why had he lied to her? And why didn't his office know where he was, if it came to that?

'Well, I think I have a clear enough idea for now. There are probably some more questions I'll have to ask you eventually, but that will do for the moment. Do you feel ready to come and identify the body?'

'You think I'll be able to?'

'I really don't know, but since this is your home it is a reasonable assumption that you'll know who it is.'

'Don't you want to ask me what I was doing yesterday?' Kate realised that she was putting off the moment when she would have to go to the mortuary.

She wondered what the Inspector would think of someone who volunteered information like this.

'I thought you were away on a book tour. Isn't that what Harley told us?'

'Yes, I was. I can give you the name and address of the book shop, if you like. And the name of the pub where Devlin Hayle and I went to eat afterwards.'

'Devlin Hayle? "The Man Who Understands a Woman's Heart"?'

'Yes, that's the one. Do you want me to get you his autograph?'

'Would you? That would be great.'

'No problem.'

They were out of the house and Kate was getting into the back of the police car. It was not very far to the mortuary.

'Well?' asked Inspector Cartwright. 'Do you know who it is?'

'Yes,' said Kate. 'I do.'

'Can you give me his name?'

'It's Andrew Grove. My friend. Andrew.'

'And you're absolutely sure?'

'Yes.'

Inspector Cartwright nodded to an attendant, who started to slide the drawer back into its refrigerated niche. 'Let's get out of here,' she said. 'We can go up to my office and I can start filling in forms.'

'Just a moment. I'd like to stay a minute or two with my friend, if you don't mind.'

She stood for a while, looking at the scrubbed steel surfaces, breathing in the chemical smell of the place, which reminded her of long-ago science lessons at school. Then at last she brought herself to look down at the still form in its metal container. Someone had cleaned him up, she imagined, before she was asked to look at him. There was something unnatural about the angle of his head, however, as though ... no, she wouldn't think about that. She would try to remember him as he was when she had last seen him. Andrew was gone. This pallid figure was just an empty shell. She had heard it so often, and read it in books, but she had never before realised just what it meant.

'Goodbye, Andrew,' she said.

Chapter Seventeen

'Could you bring Miss Ivory a cup of tea, please, Dave?' said Inspector Cartwright.

Miss Ivory would rather have had a large brandy and a packet of Kleenex, and then she would have liked to be left on her own for a few hours. Instead, she was sitting in Inspector Cartwright's uncomfortable visitor's chair, in Inspector Cartwright's cluttered office, putting a brave face on it.

'How did he die?' she asked.

'I haven't got the full details yet, but it looks as though he was hit on the head with something heavy: a large spanner, a tyre lever, something like that.'

'I see.'

'He would have died instantly. He wouldn't have suffered.'

Kate had an idea that they always said that, whether it was true or not.

'Now, what can you tell us about Mr Grove?'

'In addition to what I've told you already? Not very much, really.' How could you sum up a life in a few words? He could be pompous, he enjoyed his food, he felt at home in her house. What would any of that mean to an outsider?

'Had he any close relatives?'

Kate racked her brains. Hadn't he mentioned an ancient mother in a nursing home somewhere? She told Inspector Cartwright about it.

'We can check on that. There should be an address for her among his papers in his flat.'

'I'm not sure she's all there. I believe that her memory was going to pieces. She didn't always recognise Andrew when he went to see her.'

'That's a pity. It doesn't sound as though she'll be able to tell us much.'

'Probably not.'

'Do you know whether Mr Grove had any enemies?'

'I shouldn't think so. He was quite tough with the undergraduates when it was needed, but otherwise he was an easy-going man. He liked going to concerts and to the opera. He enjoyed sitting at home listening to his CDs. He spent time reading. I believe that he occasionally played real tennis. I can't imagine that he had an exciting enough life to make enemies.'

'What sort of enemies does a librarian make?' mused Eva Cartwright. 'You don't usually murder the man who fines you thirty pence for returning your library book a week late, do you?'

'At the Bodleian you don't even get fined for that,' said Kate. 'They don't let you take their books off the premises in the first place. Not even if you're King Charles the First.'

Eva Cartwright looked as though she needed an explanation of that last comment, but Kate failed to give it to her.

'Had he ever been married, do you know? Did he have any children?'

'I don't think he liked the sort of women who made good wife material. And he hated children, so I'd be very surprised if he had ever fathered one.'

'Who knew that Mr Grove would be at your house?'

'Not many people. Harley, certainly. And Paul. I don't know whether Andrew told anyone, but I don't see that it would have come up in casual conversation. I suppose anyone who recognised his car would have seen it outside my house and guessed that he was there.'

'But his car wasn't outside your house.'

'Really? Well, perhaps he was planning to stay overnight in my spare room and walk in to work today.'

'Didn't he usually drive over, then?'

'Usually, yes. But recently he'd taken to walking if the weather was fine. It's only two or three miles. Have you found his car?'

'It's parked outside his own house. I just wanted to make sure that this was normal behaviour for him.'

'Quite normal.'

'So, except for the people who knew that you would be away, anyone visiting the house would expect to find you in, rather than Andrew Grove.'

'I suppose that's right.' She hadn't thought of that before.

'When was the tour arranged?'

'Last week.'

'Isn't that rather short notice?'

'I think someone dropped out, and they asked me to fill in.' Oh dear, it did make her sound feeble.

'Just one more thing.'

'Yes?'

'Can you write down for me a list of Mr Grove's friends? We'll check with his colleagues at the Bodleian, of course, and we'll see if he belonged to a real tennis club, but your knowledge of his private life would be of great help to us.'

'I'll do my best.'

'Anyone you can think of. Any contact of his.'

'Like the name of the pub where he played darts?'

'Yes. That's the sort of thing. Thank you. I know this must be difficult for you.'

'Do you want me to do it now?'

'If you feel up to it. You can always add on any names that you've forgotten later.'

'I'd like to do anything that helps to find who killed Andrew.'

'And something else. Did the house look as though a burglar had been in?'

'It looked just as I left it. Tidier, possibly.'

'That's what we thought. But that is one idea: that a burglar thought the house would be empty and was surprised by Mr Grove, panicked, and hit him too hard.'

'It seems the most likely story. Likelier than thinking up homicidal enemies for him, anyway.'

'So could you look around when you get home and see if anything is missing, or even if anything looks as though it has been disturbed. The usual method is to throw everything out on to the floor – drawers, shelves, cupboards – and then look through it to see what is worth taking.'

'That certainly didn't happen. But I'll let you know if anything is missing.'

'Thank you. Well, I'll leave you now. Dave will give you a lift home when you've finished writing your list.'

'Will you tell me how he died when you know the answer?'

'Very well.'

'And do you need me here for the next week? My publishers are anxious that I should continue with the book tour.'

'Just make sure that we know how to contact you at any time. But I think you've probably told us all that's necessary for the moment.'

Kate was left with the impression that she would be the one giving any information that was going. Inspector Cartwright was unlikely to let anything out.

When Kate arrived in Agatha Street, she couldn't face going back into her house. Her bags were still packed and in her car, and she wondered whether there wasn't some friend she could stay with that night.

But first she had to see Harley.

She knocked on the Venns' door. Little Toadface had disappeared from the window and was presumably watching his latest horror video in the front room.

Jace opened the door. He didn't smile at Kate. She

didn't think he smiled at anybody. 'Is Harley in?' she asked.

'Yeah.' Then he called into the house: 'Trace! It's the Ivory woman, looking for our Harley.'

Tracey appeared, her hair newly bleached, possibly so that she would show up on the television news.

'Yeah?'

'I'd like to speak to Harley if he's in.'

'No, I don't know about that. You've got him mixed up in this murder business and it's not very nice, is it? It's not the sort of thing we like. He was proper upset when he come back from school. Well, he would be, wouldn't he, finding a dead man like that.'

'I'm very sorry about that, Mrs Venn.' They had been on Tracey and Kate terms before, but Kate felt it was diplomatic to be more formal in this situation.

'Well, it's not as though he passed away from natural causes, is it? Someone had bashed his head in, so our Harley says. And there was blood and brains and that all over the carpet. Well, that's not nice for a kid to find.'

'I'm really sorry about that, Mrs Venn.' She was getting upset about it herself, and she hadn't seen the body in that state, the way Harley had.

'No, I think it's best if he just sits here and watches his video,' said Tracey. 'He needs something to take his mind off of it for him. It wouldn't do him no good to be talking to you.'

At this minute, Harley appeared, silently, behind Tracey's back and gestured to Kate over his mother's head. Kate interpreted his sign language as 'Meet me in the rec. in five minutes', but she went on nodding at Tracey, and agreeing with everything she said.

'It's bad enough us having to have that dog back in the house,' she was saying. 'Jace just don't like dogs. It's not in his nature to like them. There's nothing he can do about it.'

'Don't worry, Mrs Venn, just as soon as I can, I'll be looking after Dave again and you and Jace won't have to bother about him.'

'And who's going to pay for his food in the meantime, I'd like to know? I can't do it on my housekeeping money, and Jace isn't going to give me extra to feed a bleeding dog, is he?'

'No, of course he isn't. There are lots of tins of dog food in my kitchen, Mrs Venn. I'll make sure that they're brought round here for Dave.'

Tracey seemed to have run out of steam for the moment. Harley had disappeared from behind her. So Kate said, 'Well, I'll say goodbye now, Mrs Venn. I expect I'll see you again soon.'

'Yes, well then. You just watch out,' said Tracey. Though who or what Kate was to watch out for, she didn't say.

Kate found Harley sitting on one of the swings in the recreation ground in Fridesley Lane.

'How did you get out?' she asked him.

'I said Dave needed a crap,' he said. 'He did, too.'

'Where is he now?'

'Over in those bushes. He'll come back when I call him.'

Kate nearly asked Harley whether he had done his homework yet, but it seemed unimportant compared with everything else that had happened. Perhaps soon there would come a time when things like homework would matter again, but for the moment Andrew's death took precedence.

It was growing dark, the way it did in February, with the temperature dropping rapidly as the light left the sky. But they sat, each on a swing, and stared at the featureless green grass, not saying anything for a while.

'How are you doing?' Kate asked at last.

'All right.'

They both swung backwards and forwards for a while longer.

'Do you want to talk about it?'

'If you like.'

'I was more concerned with what you wanted, Harley.'

'It turned me up when I found him.'

'Yes, it would have done the same to me.'

'Do you know for sure who it was?' asked Harley.

She hadn't realised that he wouldn't have been told. 'Andrew,' she said.

'Yeah. I thought it must be. I didn't like to get too close, but when I thought about it after, that's what I reckoned.'

'Can you tell me a bit about it? I'd like to know as much as possible, even if it is unpleasant.'

'Well, I come in through the front door as usual,' said Harley.

'You used your key? The door was locked?'

'Yeah. And it's the first thing I see. Laying there on the carpet, all crumpled up.'

'Which way was he facing?'

'It was like he'd been looking towards the sitting room. But there was all blood and that.'

Kate didn't ask him to specify what 'that' was. Harley's face was white in the near darkness.

'Did the police ask you if you knew him?'

'Yeah. And I tell them I dunno.'

'You hadn't heard anything before? Yesterday evening or during the night?'

'Screams and that?'

'The police think he may have disturbed a burglar. I looked around the house and couldn't find anything missing. The television and video recorder are still there, and so is my computer. Nothing looks as though it's been touched. Did you hear anything at all from next door?'

'Nah. Nothing.'

'And Dave didn't bark?'

'Nah. But he wouldn't bother to bark at anyone, would he?'

'No, I suppose not. He just wags his tail and grovels on the floor.'

'Stupid bugger,' said Harley affectionately.

'Oh, by the way, you can collect Dave's food from my kitchen cupboard as soon as the police will let you go into the place. Your mother is a bit worried about how to feed him while he's at your place. You've still got your key?'

'Yeah.'

'I suppose we'd better be getting back.'

'Yeah. Kate?'

'What?'

'Is Paul back yet?'

'I wish he was. I tried to get hold of him, but no luck. I've left messages for him to phone back but I don't have much hope he'll get them. He's due back tomorrow, but I don't suppose he'll be able to talk to us about the case. What's up? Do you need help with your maths?'

'Nah, it's not that. It's just that— '

But at this moment there was a shout from Agatha Street: *'Harley!'*

'That's my mum,' said Harley.

'Harley! Get yer arse back 'ere, yer little bugger!'

'I think she wishes you to return home,' said Kate.

'I reckon she does,' said Harley.

He whistled for Dave, who appeared as if by magic at his knee, and loped off towards home.

'See ya!' he called out of the dark to Kate.

'See ya!' she called back.

Chapter Eighteen

The first person Kate thought of when she needed a bed for the night was her friend Camilla. Camilla lived just round the corner in Fridesley Lane, and she and Kate still went jogging together when they were both in the mood for some exercise. Camilla made a big fuss about her size and weight, but really they were nothing out of the ordinary.

She knocked at the cottage door. No reply. Surely Camilla couldn't be away from Fridesley during term time? She was headmistress of a posh girls' school and needed to be at her post, making sure that her charges were not doing anything their parents would disapprove of. She and Kate had been friends since the age of twelve.

Kate knocked again on the cottage door.

A light came on in the porch and the door opened.

'Hello,' said Camilla. 'I thought it would be you. Sorry I took so long, I was sorting out the paper for recycling. What's been happening in Agatha Street? The place has been thick with the fuzz.'

'Can I come in?' asked Kate.

'Of course,' said Camilla.

'I'm not disturbing anything? Carey isn't here, is he?'

'No, he isn't. And all you're disturbing is the writing of a hundred and thirty reports. So what the hell!'

'I need somewhere to stay tonight.'

'You know you can have my spare room.'

'I'll bring my overnight bag in.'

Good old Camilla. She had the right priorities in life, like giving Kate a roof over her head when she needed it. She would ask questions afterwards. Kate had parked her car outside the cottage, just off the road, and now she fetched her bag.

'Carey's in London,' said Camilla. 'I know you wanted to ask but were too polite to do so. He hasn't left me yet. He's visiting his mother for a couple of days. He's probably borrowing money from her, if truth be told, but that's their affair.'

Carey was Camilla's toy boy. No, she mustn't think of him like that. Camilla and Carey had been loosely 'together' for nearly four years now, which was longer than a lot of marriages these days. And when had she, Kate, had a satisfactory relationship for that long? But Carey was young and good-looking, and had an irresponsible attitude to life that was at variance with Camilla's own solid and respectable state. He was about twelve years younger in years, but a whole generation in attitudes. And it was this difference, rather than their ages, that made the relationship such an odd one.

'So, why were all those bluebottles crawling over your house in Agatha Street?' asked Camilla.

'You noticed.' Perhaps young Carey was having an influence on her speech, at that.

'Couldn't fail to. And Mrs Clack has been glorying in it all day. There have been some very lurid stories passed around, I can tell you. What is it all about?'

'Well, you know that I've been away for a couple of days on a book tour.'

'No, you didn't tell me about it.'

'It was only arranged last week.'

'That was short notice.'

Kate was tired of telling people, even Camilla, that she was an afterthought, a second-best choice, so she ignored the comment and went on with the grim facts. 'Harley let himself into the house this morning to feed Dave and take him for his early morning walk, and he found Andrew dead in the hallway.'

'Good God! What was it? A heart attack? He had been putting on a bit of weight recently, hadn't he? Poor old bugger.'

'He wasn't very old. Only forty-six. And no, it wasn't a heart attack. He had been beaten over the head with something like a large spanner.'

'How awful! Whoever would do that to Andrew?'

'That's what we'd all like to know.'

'And *why*, for goodness' sake?'

'Another question it's impossible to answer.'

'I just can't take it in. Dear old Andrew, of all people!' She stood up. 'Should I get us cups of sweet tea, or do you want something stronger?'

'Stronger, definitely.'

'White wine?'

'Fine.'

Camilla disappeared into the kitchen and returned with glasses and a misted wine bottle. She poured them each a generous measure. 'I know it's a ridiculous thing to say, but when we met at your house a couple of weeks ago, he was so *alive.*'

'I can't get used to the idea, either. He was in and out of my house all the time since he and Isabel broke up, cooking food, filling in the crossword puzzle in my newspaper.'

'He cooked the night Carey and I last came round. And delicious it was, too. And ambitious.'

'Do you remember how tight-lipped he was when he first met you and Carey together?'

'Carey was at his most outrageous, and I had come straight from a parents' meeting and was wearing a matronly blue suit.'

'Carey saw the effect he was having, so he started to demonstrate his skill at juggling, and told Andrew how easy it was to make money busking.'

'He was wearing artistically torn jeans and a shirt that he bought in Turkey.'

'And his amazing sun tan.'

'I tried to tell Andrew that Carey was a post-graduate student rather than a street person, but that only made it worse. I'd forgotten that Carey's father was Warden of Andrew's own college. He was so upset when he found out.'

'Poor Andrew! He was so easy to wind up,' said Kate. 'We shouldn't have done it so often.'

'Don't worry about it now. I expect he saw it as a mark of affection.'

'Do you really think so?'

'Of course. He had a lovely time at your place, pretending to be Harley's father, cooking you lovely meals. Which reminds me, have you eaten?'

'Not for a very long time.'

'Well, come into the kitchen and finish your wine while I throw something together. You probably need comfort food after news like that.'

'Have you got any chocolate biscuits?'

'The tin's over there on the dresser. Help yourself. There's ice cream in the freezer, too, for serious comfort eating. And an aerosol can of cream to squirt all over it.'

'Sounds wonderful. But I need to make a couple of brief phone calls first.'

'Use the phone over on the wall, unless you want to be private.'

'This one's fine.'

Kate called Aisling at the Barnstaple number she'd been given by Devlin. God! That seemed so long ago!

'It's Kate. You were right, Aisling. I don't want to stay here any longer than I have to. There's nothing much I can do to help, anyway. Who was it? An old friend of mine, actually. He was hit over the head with a heavy implement of some kind. But I feel uncomfortable in that house and I'd like to get away. I shall join you in Sussex tomorrow. I've got the name of the book shop and the address. Four o'clock? Fine.'

The she rang the police station and gave a sergeant

the information that she was going away from Oxford, and read out the list of places she would be visiting and the phone numbers on which she could be contacted if necessary.

'I don't suppose there would be much you could do here, Miss,' the sergeant said. 'It will do you good to get away. You enjoy yourself.'

Kate wasn't sure she could manage that, but it would be good to get away, certainly. Then, on an impulse, she made another call, this time to Paul's office.

'I'm trying to get in touch with Paul Taylor,' she said. 'Do you know where he is?'

'I'm sorry, madam, I don't have that information.'

She was sure it was the same man as before. 'You gave me a telephone number earlier,' she said, 'but when I rang they said they hadn't heard of him. Do you think you could try again to find a contact number for me?'

'I'm sorry, madam,' he repeated. 'I have no way of contacting him at present, but I think you will find that he will be back tomorrow.' Under the polite veneer, she sensed that he was highly amused that this unknown female was chasing after Paul.

'Goodbye.' She tried hard not to slam the receiver back into its rest.

'Now,' she said to Camilla. 'Lead me to the comfort food. Have you got any doughnuts?'

In fact, Camilla produced pizza and green salad, and then let Kate pig out on the ice cream. She poured wine into their glasses at frequent intervals. Kate needed to relax and get a long night's sleep, she thought.

Eventually Camilla said, 'Was it a thief, do you think?'

'The police asked about that. But I checked to see if anything was taken, and all the obvious things like the video recorder and the computer were still there. Nothing had been disturbed as far as I could see, but with Harley, Paul and Andrew in and out of the house all the time, it is possible that something had been moved. Actually, there was one small thing that didn't seem quite right. It's been niggling me, but I can't quite put my finger on it.'

'I expect it will come back to you if you get a good night's sleep,' said Camilla, getting out camomile tea and making them both a cup. 'Do you know when it happened?'

'It must have been yesterday evening, I believe. The police are giving very little away, but Andrew would have gone home before his bedtime, I know. He wouldn't have stayed in my house unless he had a clean shirt and a change of underwear with him, and I didn't find anything like that in the spare room.'

'Are you a suspect?'

'I can't be. I've told them where I was and who I was with. They can check on that, no problem.'

'What about the funeral?'

'I didn't ask about that. I suppose I should have done. As far as I know he had no close relations, so it's up to his friends to arrange it. Goodness knows when we can hold it. I suppose the police will let us know.'

'You'll just have to leave it to them now. There's nothing else you can do, is there?'

'No, you're right. Is there any more of that chocolate ice cream?'

'Yes. And there's the one with lumps of morello cherries in, too.'

'That is definitely what I need. What is this stuff we're drinking?'

'Camomile tea, to make us sleep.'

'It tastes disgusting.'

'Drink it up. It's good for you.'

There were times when Camilla sounded just like a schoolmistress.

Kate felt a lot better the next morning. For a moment, just after she woke up, she felt happy. Then she remembered what had happened, and the dark cloud descended again. But the day was cold and bright, with a frost that coated the recreation field and dusted the hedgerows. It was a morning that made you feel good to be alive, and she stood at the window thinking about the friend of hers who would never see it.

Identifying his body had made his death a reality for her. She had no feeling that he might walk through the door at any moment, offering her some delicacy he had just prepared in the kitchen. The face she had seen in the mortuary had been carefully presented to her so that she wouldn't be upset by the sight, but it had looked like a mask of Andrew, not the real person. Everything that made him Andrew had long departed.

She went downstairs to make herself some breakfast.

Camilla had gone to school and left a note for her, saying goodbye. When she had eaten and drunk enough coffee, she stripped her bed and put the sheets through the washing machine. Camilla had a hard day at school and, anyway, was not too keen on housework at the best of times. She washed up her breakfast things and packed up her nightshirt and toothbrush. Then she checked the route down to Sussex.

Back to the grindstone, she told herself, as she belted herself into the car. But if truth were told, she was only too glad to leave Oxford behind, whatever might lie ahead of her.

She had nearly a hundred miles to drive, and now that she really had the car to herself, she had time to think and to reflect. She was in no hurry. She could sit in a lay-by or a roadside café if she wanted, and think without any interruptions.

The interview with Inspector Cartwright, although painful, had been useful. It had clarified her own ideas. She made a mental list of the points she had thought about.

First of all, was Andrew the intended victim? Or was someone else? And if not Andrew, then who?

Was Andrew killed because he interrupted something or somebody and if so, what or who?

The uncomfortable answer to her third question was that she, Kate Ivory, must have been the intended victim, and that Andrew was killed by mistake. Or because he was in the way. Or just because he was there. But in any case it was she who should have been lying there on the floor. For who else could the murderer hope to meet in her house?

She looked at this thought for a while, then pushed it away again. It was too difficult to contemplate the idea that someone wanted you dead. And wanted it so much that they travelled to your house and hit you over the head with a large metal object. Except that they didn't. It was a good friend of yours who was killed in your place. She felt sick.

For a few miles she enjoyed the view of sodden brown countryside and made sure that she followed the route she had written out. It kept her mind off the subject of dead bodies.

Fifty miles further and another thought entered her mind. The Sussex town where she was rejoining the others was not far off, and nor, therefore, was Devlin. She couldn't help feeling that he had something to do with Andrew's death. As far as she knew, the two had never met, and had very little in common. So what had Devlin got to do with it?

It was a question of what Devlin was. He was a man who went round making enemies, putting backs up, often without even noticing the effect he was having on people. In fact, this insensitivity to others was one of the most irritating things about him. That and his arrogance. And his vanity. And the way he looked at your legs. She could understand if someone hit *him* over the head with a heavy instrument. She had frequently felt like doing so herself, and she was a sweet-natured, easy-going person, after all.

She ran through the people he had told her about: the two thugs from Central America – or from the Arabian Gulf, depending on which story you believed. Edmund (could you have a murderer called Edmund? She didn't think so). Melanie's husband. Rodge. Someone called Joe, whoever he was. And then there were all the others, probably scattered throughout the length of the country, who had it in for Devlin Hayle. But who could mistake Andrew for Devlin? They were both male, certainly – though no one she knew exuded quite as much testosterone as Devlin. But Devlin was taller, wider and darker than Andrew. Even in a bad light you wouldn't mistake one for the other. And why should the murderer expect to find Devlin in Kate's house? It didn't make sense. Devlin couldn't be the intended victim.

But there was the incident of the fire in his room. (The room that was meant to be hers, however. And the excuse that Devlin had given for the swap was quite spurious.) Had she really heard the front door click shut? And then again there was the attack on Devlin in the car park – if it really was an attack and not just a drunken fall. Perhaps it had been due to the rampaging Cottam lads, as Kim had suggested, and nothing to do with Kate and Andrew, or even Devlin himself. But she was left with the fact that there had been two potentially fatal attacks on Devlin, followed by the successful attack on Andrew. It was too much of a coincidence, but still it made no sense.

She couldn't sort it out by herself. The ideas chased themselves round in her head and she got nowhere. She would like to talk it over with Paul. She just wished that he was there with her. He would be back in Oxford today and she wanted to ring him up and ask him to drive down to Sussex to meet her. But then, she doubted whether his high principles – let alone Inspector Cartwright – would allow him to discuss the case with her.

Which left her with Devlin. He might be a very poor substitute for Paul, but he might, too, hold the clue to the whole mystery. She must try to keep him sober for long enough to prise it out of him. Devlin, Paul, Andrew, and herself, Kate: they stood at the four sides of a knot. Pull the ends tight and what would you have?

She turned south on to the A284. She was nearly there. She must concentrate and find the book shop. She pulled into a lay-by and checked the instructions that Aisling had given her. Then she drove slowly into the small town.

Chapter Nineteen

Aisling was delighted to see her. So delighted, in fact, that Kate was suspicious. Why was she suddenly so popular? Her first reaction was to wonder what Devlin had done.

'Come and meet the book-shop owner,' gushed Aisling. 'Dolly, this is Kate Ivory. One of our favourite authors.'

First time I've heard that, thought Kate. Dolly was small and round, with grey streaked through her dark hair. She, too, looked relieved to see Kate and shook her hand warmly.

'We've had several enquiries about you,' said Dolly. 'People wanted to be sure that you'd be here.'

'And I have another couple of letters for you,' said Aisling. 'You're one of our most written-to authors at the moment!'

'I heard about your little problem, dear,' said Dolly, dropping her voice and looking solemn.

Kate wanted to say that the dead body wasn't so little, more like five foot eight and thirteen stone, but it seemed too flippant.

'Can I get you a cup of tea?' asked Dolly, in the same funereal tones.

'That would be lovely,' said Kate. 'And I don't take sugar.' She was afraid that Dolly would heap it in, otherwise, as being 'good for her'.

'Come and sit down,' said Aisling. 'Tell me all about it.'

'I'd rather not,' said Kate. 'Tell you all about it, that is. I've thought and spoken about little else for the past twenty-four hours, and now I'd like to get back to work, please. What has been happening here? And where's Devlin?'

If Kate had ever wondered what a pregnant pause sounded like, she knew now.

'We're not entirely sure,' Aisling said. Kate noted with interest that her face had turned pink.

'When did you last see him?'

'After lunch.'

'That's not so long ago. I don't suppose he's gone far.' It was now approaching half-past three. 'You've got a couple of hours or so before you need to worry about him turning up.'

'On the whole, I hope he doesn't turn up,' said Aisling.

'What's he done?'

'When you've drunk your tea, I'll take you to your digs,' said Aisling obliquely. 'I'm afraid that I couldn't find a decent B & B open at this time of year, so I've booked us all into a very nice little inn that lets a few rooms.'

'Inn? Do you mean it's a pub?'

'A very nice sort of pub,' said Aisling.

'With a bar stacked to the rafters with Bushmills and brandy,' said Kate. 'All just waiting for Devlin.'

'Exactly. I had no control over him, so he drank solidly throughout the lunch-time opening hours.'

'He's probably sleeping it off in his room now.'

'No, he isn't. I've already checked.'

Then he might be sleeping in a ditch, but she didn't want to upset Aisling further, so she didn't mention this possibility. 'What else has he done?' If both Aisling and Dolly were in a state, the man must have done more than get drunk.

'Did you know that there was a racecourse a few miles away?'

'I believe I did drive past it.' Races. Devlin. Had he mentioned that gambling was another of his little weaknesses? Possibly not, but it would fit in with what she already knew of his character. She could imagine that he would happily go and put the month's house-keeping money on a likely horse and then be amazed when it came in last.

'Apparently there's a National Hunt meeting there this week.'

'That's one where they jump over fences and hurdles, isn't it?'

'How should I know? What it does mean is that our nice little pub was full of dreadful racing types – common little men with tweed caps and binoculars. Last time I saw Devlin, he was sitting in the bar talking to a group of them. He towered over them – they were all about four feet tall – and they were nudging him in the ribs and telling him about this good thing they knew about for the three-fifty. It was all quite hilarious, apparently. They seemed to be pouring in pints of Guinness with whisky chasers at Devlin's expense, so I'm sure they were only too delighted to let him join them at the racecourse. Oh, what shall I do, Kate?'

'Do you think he was charging the drinks to the Fergusson account? Will they fire you when it reaches four figures?'

'Oh my God. It won't! Not really?'

'I should make sure the pub knows that he has no authority to drink at your expense if I were you.'

'And how am I going to get him to the book shop in time for his talk?'

'I suppose we had better drive out to the racecourse and try to find him.'

'Won't it be enormous and swarming with thousands of people?'

'I doubt it. As far as I know, it's a ratty little outfit that only keeps going because of the bookies. They need to keep the punters sitting in their betting shops watching horses gallop past on the TV screens without too many gaps between races. There'll probably be a few ageing types in Barbours and green wellies and a load of second-rate horses.'

'It sounds awful. Why did we ever come to turnip land?'

'I seem to remember that it was your own idea, Aisling dear.'

'Do we have to go to this racecourse?'

'What else do you suggest?'

Aisling was silent.

'More tea?' Dolly had joined them, still looking harassed.

'No, thank you. Aisling's going to take me back to the digs, and then we're going to find Devlin for you.'

'You don't need to find him for me,' said Dolly. 'I don't mind if I never see that man again.'

'What did he do? Pinch her bottom?' asked Kate when Dolly had gone to serve a customer.

'It must have been something like that. Or worse. He was only with her for a couple of minutes before she went all tight-lipped.'

'He probably thought he was doing her a favour,' said Kate.

'It's known as sexual harassment,' said Aisling severely.

'Not to Devlin, it isn't.'

'Have you finished your tea? Shall we go now?'

'I'll follow in my car if you'll lead the way.'

The pub was a very nice one, and although it was closed at this time of day, it would probably be crowded with locals and a few racegoers later in the evening.

'Give me ten minutes to settle in and then we'll go Devlin-hunting,' Kate said to Aisling.

Her room was small but adequate and at least had its own bathroom. It looked out on to the pub's car park, and Kate scanned the open space in case Devlin had once more come to grief at the hands of the local tearaways. There was nothing to see but a few crisp packets blowing about in the chilly breeze.

*

It was nearly four o'clock as they drove away from the pub in Aisling's car.

'Stop a moment!' said Kate, as they passed through the village. Aisling drew up outside the small general shop.

'What were you buying?' she asked in surprise when Kate returned.

'A newspaper. We might as well find out what's happening here this afternoon. Now, where's the racing page? Here we are. Framwell. The three-fifty is probably just finishing. Last race four-thirty.' She looked at her watch. 'We should make it in time to find Devlin placing his final bet.'

'What happens if we can't see him?'

'We'll deal with one problem at a time, shall we? Pull into this lay-by,' said Kate. 'I want to look at the map.'

Aisling did as she was told.

'Here's the racecourse,' said Kate, pointing. 'And we're on this road, *here*. If Devlin is coming back to the pub, he ought to come down this road, *here*. We'll have a quick look round and then if we haven't found him we'll turn left at the crossroads *here* and pull up at the T-junction, *here*, and then we should intercept him.'

'It looks like a very remote chance,' said Aisling.

'Have you got a better idea?'

'No.'

'We'll give it an hour, seventy minutes at the outside, then I'll have to go back to change for the signing. The punters don't want to see their Famous Author in faded jeans and a sweatshirt!'

'You look very nice in them,' said Aisling.

'Thanks, but I think I'd better put the little black suit on, just the same.'

The racecourse had the down-at-heel, depressed appearance of an enterprise that is losing money and won't be in business much longer. They were charged a ludicrous sum to park the car in a muddy field, and Kate was glad that she had stuck a pair of wellies in the boot before leaving the pub. Aisling was wearing the sort of walking shoes that are fine for strolling down Piccadilly, but which are inadequate for anything to do with mud. They made their way carefully towards the stands.

'It should be easy enough to see him if he's here,' said Aisling, taking in the sparse collection of unenthusiastic racegoers dotted around the seats.

'Do we know what he was wearing?' asked Kate, wishing she had a pair of binoculars with her.

'I suppose it was that awful mud-coloured coat of his,' said Aisling.

'It wouldn't stand out in this company,' said Kate. 'But maybe we'll recognise him by his size.'

'No luck,' said Aisling after a while. 'There's no one who looks like Devlin.'

'Maybe not,' said Kate slowly. 'But there are some people over there I recognise.' She pointed to a small group in tweeds and mufflers waiting for the last race to begin.

'Who on earth are they?' asked Aisling.

'Put your best smile on,' said Kate. 'Those are buyers of books, enthusiastic fans, would you believe.'

'Come on then!' said Aisling, setting off towards them. 'Anything to get me out of this place.'

'Oh, look! It's Kate Ivory!' cried a female voice as they drew near.

'Our fanciable lady author,' added a male voice.

'Aisling, you remember Joy and William Brent, and Jim and Jessie Russell,' said Kate.

'How lovely to see you again,' said Aisling, smiling as if her life depended on it. 'You know Devlin Hayle?'

'Of course we do!' cried Joy, whose pink nose indicated that she had been cheering herself up by supping on her hip flask.

'Have you seen him?' asked Kate. 'This afternoon? Here?'

'Oh yes! He was in fine form,' said Jessie. 'I do believe he had been celebrating with a group of friends. He was in a very jolly mood when we met him.'

'Any idea where he is now?' asked Aisling.

'You could try the bar,' said Bill, who looked as though he wished he were there himself.

'And what are you two doing here?' Jim asked Kate.

'Looking for Devlin. Whenever you see two fraught women combing the bars of the countryside, they are probably looking for Devlin. How about you?'

'Young Julian Brent, Bill's son, is at university not far from here. We thought it would be fun to combine a visit to him at college with one to the races.'

'We were wrong, however,' put in Jessie. 'This is a

bloody awful place, and your friend Devlin has provided the only entertainment of the afternoon.'

'Don't bother to ask how,' said Kate to Aisling.

'Mind you, the afternoon has improved now that you're here,' said Bill gallantly.

'Yes, dear Kate, the author we would most like to share a bedtime story with,' added Jim.

'I think we should be moving on,' said Kate.

'I think we should start checking out the bars,' said Aisling.

'Lovely to see you all! Thanks so much for your help!' called Kate.

'We'll see you again. Soon!' called back Joy.

'Please God he's still sober enough to stand upright,' said Aisling as they hurried off towards a sign saying Bar. 'Or at least sit in a chair without falling off it.'

But there was no sign of Devlin in the bar or anywhere else. The whole place was small enough to search in the time that remained before the last race, but there was still no Devlin.

Aisling opened her mouth to speak.

'No,' said Kate, before she could do so. 'No, I am definitely not going to search the Gents for the man. Not even for my beloved publishers. Any other suggestions?'

'I think we should get out of here before everyone else tries to leave,' said Aisling. 'It's not much of a crowd, but it's big enough to jam the narrow roads round here.'

'Good idea,' said Kate. She kept looking around her as they made their way back to the muddy field where the car was parked. 'Aren't those two familiar?' she asked, pointing towards the area where the bookies were taking bets.

'I don't think so,' said Aisling. 'Are they more fans of yours?'

'Eyebrows,' said Kate.

'I can't see him,' said Aisling.

'Maybe I was mistaken. Let's get on with Plan B.'

'How do you think he'll be travelling?' asked Aisling. They had pulled up on the verge by the T-junction, with a view of the road in each direction.

'That depends on what's been happening. If he's been winning, he could be riding in a Roller. If he's lost, he could be on foot or in a bus. He might have thumbed a lift. If he's fallen in with a like-minded crowd, he could be in the nearest bar. If he's lost and failed to pay his losses, he could be running, pursued by thugs. Or, alternatively, he could be tied up in the boot of someone's car.'

'How would we know?'

'Look out for air holes,' said Kate.

Ten minutes later Aisling said: 'This was a bad idea.'

Kate was inclined to agree. There was a lot of traffic on the road, but it was impossible to check out all the passengers in all the cars as they went past. A few people were on foot, but on the whole they were younger and fitter than Devlin.

'Shall we give it another five minutes?' asked Kate, eventually.

It was practically dark now, and they would be hard put to recognise Devlin even if he did come walking down the road.

But just as they were giving up, and Aisling was waiting for a space in the line of traffic so that she could turn round, Devlin found them.

A car drew up, bringing chaos to the traffic behind it, and a dishevelled figure fell out of the passenger seat on to the grass verge.

'Goodbye, my old mate!' he shouted to the driver, who waved farewell in return, before driving off to a fanfare of car horns. 'See you next year!'

'I think he's been winning,' said Kate.

'I just hope the driver wasn't as drunk as Devlin.'

'Aisling! And Kate! My own two loves!' And Devlin climbed into the back of the car. 'What a lucky thing that I found you. Wasn't I clever!'

'It wasn't luck,' said Aisling. 'It was brains and persistence on our part.'

'He's pissed,' said Kate.

'As a newt,' agreed Aisling.

'He smells like a brewery on a hot day,' said Kate.

'Brewery!' exclaimed Devlin, catching this last insult. 'I'll have you know I've been drinking the finest single malt Scotch whisky.'

'What are we going to do with him?' asked Aisling.

'We'd better get him back to the pub and then see what he's fit for,' said Kate.

'To the pub! What a splendid idea! A tottie after my own heart!' said Devlin.

'Can we gag him, do you think?'

'I'll drive as fast as I can,' said Aisling. 'And it's an odd thing, but there's a car that's been sitting on my tail since we left the T-junction.'

Kate looked over her shoulder, past the swaying figure of Devlin. She couldn't see the car behind them, only the headlights, and the fact that there were two people inside.

'Devlin, did you meet with your friends from Swindon at the races?'

'Evan and Stith?'

'So you know them. Why didn't you tell us that before?'

'You're so tight-arsed about things like that.'

'Things like what?'

'Gambling. Putting money on the gee-gees.'

'I imagine you mean losing money.'

'I do owe Joe a bit at the moment.'

'Joe?'

'My friend the Swindon bookie.' Devlin started to sing, tunefully but rather too loudly for comfort in the car.

'Shut up!' said Aisling. Devlin did, to Kate's surprise. Aisling was concentrating on her driving and was maintaining the distance between the BMW and the car following them.

'How much do you owe him?'

'About twelve.'

'Pounds?' This didn't seem impossible to deal with after all.

'K,' said Devlin.

'He means twelve thousand pounds,' said Aisling.

There was a short silence while Kate thought about it.

'Or it might have been fifteen,' said Devlin. 'Something like that, anyway.'

'Let me get this straight,' said Kate. 'You have run up gambling debts to the tune of fifteen thousand pounds with a bookie in Swindon, and he, tired of waiting for his money, has sent his friends – Evan and Stith, did you say? – round to your place to collect it.'

'Very good. Very conshithe.'

'And then, you disappear off to the races, and who should be there but your friend Joe the bookie and his two heavies.'

'Joe wasn't there himself. He sent his assistant. And his heavies.'

'And you were winning here at Framwell?'

'It was my lucky day!'

'Did they see you collect your winnings?'

'I wasn't looking for them. But they might have. Bet they were glad I hadn't put my hundred on with them.'

'No doubt. But they might have wondered why you weren't using at least part of your gains to pay off your old debts.'

'Don't be so boring!'

'It's boring being beaten up by Evan and Stith.'

'Shall I lose them?' asked Aisling.

'I think that would be a very good idea.'

Aisling must have been a rally driver manquée, Kate thought, as they slid round corners and turned left and right without indicating or giving any warning. Now she saw why Aisling drove such a powerful car.

The woman was a demon! She had serious delusions of power, obviously. She was splendid, Kate thought, as Aisling executed a perfect handbrake turn and screamed past Evan and Stith at eighty, travelling in the opposite direction.

They hit a long, straight stretch of road, with no traffic visible for a couple of miles. 'I'll kill the lights,' said Aisling. 'That'll confuse them.'

'It's terrifying me,' said Kate, as Aisling tore blindly through the gloom. But then, being stopped by two thugs was possibly a worse fate.

'I think we've lost them,' said Aisling, checking the mirror and slowing down. She pulled off the road and they sat there in the silence and the darkness. She pulled a small torch from the glove compartment. 'Let's have a look at the map. I don't want to switch the lights on, but I can see with this. We'll have to find our way back to the book shop somehow or other.'

It was a quarter to six when they drew up in the pub car park, which meant that Kate had about twenty minutes to shower and change and return for the signing. And first they had to manhandle Devlin into the pub.

'It's a pub,' coaxed Kate. 'Full of marvellous single malt Scotch whisky, Devlin. All waiting for you.'

'Will you be waiting for me, Kate?' he leered at her.

'I'll be keeping the punters happy,' said Kate, pushing his broad behind through the side door and trying to keep the momentum going until he was upstairs and in his room. 'I'll join you later, Devlin.'

At last they had him penned in his room and Kate

left Aisling persuading him to lie down on the bed until he was feeling better. He seemed eager to do so only on the condition that Aisling joined him. Kate grinned, and went to turn herself from frazzled wreck into confident and groomed Famous Author in under fifteen minutes.

'The little black suit certainly looks good,' said Aisling.

'Thank you. I'm fond of it myself.'

The audience was ranged in a semi-circle, three or four rows deep, looking eager. Kate smiled her confident smile at them. Her teeth looked particularly good next to shiny scarlet lipstick, she always thought. She looked at the audience. She must ask Aisling some time whether Fergusson were shipping the same rent-a-reader crowd from one venue to another. She was sure that some of the faces looked familiar, even though she had never been to this town before. She looked again, just to check that none of them was Evan or Stith, but they all looked wonderfully middle-class and respectable.

'I should like to introduce Kate Ivory,' said Dolly, raising her voice to a level that made her sound like the Queen. 'Though of course she needs no introduction from me.' Pause for brief but polite laughter. 'She will be speaking to you for a few minutes about her life and work, and then she will read a short passage from her new book. After that, Kate will be pleased to answer questions and sign copies of her new hardback – and any others of her books that we have in stock – for customers.' She ran out of breath and sat down.

Without Devlin there, Kate was on very good form. She smiled, she established eye contact with the front row, she was amusing and informative. She read her work as well as any actor could. She sat down to applause, and waited, smiling, for the questions.

'Can you tell me how a woman can fit her family commitments in with a writing career?' asked a youngish woman at the back.

Before Kate could answer, there was an interruption.

Chapter Twenty

There was a noise in the shop as though breath was being drawn in sharply past thirty sets of false teeth. A sort of hissing noise, Kate noted dispassionately, with a hint of a whistle in it.

She knew, without turning round, that Devlin Hayle had entered the shop. The door was behind her, and she couldn't yet see him, but a cold draught had hit the back of her neck which had brought with it the smell of a Scottish distillery advancing into the room. She could see the look of horror on Dolly's face. Perhaps it was an axe murderer, but on the whole she thought it was more likely to be Devlin.

The distillery pulled up a chair and sat down beside her. He nudged her black-clad knee with his own and said, 'Hello there, Katie. Bet you're surprised to see me!'

She tried muttering, 'Piss off, Hayle!' at him, but with no noticeable effect. So she stood up, still smiling, and said, 'Ladies and gentlemen, I should like to introduce my fellow author, Devlin Hayle. He is well-known to you all, I am sure, as "The Man Who Understands a Woman's Heart", and you will all have enjoyed his full-blooded historical adventure stories.' Then she sat down again and waited to see what would happen. Next to Dolly, Aisling was staring at her, the smile wiped off her face. She bowed her head and Kate thought she heard a small moan escape from her. No one noticed. They were all looking at Devlin.

Devlin rose to his feet and swayed. He had not changed out of the tweed jacket that he had been wearing to the races, nor had he removed the tweed cap that went with it. It looked as though he had been sleeping in both of them, and he probably had, at that. She saw from his tie and the front of his shirt that he had eaten something with tomato sauce on it for his lunch, and followed it with a chocolate ice cream.

'Ladies and gentlemen!' exclaimed Devlin. 'Members of the great reading public. That's you, isn't it?' Spittle flew from his lips and his finger jabbed in the direction of each member of the front row. They cowered back in their seats. They would have left the shop, Kate reckoned, if that hadn't involved edging their way past Devlin to get to the door. No one was going to risk that.

'Fancy yourself as literary connoisseurs, don't you?' Devlin was saying, scowling at the audience. 'Think you know all about it. You, the fat lady in the chamber pot hat! You think you're quite something, don't you? And the little wimp of a man next to you, in the dogshit brown tweed, you like to give an opinion on works of fiction, don't you? You think you know what it's about? Well, *you don't*! You know fuck all!'

Please, thought Kate, make the man shut up. Before

there is a riot and these nice, kind people tear him limb from limb. Send down a thunderbolt and strike him where he stands. Make a hole appear in the tasteful blue carpet and swallow him up. Or me up. How can I get out of here?

Devlin was getting into his stride. Although his audience was now growing restive and murmuring to one another, his beautiful voice rose above the background noise and reached every corner of the shop. 'You've got no taste. You've got no sense of adventure. All you want is the same bland pap that feeds your prejudices. The same boring crap year after year. You wouldn't recognise a literary giant if one arose in your midst and started prophesying! If Dickens, or Tolstoy or Hugo walked in here now, you'd turn away in embarrassment. Hah!'

Devlin suddenly put his hand to his forehead, all the bombast gone. 'I've got an awful headache, Katie,' he said and sat down abruptly, 'And I'm feeling a bit pukish.'

'I think we'd better get you out of here, don't you? Come on, Devlin. Off we go. Aisling will find you a couple of aspirins and we'll get you back to your bed.'

Now that Devlin appeared to be tamed, one of the men in the audience helped them to get him out on to the pavement. Kate returned to see whether anything could be salvaged from the evening. As she entered the shop she could hear the sound of vomiting in the background. She hoped that Devlin had made it as far as the gutter, and wasn't puking all over Aisling's car.

She heard a wail from the street: 'Katie! I want Katie

to go with me!' She ignored it. 'Katie! They're coming to get me! Help!' She closed her ears and hardened her heart.

It was obvious that people were unwilling to part with their money after such a speech. Kate smiled, and chatted to people, and one or two did come up and ask her to sign the copies of her books that they had just bought. She brought out a gold-nibbed pen to show how grateful she was, and signed title pages for Val, for Jim, and for Astrid with best wishes. But in general people were humming with embarrassment and obviously longing to leave as soon as they were sure that the pavement was clear of Devlin.

Dolly was pressing Australian Chardonnay on people, and small cucumber sandwiches. Kate joined a group of customers standing over by the gardening section.

'Hello again.' It was Joy Brent.

'Oh, hello.' She looked round. Yes, William, Jessie and Jim were all there.

'Thanks so much for signing my book,' said Jim.

'Thank you for buying it,' said Kate.

'I do admire the way you coped with Devlin,' said Jessie.

'Disaster management, we call it,' said Kate.

'I must say I didn't expect to see him after his celebrations at the racecourse this afternoon,' said Joy.

'I'm afraid that none of us expected to see him,' said Kate. She didn't add that if they had, they might well have stationed a large bouncer on the door to keep the man out. 'And I can only apologise for the insulting way he spoke to you all.'

'It wasn't your fault,' said Jim. 'In fact, without you, it could have been worse.'

How? wondered Kate. Well, the man might have puked all over them, I suppose, after ravishing one or two of the younger ones on the carpet.

'Thank you very much. Would you like another glass of wine?' she said.

'Yes, please,' all four of them replied.

Kate buttonholed Dolly and relieved her of five glasses of Chardonnay. If you had four fans, it was as well to keep them happy.

'That horrible man,' said Joy. 'I thought he was quite amusing when we had that Italian meal together. But tonight he went much too far. We all know that writers haven't the same standards of morality as the rest of us, but that was past all believing. How could you sit at the same table with him? I saw him touching your knee with his great hairy hands!'

'Perhaps Kate is a close friend of his,' said Jim. 'You must be careful what you say!'

'We hadn't met until this week,' said Kate. 'I must say that I found him quite an amusing companion for a lot of the time, but he did go too far tonight.' But now she looked at it, that fat woman's hat did look like a chamber pot.

'Well, we mustn't keep you from your other admirers,' said Jessie.

'We might see you again, you know,' said Joy.

'No!' It popped out before Kate could stop it. 'I

226

mean, my goodness, how extraordinary, three times on a single tour.'

'Just think of us as your groupies,' said Jessie.

'Or your supporters' club, if you prefer,' said Jim.

'Just don't let that man Hayle anywhere near us next time,' said Bill.

'I'll do my best,' said Kate. 'But the man takes little notice of other people's wishes, I'm afraid.'

The room was clearing, but she spoke to three more elderly fans, and thanked them for coming out on a February night to meet her. She smiled and she apologised for Devlin's behaviour.

'Where is he?'

'I beg your pardon?'

'That man Hayle. What have you done with him? Where's he hiding?'

'I imagine he's back at our digs, sleeping off the bottle of whisky and the pints of Guinness by now.'

Kate looked at the man who was speaking to her. Short, stocky, red-haired.

'Rodge?' she enquired.

'Too right. And I'm looking for Hayle. Where's he staying?'

'I don't think I can give you that information.'

'Who are you? His latest tart?' Rodge had angry red eyes to match his hair.

'I'm just a poor, inoffensive novelist, trying to earn a crust and spending half my time apologising for Devlin.'

'Devlin! His name's Dan.'

'The literary pseudonym has a long history,' said Kate.

'I don't give a—' said Rodge. 'But I think I see someone over there who can tell me where to find him. And just you watch out for yourself in that man's company.'

'Can't you get rid of Hayle for the rest of your tour?' It was Jim Russell again.

'It's not up to me, I'm afraid.'

'He certainly adds to the unpredictability of life,' said Jessie. 'Is that a bad thing?'

'I quite like the old bugger,' admitted Kate. 'And now I think I should go and have a word with Dolly, don't you think? She looks as though she's still in a state of shock.'

'Thank you, Kate, for what you've done,' said Dolly. 'I don't know what I should have done without you. I shall create a special window display of all your books and make sure that my assistants recommend them to my customers.'

'That's very good of you,' said Kate, impressed. This was what one liked to hear from a book-shop owner.

'And as for that Hayle man, I shall never have him in my shop again. And I shall return all his books to Fergusson. Luckily he hasn't signed any of them. I don't want them polluting my shelves any longer.'

'Isn't he in great demand? I thought he was a best-seller.'

'He used to be, but his sort of thing is getting very old hat. In spite of what he said, the public wants some-thing new every couple of years, they don't want that pirates and ravished maidens rubbish dished up every year.'

'I see.'

No wonder Devlin was having trouble paying his bills.

'Time to go?' asked Aisling, appearing at Kate's elbow.

'You've disposed of Devlin?'

'For the moment. But he's like a character in a horror movie who keeps coming back every time you think the hero's bumped him off.'

'Poor old Devlin. He's going to have a terrible hang-over tomorrow. And Sussex seems to be full of people who wish him harm. Have you any idea what Edmund looks like, by the way?'

'Who?'

'Never mind. For Devlin's sake, let's just hope he isn't here too.'

'Don't waste your sympathy on the man. And now let's make our getaway.'

Really, thought Kate, if it had been Devlin who had been killed, it would have made a lot more sense.

Chapter Twenty-One

The trouble with staying in a popular rural pub during a race meeting was that the place was noisy, Kate found. And since they were not in the town, and not even in the centre of the village but on its outskirts, the landlord was not too fussy about the time he closed. Normally, Kate would have joined Aisling in the bar and had a convivial evening, but after the events of the past couple of days, all she wanted to do was lie on her bed, close her eyes and go to sleep. She had tried to phone Paul, but still hadn't found him at home.

She had watched some anodyne television, she had had a warm bath. She had even read the rest of the newspaper she had bought for the racing. She lay on the bed and closed her eyes, but gusts of laughter and loud conversations kept beating against her door. The pub's customers must have been as lucky at races as Devlin by the sound of them.

Of Devlin there had been no sign nor sound. Kate had thought about popping in to see him, to make sure that he was all right, but she was too tired and too low-spirited to do more than think about it.

She was drifting off to sleep when she was awakened again by car doors slamming outside her window. More loud conversation. More door-slamming.

She heard footsteps in the passage outside her door, and hoped they didn't belong to Devlin, awake and off on the rampage. She wondered about locking her door, but there was no key. They were trusting souls out here in turnip land, apparently.

The quiet footsteps went past her door again, making for the stairs this time. Perhaps it was the landlady, fetching clean glass cloths. Perhaps it was a burglar. Perhaps it was Edmund. Or Rodge. Perhaps it was someone creeping round the pub with a large metal implement, looking for someone to bash over the head.

She knew she was being ridiculous, but she also knew that she wouldn't be able to sleep unless she went out to see what was happening. Suppose someone – Evan and Stith, for instance – had traced Devlin and set fire to his room again. It couldn't be that difficult to find out where he was staying. A phone call to the Fergusson publicity department would do it, no problem. 'Could I speak to Aisling. Oh, it's really urgent, can you give me a number for her?' would probably get you the number of the pub. And a call to the pub would get you its address. She turned on her bedside light and crossed the room. She opened the door an inch or two and listened. Another gust of laughter from downstairs. Nothing from anywhere nearer. She left her room and started exploring down the corridor.

'Aisling!' she called softly. 'Devlin!'

Aisling appeared in a doorway, fully dressed.

'What's up?'

'I thought I heard something. I wanted to check.'

'Devlin?'

'I haven't looked yet.'

'I'll come with you. He might consider that T-shirt an invitation.'

They tapped on Devlin's door. Nothing.

Aisling tried the handle. It turned.

'Devlin?'

Still no reply, but Kate could see a substantial form on the bed. She could smell whisky but she heard no breathing.

'Do you think he's still alive?' she asked Aisling.

Aisling switched the light on and they both went over to the bed.

'Call an ambulance,' said Aisling.

Devlin was lying face up, very still. He was blue around the mouth and there were pinpoints of red, like a rash, around his eyes. Kate could see no movement of his chest.

'Call an ambulance,' repeated Aisling. 'Then come back here and help me with CPR.'

Kate ran. She phoned for the ambulance, warned the landlady what was happening, and told her to send the paramedics straight up to Devlin's room. Then she went back to help Aisling.

'It worked. He's breathing again,' said Aisling, sounding relieved. 'Help me get him into the recovery position.'

They rolled him on to his side and put his arms and legs in the approved positions.

'What do you think happened?' asked Kate. 'Was it just too much booze, do you think?'

'Could have been, I suppose.'

They were both silent for a moment, while Kate remembered the quiet footsteps moving up and down the corridor.

Aisling said, 'Where's his other pillow?'

There were two pillows on her own bed, certainly, Kate remembered. She looked underneath the bed.

'It's here, on the floor,' she said. 'Why?'

'I used to edit crime fiction,' said Aisling. 'I read hundreds of the things, good and lousy. But I did pick up one or two points along the way. One of them was that people who have been suffocated – by holding a pillow over their face, for example – get these pinpoint marks round their eyes, where the blood vessels have broken.'

'And you think that's what happened to Devlin?'

'It's a possibility.'

'Maybe he likes to sleep with only one pillow. Maybe he chucked the other one out.'

'But it would land on the floor next to the bed, wouldn't it? Not underneath. That would take quite an effort, and I don't think Devlin was capable of anything when I brought him back here earlier.'

'Should we tell someone?'

'Let's wait and see what the medics think.'

Shortly after this the ambulance team arrived,

commended Aisling for her efforts, and removed Devlin on a stretcher.

'Do you know anything about his medical condition?' one of them asked.

'He was pissed out of his mind,' said Aisling. 'Apart from that, I think the man is as strong as a bull.'

'Shouldn't that be ox?' asked Kate.

'Not in Devlin's case.'

'Should we tell Jacko what's happened?'

'Do you think she will rush to his side with flowers and chocolates?'

'No.'

'We'll go and visit him ourselves tomorrow morning, instead. He'll probably be just as pleased to see the two of us as he would Jacko.'

Kate was glad to find that the noise was subsiding downstairs and there were only a few cars left in the car park. She lay on her bed with her eyes closed, doggedly refusing to consider all the possibilities that led from this latest attack. And within twenty minutes, she was asleep.

Next morning, over a breakfast served in the pub's small dining room, Kate opened the two letters that Aisling had given her the previous afternoon and which she had forgotten until now. Aisling herself was not yet down, and Kate was alone in the room. She was grateful for the solitude. She didn't want to make polite conversation just yet.

She opened the first envelope. Funny the way these letters always seemed to be in the same handwriting.

> Dear Miss Ivory,
> I have been reading one of your books, *Silver Song and Green Willow*. In this you make a reference to Helen of Troy, comparing your heroine to her in terms of beauty. But I have to tell you that you made a mistake in this passage. Helen was the daughter of Leda and Jupiter, and was the wife of Menelaus, King of Sparta . . .

Kate skipped down to the bottom of the page. It was more of the same. The woman didn't even like her books. She opened the other letter.

> Dear Kate Ivory,
> I am still waiting for a sign from you. I have done all you have asked of me, and yet you keep me waiting. What else should I do?
> And you haven't mentioned the present I sent you.
> Yours devotedly,
> J. Barnes

Another nutter, thought Kate. I can't make out what J. Barnes is on about. She put the letter down and helped herself to more toast and marmalade. I can do without this now.

'Good morning.' It was Aisling, wearing lime green and royal blue, much of it in stripes.

'Good morning. Shall I pour you some coffee?'

'Thanks. Have you rung the hospital yet?'

'I was waiting for you.'

'We'll do it after breakfast.'

Aisling took toast and spread it with butter. 'Were they good letters?'

'No, I'm afraid not. One of them pointed out my mistakes, the other I simply couldn't understand.'

'Let's have a look at it.'

Kate handed over J. Barnes's letter. Aisling read it through.

'Have you heard from J. Barnes before?'

'It's possible, I suppose. Like you said, I've been getting a lot of letters recently, and I can't remember everyone's name.'

'Have you had a present?'

'Yes. It turned up with no card, no message. No clue as to who had sent it.'

'What was it?'

'A gold ring. One of those knot-rings that take apart.'

'Where is it now?'

'It's at home in Fridesley.'

'Do you think that's what J. Barnes sent you?'

'It must have been.'

'Did you say gold?'

'Yes.'

'Real gold?'

'Yes. Nine carat, Paul said.'

'Not eighteen? Pity. But it's still a very odd present

to send someone anonymously. And it's even odder for a fan to send such a gift to an author.'

'I suppose pop stars get sent things like that every day.'

'It's possible. But you're not a pop star.'

'Life at the moment is full of mysteries.'

After breakfast Aisling rang the hospital to find out how Devlin was getting on. He had passed a comfortable night, apparently, and was sobering up nicely. They wanted to keep him in for another twenty-four hours, though it would take longer than that to dry him out properly. And yes, Kate and Aisling could come and visit him this morning, if they liked.

The hospital where Devlin had been taken was in a town ten miles away. They found him in a small ward of four people. He did look very pale, and there were still odd marks round his eyes.

'How are you feeling?' asked Kate, curious to see how Devlin would play this one.

'I have felt better,' said Devlin with a wan smile. Ah, thought Kate, we're the brave soldier, smiling in the face of pain, are we?

'Have they told you they want to keep you in for another twenty-four hours?' said Aisling.

'I believe someone did say something, but I was in no state to take in information.'

'Just how much whisky did you drink yesterday?' asked Kate.

'I may have had a dram or two, that's all.'

'It took more than a dram or two to produce that scene at the book shop,' said Aisling acidly.

'Scene? What scene?' asked Devlin. 'I remember only retiring to bed early because I was feeling somewhat under the weather. I don't believe I was well enough to attend the scheduled event at a book shop.'

'That's what you think,' said Kate. 'Thirty-five startled customers can tell you something different.'

Devlin turned his head away as though wracked by a spasm of pain.

'Are you all right? Should I call a doctor?' asked Aisling.

'Don't worry about me,' said Devlin weakly. 'I'm sure they have much more urgent cases to deal with.'

'I expect they have,' said Kate.

'And I believe I have you to thank for saving my life, Katie darling,' he said.

'I'm afraid not. It was Aisling who was the efficient one and who brought you back to life with her first aid skills.'

'Oh, Aisling.' He sounded disappointed. 'Did you give me the kiss of life?'

'I used various techniques,' said Aisling crisply. 'Whatever seemed appropriate.'

'Well, thank you, thank you,' he said fervently. 'Thousands of fans of my historical adventures will want to thank you, Aisling.'

Wasn't this going a bit over the top, even for an old ham like Devlin?

'I think we'll go and talk to someone about your condition now,' said Aisling.

'Get me away from the old fraud,' she said to Kate as soon as they were out of earshot. 'His thousands of grateful fans, indeed!'

They found a nurse who told them that Devlin still had large amounts of alcohol circulating in his blood.

'He'll be all right though, won't he?' said Aisling.

'He'll damage his liver soon if he doesn't ease up on his drinking,' she said. 'Have you talked to him about safe levels? Twenty-eight units? Does he even know what a unit is?'

'I'm sure you're a very brave woman and will tackle him on this subject yourself,' said Aisling. 'And do you think you could keep him in for forty-eight hours rather than twenty-four?'

The nurse looked surprised and said that it was up to the doctor. Perhaps they could telephone again later to find out what the doctor had said when he had done his rounds. She would also ask the doctor to bring up the possibility of Devlin's contacting AA.

'He'll think you want him to join a motoring organisation,' said Kate.

'Hmph,' said the nurse. 'And one other thing,' she said. 'Do you know how Mr Hayle's accident happened? He didn't seem very clear about it himself.'

'I'm afraid not,' said Aisling. 'We do know that he had been drinking very heavily during the day, after a win at the races, and we just popped in to make sure that he was all right. When we found him, his face was blue and he didn't appear to be breathing. The rest you know.'

'It's all rather mysterious then, isn't it?' said the nurse.

'Life is full of mysteries,' said Kate. 'Can we go now?'

Out in the car park, they made a plan of action. First they would return to the pub to load their luggage and pick up Kate's car. Then they would set off for their next book shop.

'Where's our next appointment?' asked Kate, who was losing track of days.

'Essex,' said Aisling.

'Isn't that quite a distance away?'

'I thought it must be close to Sussex,' said Aisling, confirming Kate's opinion that she rarely moved outside SW3.

'I hadn't planned to be with you today, but with all the mishaps that keep occurring, I feel I should stay and look after you. Let's work out a route, and then we can meet up for lunch halfway.'

'What about Devlin?'

'Sod Devlin. He's well looked after for the next twenty-four hours. And with any luck they'll find something seriously wrong with him so that he has to stay in for the rest of the week.'

'Is that a representative of his ever-loving publisher speaking?'

'It's a seriously pissed-off publicity person,' said Aisling. 'You're not the one who had to give him mouth-to-mouth resuscitation last night.'

Chapter Twenty-Two

There were luckily no race meetings in the part of Essex they were travelling to. Aisling had booked them a very pleasant bed and breakfast place, and took for herself the room that had been reserved for Devlin.

'Isn't it a relief to be without him,' said Aisling.

'Oh yes.' But Kate had to admit that it was duller when Devlin wasn't there. There was always something unexpected around the corner when Mr Hayle was with them. 'I could miss him just a little, though.'

'I wouldn't miss him if I never saw him again in my life.' Then she remembered who she was. 'You won't tell anyone I said that, will you?'

Kate laughed. 'Your secret is safe with me.'

'We are not supposed to say things like that about our authors outside the confines of the office.'

'You must admit you enjoyed the car chase in Sussex. Where did you learn to drive like that?'

'My brothers gave me a course in advanced techniques with a specialist school for my birthday one year. I rather took to it.'

'I'll say! Well, thank your brothers for me next time you see them.'

'I had thought of thanking them on my own account, but I don't think they'd believe me if I told them the circumstances.'

'You should enjoy yourself like that more often,' said Kate.

'But next time without Devlin in the car. Well, now I'm going to have a little nap before we start our labours this evening,' said Aisling. 'Last night's sleep was somewhat fractured.'

Kate was about to do the same, when their landlady called her. 'There's a telephone call for you,' she said.

It was Paul. She was so pleased to hear his voice that she found her eyes filling with tears. She sniffed.

'Are you all right? Are you getting a cold?' he asked.

'Just a touch of hay fever,' she said.

'How are you managing?'

'Fine, really. I'm keeping so busy that I don't have time to brood.'

'Good.'

'Is Harley all right? You know he found— '

'I know. We've talked about it.'

'You will keep an eye on him, won't you? I don't think Tracey knows how to deal with him at all sensitively. And Dave needs you, too.'

'Stop worrying about us all. It's under control, believe me.'

'Is there any news?'

'Not about the investigation, but there is about Andrew.'

'What?'

'The police have released his body for burial. They

traced his mother, and you were right, she's in no state to understand what's happened. He doesn't appear to have any other relatives, except for a cousin in Canada, and they only met once, fifteen years ago, so he isn't very interested.'

'So it's up to his friends.'

'That's right. As soon as you get back, you can arrange something. Was he any sort of believer?'

'I don't think he had any religious convictions, but there were plenty of things he believed in. I think it would be best if we could hold the funeral service at his college.'

'Do you know which that was?'

'Yes, Leicester. I'm sure the chaplain would officiate and let us hold the service in the college chapel. And the college must be used to services with the minimum of religious content. They must have a room we could use to invite people back for sherry and ham sandwiches, too. I'll think about it, and about the people we should invite, during the next twenty-four hours. I'm sure I could fit in a trip to Oxford between these shop visits, and then I could start doing some phoning.'

'It's good to hear you back on form again.'

'I'll see you soon, then.'

'Yes.'

'Have you been feeding my cat?'

'Of course. And Harley does it when I'm not there. I told you, don't worry.'

'I can't help it. I miss you.'

After a pause, he said: 'I miss you, too.'

When they had hung up, Kate spent the next half

hour wondering what the pause meant. Then she fell
asleep.

For that evening's session, Kate returned to her yellow
jacket and black skirt. She chose some dashing ear-
rings, put on a layer of make-up, and went to meet
Aisling. Aisling, she found, had changed from lime
green to shocking pink. Kate wondered whether she
could ask her to mute her colour schemes, but she
didn't have the heart. She was warming to Aisling who,
with her driving and first aid skills, was revealing
hidden depths.

'By the way,' said Aisling as they were leaving, 'it
isn't a shop this time, it's a public library. But I've
brought copies of your books so that people can buy if
they wish.'

'I thought the point of a library was that you bor-
rowed rather than bought.'

'The two things are not incompatible,' said Aisling,
driving through a narrow opening into a car park that
displayed a large notice saying 'Council Employees
Only. Other Vehicles Will be Clamped and Towed'.

'Aren't you afraid of being towed away?' asked Kate.

'Not at this time of day,' said Aisling airily.

'I do hope you're right.'

They were met inside the main entrance by the
head librarian and taken through to the room where
Kate would be giving her talk. There were about fifty
chairs set out.

'You're expecting a good turn-out, then,' said Kate.

'Not really. We always put out this many chairs, but there's something on the television this evening – some crime series, I believe – and we're not sure how many people will turn up.'

'Maybe they'll set their videos,' said Aisling.

'They might do. But with one of the speakers missing, they probably won't.'

'Do you think I could wash my hands and comb my hair?' asked Kate.

'The rest rooms are locked at five o'clock,' said the librarian.

'Would it be possible for someone to unlock them?'

'Glenys!'

'Yes, Miss Burcot?'

'Would you fetch the key to the ladies' rest room and accompany these ladies who wish to use the facilities. You can wait outside until they have finished and then you can lock it up again.'

'Just as long as it isn't too much bother,' said Aisling.

'Glenys doesn't mind. And if you need to use the facilities again during the evening, then Glenys will accompany you to the rest room.'

'Thank goodness we haven't got Devlin with us. He could cause mayhem with a system like that,' said Aisling when they were both out of earshot.

'I might have enjoyed watching him,' said Kate.

When they returned to the room where the talk would be given, a few readers were starting to filter in.

'Would you like to go in now, or do you wish to make an entrance?' asked Miss Burcot.

'Why don't we all go in and watch the punters as they come in,' said Kate.

'Punters?' asked Miss Burcot.

'Customers. Readers. The audience.'

'Oh, I see.'

The awful thing about librarians, thought Kate, was that they so frequently lived down to one's worst expectations. She and Kate took seats to one side, though it was difficult for Aisling to be unobtrusive while wearing shocking pink.

Miss Burcot was right about the size of the audience. Sparse was the word that Kate used to describe it. One or two of them came up and read through the details on the showcard and examined the photograph of Kate. Nobody appeared to recognise her from her photograph, she noticed. Perhaps it really was time that she had a new one taken.

'Have you heard of her?' she heard someone say.

'No, dear. But you have to get out of the house sometimes, don't you?'

'And it is free.'

The audience was older than the ones in the book shops had been, but otherwise it contained similar types. Kate looked around to make sure that Evan and Stith were not there. They weren't. They would have stood out quite clearly in this company. If they were after Devlin, they would be staking out the hospital in Sussex.

'Hello, dear.' It was one of the elderly women from the audience. White hair and a green knitted hat like a tea cosy.

'Hello,' said Kate.

'I wrote to you, you know.'

'How very kind of you. What would it have been about?'

'I asked you about my old schoolfriend, Edna Burbage.'

'Yes, I remember it well.' She didn't say that she had thought the letter was a practical joke sent by one of her friends.

'Well?'

'I'm afraid that the character in my book was an invention. I made her up. It's just that I happened to choose the same name as your friend.'

'You mean it was all lies?'

'Fiction. That's what we call it.'

The tea cosy went back to her seat and shouted at the man next to her, 'Come along, Edmund. We're leaving. She says it's all a load of nonsense. She made it all up. It's nothing but lies.'

The man stood up, and the two of them left the room, slowly.

'Oh dear,' said Aisling.

'Two down, eight to go,' said Kate. 'Did you hear what she called him?'

'Edmund, I think.'

'Yes. I was afraid so.' If it was the same Edmund, he looked as though he was getting a bit long in the tooth for attacking people as they slept. Still, you never could be too sure.

Just then Miss Burcot called for silence and introduced Kate.

Kate gave one of her longer talks, and read more than one extract from her novels. She wasn't going to spend much time signing her new hardback, by the look of it, so she'd better fill their evening somehow.

'And now,' said Miss Burcot. 'Does anyone have a question for Miss Ivory?'

'Yes, I have,' said a woman at the back. 'Can you tell me, dear, how do you manage to look after your family and write your books at the same time?'

'Did we sell many?' Kate asked Aisling afterwards.

'Only one. And a paperback, at that.'

'Was it worth it?'

'You have to believe that all this effort pays off in the end.'

'I just wish I didn't believe it was the same half-dozen people turning up every time.'

'Really, Kate, they're not the same people. They just look the same, that's all.'

'I do hope you're right. Do you think we should ring the hospital and find out how Devlin is getting on?'

'I suppose so. They might have had enough of him by now, and I had better make arrangements either to get him back to Swindon or on to our next venue.'

'There's one good thing about his absence,' said Kate. 'We're not likely to be disturbed by arsonists or thugs tonight, are we?'

'I hope not. I've had enough excitement for one week.'

When they returned to their digs they found there

had been two messages for Kate. 'One from the gentleman who phoned you earlier today. He said he would ring back in the morning. And the other from someone who just wanted to check that you were here.'

'That's odd,' said Kate, feeling slightly uneasy.

They were sitting in the very clean, very austere front room, drinking the tea provided by their landlady.

'I'll find out about Devlin,' said Aisling.

When she came back, she said, 'He's improving, apparently. They think they'll let him out tomorrow. Devlin himself is very keen to rejoin our tour and has made a provisional plan to travel up to Birmingham by train when they release him.'

'You don't sound enthusiastic about it.'

'I'm not. I could do without the problems he causes.'

'It's somewhere near Birmingham tomorrow, is it?'

'Just a few miles away. I was going to leave the two of you on your own for a couple of days, but in the circumstances I'd better be there.'

'In that case, I'll drive back to Oxford early tomorrow morning and see to the arrangements for Andrew's funeral if I can. Birmingham's not much more than an hour away, and I'll join you before we're due at the book shop.'

'If you were Devlin, I'd be afraid that you'd get lost at a pub on the way, but I'm sure that it will work out. Have you got the address of our digs? No? I'll give it to you.'

Kate wondered whether to ring Paul back before she went to bed, but since he hadn't asked her to, it meant that he would be working rather than at home, and it would be difficult to speak to her. She would have to be patient. She just wished that he would drop everything and fly to her side. She needed him. She really was growing soft.

Before she went up to bed, she spoke to the landlady.

'You do lock the house up at night, don't you?'

'Of course, dear. I couldn't have strangers wandering around in here, could I?'

'No, of course not. And you bolt the doors as well?'

'You are a nervous one, aren't you? Yes, I bolt the back door, and Dannie bolts the front door when he comes in. It's on the Yale till then. I couldn't lock my own son out of the house, could I? But don't you worry, dear, Dannie never forgets to bolt the door behind him.'

'And have you got an alarm?'

'I'll give you a call in the morning. What time do you want to get up?'

'Seven, please. But actually, I meant a burglar alarm. Do you have one of those?'

'Good Lord, no! They're a terrible nuisance, going off at all times of night or day, just because a sparrow's farted. And then the police come round and the neighbours complain. They're more trouble than they're worth. Like those car alarms. You haven't got one of those, have you, dear? I don't want to be scared out of my bed by that thing screeching in the middle of the night.'

Kate assured her that her car was too old to boast an

alarm. She couldn't speak for Aisling, but she was sure that Aisling's alarm would be in full working order.

'But don't you fret yourself,' said the landlady. 'It's not like London here. We're still safe in our beds at nights in this little village.'

Good old turnip land, as Devlin would say. Kate, more or less satisfied, went upstairs to bed. It was a pity she didn't ask what time Dannie was likely to come in, because his mother would have told her that he was on nights this week and wouldn't be back until eight o'clock in the morning.

Chapter Twenty-Three

Something had woken her. A noise, but she could not identify what it was. But something. She listened, holding her breath. Nothing. This was getting to be a habit. There was no glimmer of light through the thick, lined curtains and so she sat up in bed, straining to see through the darkness, listening for the slightest sound in the sleeping house. Perhaps, her reason told her, it was Dannie, entering the house and bolting the door behind him. She scrabbled for her watch on the bedside table to see what the time was.

A hand covered her mouth.

For a moment she froze in terror. Then she tried to bite, but the hand was held too tightly against her teeth to make much impression.

'I have a knife,' a hoarse voice whispered. 'Don't make a sound or try to struggle. Nod your head to say you agree, and I'll take my hand away from your mouth.'

Kate heard her heart thumping and her eyes were open wide, trying to catch the slightest glimpse of her assailant. She nodded her head to show she understood, and after she felt the slight scrape of a blade on the skin of her neck, the hand was taken away.

'I thought you wouldn't believe me unless I let you feel it,' the voice said softly.

'What do you want?' She found that she was whispering, too. Her mouth and throat were so dry with fear that she didn't think she could make enough sound to wake anyone in the house even if she did try to shout or scream.

There was no reply, so she asked again: 'What do you want?'

'I want to know where he is.'

There was only one person he could be talking about.

'Do you mean Devlin?'

'Of course I mean bloody Devlin.'

She sighed. 'Which one are you?'

'Don't worry about that. Where is he?'

'In Sussex.'

'What? But I checked. He was booked into this place, and so were you. But then the big horse-faced woman turned up and took his room. So there's only one other place he could be.'

'Where?'

'Here, you stupid cow. So where is he?'

'In hospital. In Sussex.' Why wouldn't he believe her and leave her alone? He was whispering still, but she thought she was starting to recognise the way he spoke.

'Rodge?'

'Never you mind who I am.'

'I'm right, aren't I?'

'Maybe.'

'Let me get this straight.' She was feeling bolder now that she knew who it was, even if he did go in for body-building. 'You believe that I am the last in a long line of women that Devlin's been bonking.'

'Yeah. Of course. It's obvious.'

'And you think he is sharing this room with me?'

'Yeah.'

'Well, where is he? In the wardrobe? Sleeping in the bath?'

'He could be.'

'Why don't I turn the light on and let you search?'

Short silence. 'All right.'

She switched the bedside light on. Rodge was wearing black trousers and jacket and a balaclava helmet. 'Go on then,' she said.

He prowled round the room, peering under the bed, into the cupboard, in the bathroom.

'Well?'

'He's not here.'

'That's what I said. You'd better check outside the window, too, in case he's hanging on to the windowsill by his fingernails.'

'All right, I believe you.'

'Now, to get back to the central problem, you think that Devlin should give up all his other women and marry your sister.'

'She was a fool to get involved with him. But after five kids they ought to do the right thing.'

'I agree.'

There was a short silence. 'You do?'

'Yes, of course. And no, I met Devlin for the first time, or nearly so, last Monday. We are not having an affair. I have my own, very passable, bloke in Oxford and I can't wait to get back to him.'

'Are you sure?'

'Absolutely. Devlin is not my type and never has been, and I completely agree with you about his responsibilities towards Jacko. I also think, for what it's worth, that he should give up drinking and gambling.'

'Maybe, but a man needs some pleasures in life.'

'I don't think Devlin stints himself on those.'

They were getting positively cosy.

'How did you get into the house?'

'It was easy. Just an ordinary lock. No one had bolted the door.'

So either dear Dannie hadn't come home yet, or he wasn't as reliable about locking up as his mother imagined.

'Do you think you could leave now? I get rather nervous when people break into my bedroom and brandish knives in my direction. I'll do all I can – not that it's likely to be much – to get Devlin to behave better.'

'I'm a fool, but I believe you.' He moved away towards the door. 'I'm sorry about the misunderstanding, but I'm glad we got it sorted out. You won't complain or anything, will you?'

'I may be a fool, but no, I won't.'

He slipped silently out of the room and she heard the door click softly behind him.

At this moment she heard a noise from the next

room. Aisling's room. She remembered now what acute hearing Aisling had: when she had called her name softly upstairs in the pub, Aisling had appeared at her door immediately. Maybe she had heard their whispered voices, or a creaking floorboard.

There was a soft tap at her door. 'Kate?' It was Aisling. 'Are you all right, Kate?' came the voice at the door.

'Yes?' Kate called out as though she had just awoken. 'Is someone there?'

'It's only me,' said Aisling. 'I thought I heard something. I was just checking.'

If she had been a sensible person she would probably have called Aisling in and told her all about her night-time visitor, then they would both have reported the incident to the police. But Kate felt sorry for Rodge, and she didn't feel like shopping him to Aisling or anyone else.

Chapter Twenty-Four

When the landlady called her at seven the next morning, Kate was still groggy with tiredness, but she managed to resist the temptation to turn over and doze off again. She sat up in bed and knuckled the sleep out of her eyes.

She looked around the little room. It looked absolutely normal. Images of a shadowy figure and a whispering voice came back to her. Had it really happened? She couldn't blame Rodge for what he had done, but by daylight it did seem out of proportion.

When she went downstairs to breakfast she found that she was alone in the dining room.

'Is Aisling not down yet?' she asked the landlady.

'I heard her splashing about in the bathroom. She must be taking a bath, even though it is a Saturday morning.'

Kate helped herself to toast.

'Wouldn't you like some marmalade on that? It's home-made.'

'Thank you.'

'I'll get you some fresh coffee. I've never met anyone like you for drinking coffee.'

Kate was on her second slice of toast and marmalade when Aisling appeared.

'Good morning.'

'Good morning, Kate.' She looked carefully at her. 'You're looking a bit pale, are you feeling all right?'

'Fine. It's just that I didn't sleep very well.'

'Any particular reason?'

'Just general stress and worry, I think.'

'Did something wake you?'

'I wondered about that,' said Kate. 'I had the impression that someone might have been walking around' – she decided to keep it general – 'but I thought it was a dream. Did you hear something in the night?'

'I'm a very light sleeper, as you've probably noticed. I thought something woke me, but then I listened for a while and couldn't hear anything. I called out to you, in case you had heard it, too.'

'I don't remember that. I must have been asleep. And it could have been our landlady's son returning, and being told off by his mother.'

'Very likely,' said Aisling. 'Is there any coffee in that pot?'

'I'll ask for some more. She already thinks we're mad for having so many baths and drinking such a lot of coffee. We might as well confirm her prejudices about us creative types.'

'What are your plans for today?'

'I'll go upstairs to pack after breakfast. The earlier I get to Oxford, the better.'

'Will you be all right, returning to your house? You won't be, you know, upset or anything, will you?'

'I expect I will. But I have to face going in there at some time. And the longer I put it off the worse it will be. I have to get it over with.'

The thought dampened her spirits as she went upstairs to pack. She would have to open the front door and look at the spot where Andrew's body had lain. Would there still be a chalk outline to show its position? Would there still – she shuddered at the thought – be a patch of dried blood on the carpet. She would have to face it, though. What she had said to Aisling was right: the longer she put it off, the worse it would be.

When she had packed, she took her bags downstairs and loaded them into the boot of her car. Then she had a word with the landlady.

'When my friend from Oxford rings this morning, tell him that I've already left and will be in my own house as soon as I can. He can ring me there later.'

Aisling came down to see her off.

'I'll see you at the book shop tomorrow evening,' said Kate. 'I won't have time to ring the hospital to find out how Devlin's getting on, so let me know how he is when I see you.'

Aisling pulled a face. 'I thought I'd arrange for him to be taken back to Swindon. My brothers have booked my first lesson in a glider, so I was going home this morning. Then I thought what havoc Devlin could wreak without me as his minder, and I've put off the lesson. I'm driving down to Sussex while you're going to Oxford.'

Kate laughed. 'You do lead a surprisingly exciting life!'

'Oh no. I think it's just that my brothers would rather watch me doing these things than try them themselves.'

'I'll be off,' said Kate.

'Drive safely,' said Aisling.

As Kate was belting herself into the car, a young man wheeling a small motorcycle came through the gate. She stuck her head out of the side window.

'Dannie?' she queried. 'Have you just got back from work?'

'Yes,' he said, surprised. 'Who wants me?'

'No, it's nothing. I was just curious,' she said.

In the Sussex hospital, Devlin was making a nuisance of himself.

He had been given a bottle of tablets to take for the next week. He had been given a lecture on the evils of over-indulgence in alcohol. When they caught him having a cigarette in the television room they gave him another lecture on the evils of smoking. Then they discharged him. It was at this point that Aisling turned up.

'I've come to drive you home to Swindon,' she said. 'Jacko will take care of you now.'

'If I were going up in flames, Jacko wouldn't piss on me to put the fire out,' said Devlin. 'The chances are she'll tell me that it was all my own fault and she's buggered if she's going to raise a finger to help me.'

'Nonsense. Of course she'll be delighted you're

back. She wouldn't want anyone else to look after you. She is your wife, after all.'

'Not exactly my wife. We never quite got round to doing anything formal about marriage.'

'Even after having five children?'

'Jacko likes to keep the idea of her independence. In a situation like this one, she's likely to say that it's nothing to do with her and I can go and find one of my other women to look after me.'

'Nevertheless, home is the best place for you,' said Aisling.

'*No!*' roared Devlin. 'I'm not being bossed about by any more women. I've had them sticking thermometers in my mouth and needles in my bum for the last couple of days. I'm not having Jacko bullying me and nagging me now. That's enough. I'm back to work. It's Birmingham tomorrow evening, isn't it?'

'A small place not far from there,' said Aisling, seeing that she was about to lose the argument. She couldn't imagine driving a protesting Devlin all the way to Swindon. She didn't like the idea of driving a complaisant Devlin to Birmingham, but at least she might be able to keep him under control and make sure that he didn't hit the whisky too heavily before the evening.

'Have you understood me?' said Devlin. 'I am not going to Swindon. I am going to Birmingham. Is that clear enough?'

'Very well,' she said, giving in since she saw no alternative. 'We'd better look at the map. Do you want to spend tonight in Sussex or in Birmingham?'

'As long as I don't have to spend the night with you, Aisling, I don't care,' he said nastily.

'Very well,' she said. 'We'll go to Birmingham, then. I believe you're an excellent navigator, so you can be in charge of getting us there. You tell me where to point the car, and I'll drive it.'

With any luck, she thought, Devlin would get them so lost that they'd end up in North Wales or East Anglia, and far from the unsuspecting book shop that they were scheduled to visit.

'What about my luggage?' asked Devlin as they got to the car.

'There was very little of it,' said Kate. 'I've put a plastic bag full of dirty laundry in the boot, and that zip-top thing of yours. You'd better find a launderette and get your washing done, or I can understand how Jacko will be less than welcoming when you turn up with it.'

'Women's work!' said Devlin. 'If you think my underpants and socks need washing, you'd better do them yourself.'

'Good try, but no. I will show you to the launderette and give you instructions, but you will do this one thing for yourself.'

Devlin looked at her admiringly. 'There's nothing I like more than a strong-minded woman.' His large paw reached across and squeezed her knee. 'Why don't the two of us slope off tonight and find a little place for dinner on our own?'

'No thank you,' said Aisling. She removed the hairy

hand from her knee and put the car into gear. 'I hope you've fastened your seatbelt,' she said.

'Hello. Joe Latch Betting Shop.'

'Is that you, Boss?'

'Joe Latch speaking. Who's that?'

'It's Evan, Boss.'

'So what you and Stith been up to the last twenty-four hours, eh?'

'Tracking Hayle. Like you told us.'

'And have you found him?'

'We found the hospital they took him to.'

'It wasn't you put him there, was it?'

'No, Boss. We don't know who done that. But it weren't us.'

'Well, what you doing now, then? Have you been to see the bugger? Told him I want my money?'

'We went up to see him in the hospital. I don't like hospitals myself, but we thought he'd find it difficult to get away from us if he was lying in bed. Stith bought some flowers down at the stall by the gate. We walked up through the wards but when we go there, he'd gone.'

'How do you mean, gone? Have they switched off his life support, or what?'

'No, he's gone. Someone came and picked him up. They drove off while we was in the hospital, we reckon. Just caught sight of 'em as they turned right out of the car park.'

'Who was it? Who took him?'

'It was some tart in a red BMW and an orange coat.'

'She should be easy enough to spot when you catch up with them. Why didn't you follow her?'

'We tried to, but she was driving so bloody fast she'd disappeared by the time we got to the car and drove it down the road.'

'A woman. Chances are she's from that publishers. They employ a lot of women, don't they? Let me look at the list the bloke in the office gave me. Helpful little prat he was. Sunday. They're due up near Birmingham tomorrow evening. So why don't you get in the car and catch up with them?'

'Have you got an address in case we don't catch her? I reckon you'd need a helicopter to follow that one.'

'Yes. Have you got something to write with?'

'Just a minute, Boss.'

'Here's the address, then. Mind you don't lose him this time. I want the money he owes me, understand?'

Chapter Twenty-Five

Kate drew up outside her house. She reversed the car into a parking space, taking time to place it precisely parallel to the kerb and just a couple of inches away from it. It was surprising how speedily you could do this, she noted, when you were in no hurry at all. She knew she was wasting time, to put off the moment when she would have to open the front door, but she did it anyway.

The yellow tape and the blue uniforms had gone, but she hesitated on the doorstep before putting her key in the lock and pushing the door open. She might have waited out there even longer, but she could hear the telephone ringing in the background, calling her inside. It was an excuse to pass swiftly through the hall and into the sitting room to where the phone sat on the windowsill.

She noticed in passing that someone had cleaned the carpet. There was only a faint discoloured patch where before there had been a puddle of blood and brains.

Telephone, Kate. She picked up the receiver.

'I was just giving up. How are you?'

'Paul?' She felt a rush of relief. Who had she been afraid she might find on the other end of the line?

'You sound a bit odd. Are you all right?'

'I've only just got here. The phone was ringing as I came through the door.' Mind you, if the phone hadn't been ringing, she might still be out on the doorstep. But she didn't say that.

'It must have been difficult for you, coming back into the house.'

'Yes.' She couldn't think of anything else to say.

'I'll be over in about fifteen or twenty minutes.'

'But you're at work.'

'Yes, and I'm going to take a couple of hours off. I'm sure I'll think of a good reason.'

'Thanks.'

'Think nothing of it.' And he was gone.

The thought that Paul would soon be here cheered her up. She could sit on the pink sofa until he arrived without feeling guilty. She looked around at the room. It was just the same, perhaps a little dustier. Even the houseplants were still flourishing. Andrew's cotton throw was lying over the back of the sofa and she unfolded it and draped it over the velvet. He was right: there were a lot of cat and dog hairs over it. She would have to work over it with a roll of Sellotape.

On the low table in front of her she saw the knot-ring. She picked it up and looked at it. She slipped it on to her finger: it was loose. She couldn't like the thing. She didn't want to wear it. She took it off. And if it fell apart again she wouldn't know how to put it back together again. And she wouldn't care.

The front door bell rang. Paul?

She went to open the door and wondered why he hadn't used his key. On the doorstep stood Harley.

'You all right?' he asked.

'Yes, I'm fine. Come in, Harley. I've only just got here, so I might as well make some coffee. Would you like some?'

'Yeah. All right.'

If she went into the kitchen with Harley, she would cross another invisible barrier. Soon she would be able to move all over her house without being reminded of Andrew at every step.

'Aren't you supposed to be at school?' she asked, when they were sitting at the kitchen table, munching shop-bought biscuits and making puddles on the clean surface with their coffee. It didn't matter, thought Kate. It was her table and if she wanted it in a mess she could have it that way. On the other hand, since she hated things to be messy, she fetched a cloth to wipe it up.

Harley looked at her in surprise. 'It's Sunday,' he said. 'There's no school on Sundays.'

'Of course.' She should have known, but she had lost count of the days. This was Sunday and she had to drive up to Birmingham tomorrow. That didn't give her long to get on with what she had to do.

'I saw your car outside so I knew you was here,' he said. 'You parked it really well, didn't you?'

'Just for once, yes.'

'How long are you here for?'

'I'll have to leave after lunch tomorrow. I'll be back tomorrow night.' Then she thought of arriving in the house at night, in the dark, on her own. 'Or I might stay overnight and come back on Tuesday.' That would be better. Daylight. People.

'Would you like me to bring Dave round?'

'You can fetch him now if you like. I'd like to see him.'

Mention of Dave made her remember Susannah. She hadn't seen her cat since she arrived home. She was afraid that she might have run away while the place was overrun with policemen. She went to the kitchen door and called. No response. She would have to look round the house. She didn't want to leave the kitchen, but she forced herself to do it.

She found Susannah in her workroom. 'Sensible cat,' said Kate. 'This was probably the most undisturbed room in the house, wasn't it?'

Susannah sat on a pile of papers, which Kate recognised as a couple of chapters of *Izanna's Secret*. She had made herself comfortable by scrunching up some of the pages and kneading pin holes in them. Susannah stared at her with baleful amber eyes. The wind had risen again, and the house was noisy, with rattling window frames and whistling chimneys. Susannah lashed her tail and wailed at Kate.

'You think that I'm responsible for all this wind and rain, don't you, Susie? You think I can make it all better for you. Well, I'm afraid I can't. I can't make anything better for anybody any more.' She picked the cat up and held her close. If she kept Susannah with her, she would be all right.

'Have you eaten, my love?' she murmured. 'Let's find you something delicious, shall we?'

Susannah struggled for a moment, digging her claws into Kate's shoulder, then, as they made their way towards the kitchen, she realised that food was on its way and stopped protesting.

A few minutes later the kitchen was full of Harley and Dave, and then Paul, who arrived at the same time.

After she had greeted them both, she said, 'Do you know who cleaned . . . things . . . up?'

'I did,' said Paul. 'I didn't think you'd want to face it when you came home.'

'Thank you. I was dreading the sight of the hall when I came in. You can hardly see where it happened now.'

'But you imagine it, don't you?' said Paul. 'It hasn't really disappeared.'

'Maybe I'll get the carpet replaced.'

'It might be a good idea.'

'Coffee?'

'Yes please. What are you going to do today?'

'I want to get his funeral organised. There's no one else to do it, and anyway I'd like to.'

'Yes, it will put some sort of ending on his life for you, won't it?'

'There's a lot to do. I've got to find a chapel and notify all the people who need to be notified. Thank goodness it's term time. I can find most of them in their colleges.'

'Do you know whether he wanted to be buried or cremated?'

'Cremated. I'd better contact the crematorium and see when they've got a free time.'

'I think it's time to make some of your lists. Find us some paper and I'll help you.'

'Thanks.'

They moved into the sitting room so that Kate was near the phone.

'Didn't he belong to some Oxford college?' said Paul.

'Yes, Leicester. I'll get in touch with the Warden and the Chaplain.'

'He'll want a traditional do,' said Paul. 'None of that modern English for Andrew.'

'I'll make sure they know what he would want,' said Kate. 'By the way, Paul, I tried really hard to get hold of you on Thursday to let you know what had happened.'

'Hadn't I left the number with you?'

'No. I tried your office and they gave me the number of the management course organisers.'

'That's good.'

'No. When I rang them they said they'd never heard of you.'

'That's ridiculous. Of course I was there.'

'The first time I rang they said everyone on the course was out. The second time they said you weren't there.'

'It just shows you how hopeless these management types are.'

'I'm taking Dave down to the rec.,' said Harley, bursting into the room with his dog and interrupting.

'You can bring him back here for the afternoon,' said Kate.

'Can I come to Andrew's funeral?' he asked.

'Yes, of course. He'd want you to be there.'

' 'Ere!'

'Yes?'

'That ring,' said Harley.

'What about it?'

'When I was here, just after you left last week, I was sat here trying to work out how to put that ring back together. But I couldn't do it.'

'You mean,' said Kate slowly, 'that you left it in four pieces.'

'Yeah. I didn't mean to break it. But I thought I could do it. I watched Paul when he did it, and it looked easy.'

'I couldn't manage it either,' said Kate. 'And Andrew couldn't fix it?'

'No, he said he couldn't do it and he wasn't interested in finding out how.'

'But it was in one piece when I came back on Thursday,' said Kate.

'That's why I asked you whether Paul had come home,' said Harley.

'Thursday? But I was still away then,' said Paul.

'You didn't pop back for an hour, just to make sure everyone was all right?'

'I knew they could all look after themselves,' said Paul, then stopped suddenly as he remembered that Andrew hadn't.

'So who put the ring together?' asked Kate.

They looked at each other. They had no answer.

'I think if we knew the answer to that, we'd know who killed Andrew,' said Paul. 'Are you all right on your own for a bit, Kate? I think I should get back and make a few enquiries.'

'Yes, I'll be fine.' Her heart sank even as she was saying it. But she had to get used to being alone in the house again. It was odd to think that she had just been getting used to living with her unconventional family. Now she had to get used to being on her own again. It would never be the same without Andrew there.

'I'll be back in ten minutes,' said Harley. 'Dave don't want a long walk today.'

'Don't skimp on Dave's walk,' said Kate. 'I'll manage on my own, really.'

'You could come with us, if you like.'

'I'd like to, but I think I should get on with making the funeral arrangements.'

Paul and Harley looked at her with concern, but she kept a cheerful expression on her face.

'Really,' she said to them. 'I mean it. You both go now. I'll sit here by the phone and I'll see you as soon as you get back. I'll be fine.'

The two males looked at each other, nodded, and went out together.

Kate waited until they had left the house before she allowed herself to cry. Susannah had joined her after her unscheduled meal and had jumped up on to her knees. Kate buried her face in the soft fur. Susannah didn't seem to mind getting wet.

I wonder whether the college choir knows 'Rejoice

in the Lamb', thought Kate, after a while. He was really quite fond of you and Dave, wasn't he? And we could all sing Psalm 23. I don't like Crimond much, but we could have Brother James' Air instead. If you've left me a flat piece of paper, Susie, I could start making a list.

Chapter Twenty-Six

'Well, here we all are!' said Aisling.

'Hello, Aisling. Was that a note of desperation I heard in your voice?' asked Kate.

'Kate! Lovely to see you! You're looking a little pale, though. Are you feeling all right? Do you think you should use a little more blusher?' said Aisling.

'Give me a glass of wine and I'll produce a healthy glow in no time at all,' said Kate. Somewhere on the M40 she had decided to put her personal life behind her and concentrate on giving the punters value for their £16.99s.

'Hello there, Kate.'

'Devlin, how are you?' said Kate. She found herself reaching up to kiss him on both hairy cheeks. And, oddly enough, she really was glad to see him again.

'They let me out of prison eventually,' he said. 'They said I was lucky to be alive and wanted to keep me in for at least another week, but I insisted. My public won't allow you to keep me away from them any longer, I said. They will be queuing up in Emergency and storming the medical wards. How can we possibly disappoint them? And so dear Aisling here drove me up to scenic Birmingham, didn't you, darling?'

Aisling was making faces at Kate out of sight of Devlin, but still she looked happy enough to have him there.

They were gathered in a small, independent book shop, run by a married couple, Martha and Bob Alden.

'What are we doing up here?' asked Devlin. 'Can you explain it to me, Aisling? It's miles away from our usual territory. Have Fergusson finally gone completely mad?'

'Martha and Bob are good friends of mine,' said Aisling firmly. 'I send them my popular authors for signings and talks, and as a result, they sell a lot of their books. In return, they set up events for authors like you and Kate, if I ask them to. And it increases your sales.'

'Are you saying that Kate and I are not popular authors?' rumbled Devlin.

'Of course not,' said Aisling. 'You and Kate are among my up-and-coming writers. Just another year or so and you'll both be up there with the stars.'

'I thought I twinkled quite convincingly before any of this nonsense,' said Devlin. 'Didn't you, Kate?'

Kate thought it was time to come to Aisling's aid.

'What a lovely job they've made of your showcards, Devlin,' she said. 'Isn't that a good photograph of you?' Devlin looked broodingly out of his photograph, a good ten years younger and much less careworn than he appeared in real life.

'Not bad,' said Devlin. 'Doesn't quite do me justice, of course.'

Martha Alden came up at this moment and handed them each a glass of wine.

'Australian Chardonnay?' asked Kate.

'Chilean Sauvignon Blanc,' said Martha.

'And very nice too,' said Kate after a cautious sip.

'You're right,' said Aisling. 'You're starting to get some colour in your cheeks already.'

'Now, let me tell you how we've organised things,' said Bob, joining them. They were the sort of married couple, thought Kate, who might have been brother and sister, they were so alike. Dark hair going grey, blue eyes, well-defined jawlines. Bob wore a dark blue sweater that looked like cashmere with his dark grey trousers. Martha wore a similar sweater with designer jeans. They looked like a matching set.

'We have sent personal invitations to all our regular customers, and in addition we put a notice in the local press. Anyone who came into the shop will have seen the posters on the door and in the window, and will have been offered tickets. It is a ticket-only affair, although the tickets themselves are free. It gives people the idea that they belong to an exclusive and cherished circle. We've set chairs in groups over here, so that those who want to sit down can do so, and chat with their friends. But we've left room to circulate so that you two can wander round the room meeting people and talking to them in an informal way. Don't worry about food and drink, we have slaves on hand to do the handing round and pouring.'

Kate raised her eyebrows.

'Our teenage children,' put in Martha. 'They are well-trained.'

'And reasonably well-paid,' added Bob. 'We have a good relationship with our customers, and in return they support our events. As you can imagine, there isn't much literary entertainment out here in the country, and they appreciate what we do for them. You'll find that they have met each other quite frequently over the years, and the evening will seem more like a party given for a group of friends than a commercial enterprise.'

'And what about my talk?' asked Devlin.

'At half-past seven, when the majority of people will be here, I will ask for silence and introduce you. Keep it brief, and read a few paragraphs from the new work. Kate goes first, I think, then you, Devlin.'

Devlin looked as though he was about to argue, but thought better of it. Perhaps the man was mellowing, thought Kate.

'I've put separate tables for you to sign at,' said Bob. 'One on each side of the room. That will keep the customers circulating. You'll find that there's a pile of your books to sign for stock placed ready on your respective tables, so you needn't fear that you'll be sitting there with nothing to do. I think I've covered most of it. Any questions?'

'I don't think so,' said Kate.

'There is just one thing,' said Devlin, looking a little embarrassed.

'Yes?'

'Have you a back way out?'

Bob looked a little surprised. 'Why, are you expecting to be pursued by gangsters?'

There was a brief pause before Kate put in, 'Devlin is nervous about fire. He was involved in an unpleasant incident last week and he likes to know that his exit is clear.'

It wasn't far from the truth. Bob took him through to the back of the shop and showed him where the delivery vans came in.

'The door is locked, but the key is on this side. All right?'

Devlin muttered, 'Yes,' and they returned to the main part of the shop.

'Is that everything?' asked Martha. They all nodded. 'Well, have another glass of wine, everybody, and then enjoy yourselves.'

'That's good,' said Kate to Aisling.

'They are very good booksellers,' said Aisling.

'I meant the fact that everyone is coming by invitation. It should keep out the likes of Evan and Stith, anyway.'

'Who?'

'The two we escaped from after the race meeting. The heavies. I can't see anyone offering them a ticket to a literary event, can you?'

Martha and Bob exuded such competence that she felt that she could relax for the first time in days and simply enjoy the evening. As long as Devlin behaved himself, it ought to be a piece of cake. And even Devlin looked to be on his best behaviour. Perhaps the nurses in the 'prison' had terrified him into submission.

Kate wandered round the book shop, looking at the stock. She would like to spend time here, she thought. There were plenty of books that she would like to add to her own collection. Gardening, cookery. Cookery. It made her think of Andrew and she felt her face move into downward lines. Stop it, Kate, she told herself. You're at work. You will smile and look happy. She turned back to the fiction section and picked out the new Kate Atkinson novel she wanted to read. She took it over to the cash desk. When she got back to Oxford she could relax for an hour or two with the results of someone else's hard work.

The customers were starting to arrive. They were livelier than the ones that had turned up to their other evenings. Perhaps they were a little younger. And Bob was right, they seemed to know each other, and greetings and hugs were happening all over the shop.

Kate turned to Aisling. 'Not a familiar face here tonight,' she said.

'Were you expecting someone?' she asked.

'No, but I've got used to seeing at least one of Devlin's enemies at every venue.'

'Are you talking about me?' asked Devlin at her shoulder.

'Of course,' said Kate. 'And incidentally, can you tell me what Edmund looks like?'

'Whatever for?'

'Just checking. There was an Edmund at the library talk the other evening.'

'Edmund is a tall, skinny man with a mop of hair falling over his forehead. And he wears glasses.'

'Is he in his seventies?'

'Thirty-five.'

'So it wasn't the same Edmund.' She felt a great relief. Now that she had tamed Rodge, it looked as though they would be safe from attack this evening.

From just behind her chair a soft voice said, 'Hello, Kate.'

She looked round. It was Jim Russell. She couldn't see Jessie for the moment, but Bill and Joy waved to her from the row of seats. Her groupies. It was nice to know that she was collecting a faithful following.

Bob Alden called for silence and announced that Kate would speak to them for a few minutes and then read from her latest work.

She could give this talk in her sleep by now.

I like to research my books thoroughly before I begin to write. Jim Russell had moved to a seat next to the Brents in the middle of the front row. His eyes were on her all the time, a smile on his face. It was odd how rarely you saw men smiling like that, for no particular reason. *I immerse myself in the period, so that I know what any of my characters would eat or wear or do at any time of the day.* Now, women of a certain age smiled all the time, as though it was part of their wifely duty to look happy and contented. *In some ways the research is the easiest part.* The odd thing about Jim Russell was that he had a face whose two halves, top and bottom, didn't match. The forehead was flat, broad, expansive; the eyebrows put in with delicate strokes of a fine sable brush dipped in light brown paint. His eyes were the eyes of a seer, a visionary. They were dark brown, soft as moss. He watched her through the top half of his bi-focals all the time she was speaking. She didn't see him blink. *I fill at least one notebook, sometimes two, with jottings.* His nose had a narrow bridge and started in a straight vertical. *When I get to the actual writing part, then I have to exercise self-discipline.* Before the nose reached the tip it broadened, and the nostrils flared like those of an excited horse, or a pug dog's, perhaps. His upper lip was heavy, strongly indented and was pushed outwards by large teeth so that it overlapped the lower lip. *And now I'll read you an extract from chapter one.* She could use a face like that in one of her stories, though she couldn't decide for the moment what the character would be.

After her reading, there were the usual questions, and she gave the usual answers. Bob wound up her part of the proceedings and thanked her. There was polite applause. She and Devlin were expected to circulate again for a few minutes before it was time for him to give his own talk and reading.

When everything was going well, like this, and Devlin was sober, it was a very enjoyable way to spend an evening. She could even get to like it.

And then she saw them. Evan and Stith. She couldn't possibly be mistaken. Black track suits, gleaming white training shoes, hair cut to two milli-metres, pierced lip and shaved eyebrows. They stood out in that crowd like two grannies at a rock concert. Had Devlin seen them? She looked round. Devlin was on the other side of the room, near his showcard and signing table. She didn't think he could have spotted

Evan and Stith yet. He wouldn't be looking so pleased with himself and so relaxed if he had. She must try to alert Devlin to the danger he was in. She moved across the room towards him. But as she approached, she realised that his two adversaries had also spotted where he was and were moving in his direction.

She was about to shout, 'Run, Devlin! I'll lock the door behind you and swallow the key!' when she realised that they had plenty of people on their side. Martha and Bob to start with, and Aisling. And their four groupies. Nine against two? It must make Evan and Stith pause for a moment.

Aisling was at a nearby bookshelf, absorbed in *Hang gliding for beginners of all ages.*

'We're under attack again,' Kate said.

'The two heavies?'

'Evan and Stith. Yes. Over there. Go and stand near Devlin and look large and tough.'

Aisling put down the book and did as she was told. Kate saw Bill and Joy and went over, quickly. 'Please,' she said. 'Go and join the group with Devlin. We need your help.' Wonderful people. They didn't argue. They just did what she told them. Now for the two book-shop owners.

'Martha, Bob, there's a problem with Devlin,' she said quietly. 'If you could keep that protective group round him, and simultaneously edge them all out through the back door so that he can escape, you could well prevent a messy fight in the middle of your lovely shop.'

They looked startled, but they went immediately to

join Devlin. The words 'fight' and 'shop' had galvanised them into action, she judged.

'Jessie!' She hadn't seen her before, but there she was in a navy-blue coat and rather smart red hat. 'Please. We need your help. Could you find your husband and then go and stand near Devlin, looking fierce. He needs protection.'

Jessie looked at her. 'I'm not married, but I'll go and help out if you like. Life is always so exciting when you and Devlin are around. It's the reason I'm becoming a book-tour groupie.'

'But who is Jim? I thought he was your husband.'

'Jim Barnes? I really don't know him very well, I'm afraid. He just sort of attached himself to the three of us. It's nice to have a man around, so I didn't object.' And Jessie went to join the group around Devlin.

Kate didn't have time to work out how she had made the mistake about Jim. She must have assumed that they were married because they were middle-aged and together. How stupid of her. Still, it didn't really matter now.

She looked over at Devlin. He was surrounded by an impressively large group of people. She looked across to the two thugs. They had paused and were consulting together, presumably waiting until Devlin was alone and vulnerable before making their move.

'What's wrong, Kate?' It was a familiar voice just behind her shoulder. She turned to look. Jim Barnes. He was watching her carefully. So carefully that it made her think. Someone called J. Barnes had written to her. And it was the very odd letter. He was probably the one who had sent her the ring, too. He was still staring at her, as though he could follow the train of her thoughts. His voice was familiar because it had left a message on her answerphone. She felt her expression change and by the way he reacted she saw that he knew she had made the connection.

'Keep smiling and move towards the back door. We'll go out that way.'

'Why should I do that?'

'Because I have a large screwdriver in my pocket and because you are aware that I will stab it into your neck if you call out.'

Beyond a bookstack she saw someone else she recognised. Rodge. He waved to her and looked puzzled when she didn't respond. She couldn't warn Devlin now, she could only try to survive herself. She moved towards the back door, Jim close beside her. They skirted the group round Devlin. He was talking loudly and holding everyone's attention so that no one took any notice of her. Bob and Martha were nudging them all towards the back door. If they all arrived together there would be quite a traffic jam.

'Slowly,' said Jim. 'Don't draw attention to us. Keep smiling.'

She made an effort to follow his instructions. She knew that her safety depended on it for the moment.

After what seemed like an age, they were moving past the office and towards the back door.

'Unlock it,' said Jim, still in his quiet voice.

She did so and they passed through into the concrete yard at the back of the shop. Kate's mud-spattered car was parked a few yards away.

'Whose car is that?'

'Mine.'

'Walk over and open the back passenger door.'

'What are you going to do?'

'I want us to talk for a while.' She hated the quiet way he spoke.

He pushed her into the back seat and she sat there, her heart pounding, the blood thundering in her ears, wondering what was going to happen to her next.

He turned towards her and the moonlight through the car windows made his face more grotesque, like a mask. She still didn't know what was hiding behind it.

'Why are you doing this?' she asked. 'What is it all about?'

'I wrote to you many times. Why didn't you reply?'

'I received one letter from you, though I didn't know it was you until now. Didn't I answer it?'

'You sent a short, formal note. One you might have sent to anyone. And what about all the others?'

How to phrase this without giving offence? 'Are you certain that you posted them?'

'What?'

'Nothing. Just a thought.'

'And then there was the ring I sent you. Why aren't you wearing it?'

Because I hate it. 'I thought it was too valuable, too special to bring away with me. It might so easily have been lost or stolen.'

'Its place is there on your finger. If you never removed it, you wouldn't be in danger of losing it.'

'Yes, I see that now,' she said meekly. 'And I would have thanked you for it if I'd known that it was you who'd sent it to me.'

'Would you?' He didn't sound convinced. 'And then there was the way you flirted with all those other men.'

'I don't remember any serious flirting,' said Kate.

'There was that man Hayle for a start. His great hairy paws all over you, touching your legs, making obscene suggestions.'

'I don't think any of it was serious. He does that automatically to any female.'

'It was disgusting. I saw.'

'And did you try to punish him for it?' asked Kate softly.

'The man is indestructible! Why did that Aisling woman keep interfering? He would have died in the fire without her.' Without me, actually, thought Kate, but didn't say it. 'And he should have died when I put the pillow over his face. At least it kept him away from you for a couple of days.'

'And who else did you disapprove of?'

'Those men at your house. Always a different one! And at any time of night or day! They shouldn't be there. You're mine. Don't they know that?'

'You'll have to let me explain it to them,' said Kate soothingly.

'What? Don't be stupid. I dealt with one of your men friends in the only way he could understand, but there's only one way you'll belong to me for ever.'

Kate felt fear prickling down her spine. Slow beads of sweat were running down her back under her clothes.

'You should have worn the ring, though,' he said.

'We could drive over and fetch it. It isn't far to Oxford if you take the motorway.'

'You think you can talk me round, do you?'

'No, not really.' And that was the truth. She couldn't think of much else to talk about and Jim was getting restive. She had to get away from him. No brilliant plan came into her mind. She felt frozen, like a rabbit in the car headlights.

'It's time we were going.' The simple words made her stomach churn.

But at that moment she heard the shop door slam back against the wall and a jumble of shouting voices. She would have run for it then, but Jim's left hand was grasping her wrist, and in his right hand he held the screwdriver, just millimetres away from her eye.

Running feet thudded towards her.

'Don't say a word. Don't move.'

'Kate, is that you?' It was Devlin. She didn't dare to shout a warning. 'I've locked them in for the moment, but they'll come round the other way any minute. What the hell are you doing in the back of the car? And who is that with you?'

'My name is Jim Barnes,' said the soft voice. 'I am holding a screwdriver up to your friend's eyes, so I suggest that you do what you are told.'

Devlin for once had not had a drink all day and was stone-cold sober. He took in what Jim said and remained very still. His eyes searched for Kate, trying to see if she was all right.

'What do you want me to do?' he said.

'I think you had better drive,' said Jim. 'The exit is over there. And if your other friends are chasing you, I suggest you drive as fast as this motor car will go.'

'Keys, Kate?'

Jim took them from her and handed them over. Devlin climbed into the driving seat and adjusted its position. 'All right?' he asked.

'Yes, I'm fine,' said Kate. But for how long? Lovely thick clouds of stale Gauloise smoke were rising from Devlin's coat. She had never thought that she would appreciate the sour smell of the thing.

Devlin pushed the key into the ignition at the third try. He switched on, gunned the engine for a few seconds, put it into gear, then let out the clutch and put his foot hard down on the accelerator. The car moved off with a shriek of rubber and he aimed it at the narrow exit into the street.

Behind them came shouting, and a thumping noise on the car boot.

Devlin checked the mirror. 'Evan and Stith,' he said.

'Never mind them. Just drive! Turn left.'

As they moved down the street, Kate heard another car starting up behind them, and headlights glared in the driver's mirror.

'Aim for the M42,' said Jim, still in his quiet, controlled voice. 'That will be a right turn at the next T-junction.'

When they reached the junction, they saw that

traffic was heavy in both directions and Devlin sat, revving the engine, watching for a gap, however small. The headlights drew closer and stopped just behind them. 'Put it into first and just go!' snapped Jim. 'They'll make way for you if they see you're coming out anyway.'

There was a nasty grinding noise as Devlin changed gear, he put the headlights on full beam to show he meant business. He put his foot hard down on the accelerator and let out the clutch. 'Pray!' he shouted.

There was an almighty crash as they hit the car behind them.

Devlin, Kate remembered later, never could tell the difference between first gear and reverse.

The screwdriver had fallen to the floor of the car. Jim Barnes was dazed, shaking his head. Kate reached for the heavy, clublike steering wheel lock which was under her feet, and hit him with it. He subsided. She didn't care too much whether he survived the blow. This was the man who had killed Andrew.

'Get me out of here!' shouted Devlin.

There were two figures at his window and someone was trying to open the driver's door. Kate decided to stay where she was for the moment. Her car wasn't going to move far until someone had mended it. And there was blood trickling down her neck and ruining her silk blouse.

'Right!' said a new voice. 'Stand out of my way! I'll sort this out.'

It was Rodge.

'Help!' shouted Devlin. 'Get me out! Keep those gorillas off me!'

'I'll do that,' said Rodge through the window, 'on one condition.'

'I'll marry her!' cried Devlin. 'I'll go on the wagon. I'll give up gambling. Anything!'

'There are witnesses to what you've just said,' said Rodge.

'Fine! I swear it!'

'OK,' said Rodge, turning to Evan and Stith. 'Let's go and talk business. How much is it he owes you?'

'Is he rich?' asked Kate.

'There's a lot of money in the salvage business,' said Devlin. 'He's a good man to have on your side.'

'Do one thing for me now,' she said. 'Pick my mobile phone out of the door pocket and ring for the gendarmes.'

Chapter Twenty-Seven

'What's the arrangement?' asked Paul.

'We go to the college chapel for the funeral service at eleven-thirty,' said Kate. 'Then we go to one of their elegant reception rooms and mill around and drink Australian Chardonnay, or Chilean Sauvignon Blanc if we're lucky, eat smoked salmon sandwiches and talk about Andrew. While we're doing that, the coffin will be taken to the crematorium. Close friends will gather there at one-thirty for a brief service and then . . . well, I suppose the coffin disappears through the blue curtain and it's all over.'

'Is Harley coming?'

'He has the morning off school. I wrote a note to the headmaster for him and he has been given permission. He can come in our car, and I think he would like to go to the crem. afterwards as well. He won't remove his nose stud, but I think I have persuaded him into some respectable clothes.'

'Are you wearing your black suit?'

'And black tights and shoes, and a hat.'

'Isn't that overdoing it a tad?'

'The hat is emerald green.'

'That's OK then.'

They were talking to keep their spirits up, Kate knew. You didn't expect at this stage in your life to have to go to a friend's funeral.

Leicester college chapel was looking beautiful. The woodwork was dark and polished. The windows were rich with stained glass so that the light was both subdued and jewel-like where it fell on the warm golden stone of the walls. The flowers were cream and gold. The organ played softly. Kate didn't recognise the piece the organ scholar was playing, but it sounded like the sort of thing that Andrew would have liked.

The chapel was filling up. It probably held a couple of hundred people, and it must have been two-thirds full already. There were people who looked like librarians and people who looked like college Fellows. And then there were people who looked as though they might play darts at the local pub.

'Good turn out,' murmured Kate.

'He had a lot of friends,' said Paul.

'This place is old, innit?' said Harley.

'Seventeenth century,' said Kate.

'There's Camilla,' said Paul.

'And Carey. Wearing a suit, for goodness' sake,' said Kate.

'But he's still wearing an ear-ring, too,' said Paul.

'And very pretty it is,' said Kate.

'Where's the coffin?' asked Harley.

'It'll be here in a minute,' said Paul.

'Have you ever been to a funeral before?' asked Kate.

'Nah. Me gran's still alive,' said Harley.

Which was how it should be, thought Kate.

At this moment the organ music changed slightly and the college Chaplain entered, followed by the coffin.

'Is that Andrew?' whispered Harley.

'It was once,' said Kate, struck by how much smaller the coffin appeared than the man had done.

I am the resurrection and the life, saith the Lord: he that believeth in me, though he were dead, yet shall he live; and whosoever liveth and believeth in me shall never die.

'What's he on about?' asked Harley.

'Sh,' whispered back Kate. 'Have you ever been to church before, Harley?'

'Nah.'

'Well, look and listen. It's all part of your cultural heritage.'

This appeared to shut Harley up, at least for the moment.

Remember not the sins and offences of my youth: but according to thy mercy think thou upon me, O Lord, for thy goodness.

Or maybe it was that verse of Psalm 25 that chastened him, thought Kate.

Blessed are they that mourn: for they shall be comforted.

And I just hope that that's so.

The college choir sang Psalm 23, as Kate had requested, and then there were readings by men in gowns. Finally, the Warden – Carey's father, as Kate knew – stood up and talked about Andrew.

'Andrew Grove was a graduate of King's College, London University, although he had been so long at the Bodleian that he must at last have thought of himself as an Oxford person. His first degree was in theology, and then he added a qualification in librarianship. After a year running a small cathedral library and archive, he moved to the theology section of the Bodleian Library, where he remained until his death.'

It sounds so simple and so dull, thought Kate. And yet there was so much more to him than appears in this eulogy. People might wonder what difference it makes that he is no longer here, but it does matter. It matters to me, to Paul and to Harley. We shall all be the poorer because of that man Jim. And why?

'But that was not the whole man,' the Warden was saying in his rich round voice that Kate remembered so well. 'Andrew, as we can see from the congregation assembled here, had a wide circle of friends. He was a convivial man.'

You can say that again, thought Kate, remembering their sessions in the Crypt where they drank their way through bottles of pinot blanc and discussed the affairs of the day.

'Andrew was well known at his local pub, where he played darts, and indeed turned out for the pub team on occasions.'

Did he? Why didn't he tell me about it, she wondered. Perhaps he did, and perhaps I wasn't listening.

'And although he was not what you might describe as an athletic man' – slight murmur of laughter at this – 'Andrew was a keen player of the great game of real tennis.'

And I never really knew what that was, thought Kate.

But there it is, all gone now. What will they do with Jim Barnes? Shut him up in some institution, keep him away from society? And why on earth did he have to fix his obsession on *me* of all people?

They were shuffling to their feet, the organ was playing again.

'Can we sing now?' asked Harley.

'If you know the tune,' said Kate. 'The words are here in this book.'

'Course I know it,' said Harley, and sang with the rest of them.

'The day thou gavest, Lord, is ended.'

Later they circulated with their wine and smoked salmon sandwiches, talking to Carey and Camilla and to the Warden and the one or two other people that Kate recognised. It reminded her rather of her recent book tour, though the mood was rather jollier and there wasn't the constant background noise of the till ringing.

'Time to go,' said Paul eventually.

They picked up Harley, who was wolfing sandwiches.

'What's in these then? It tastes like fish,' he said.

'Smoked salmon,' said Kate. 'Learn to enjoy it, Harley.'

'If you say so.'

They said their farewells to the Warden and went to find Paul's car.

'Have you heard from the insurance company?' he asked Kate.

'Not yet. But the car was a complete write-off. They'll have to give me something for it.'

'Even though Devlin was driving?'

She sighed. 'If he hadn't been, I might not be here today. No one but Devlin could put the car into reverse and drive away with such confidence, sure that he was in first gear.'

'How's his neck doing?'

'He's still got one of those collars round it, but it's getting him major sympathy from every woman he meets.'

'I thought he had renounced all that sort of thing.'

'He and Jacko are getting married next month, with much pomp, and all the little Devlins will be attendants.'

'Good grief!'

'I'm invited. Do you want to come with me?'

'Maybe I'd better. You need a minder when Devlin's around. And how's your back holding up?'

'It's not too bad. There's nothing much they can do for it. It's just a matter of time, they say.'

They were in the car by then and driving the few miles outside Oxford to the crematorium. Kate was wearing a silk chiffon scarf round her neck to hide the stitches she had had put in when Jim's screwdriver had sliced into her neck when they hit Evan and Stith's Volvo. It was, luckily, only a flesh wound, as the weapon had slipped sideways rather than going straight in, and she didn't like to think about what would have happened if it had entered her eye. Jim was lucky, too, suffering only concussion and bruises as a result of the impact and her attack. He would stand trial for Andrew's murder, but he would probably not go to prison, Paul had told her. The man was completely off his trolley.

'You mean he'll get away with it?' Kate had said.

'No. He'll go to Rampton or somewhere like that. And they won't let him out until they're sure he is of no further danger to the public.'

'That's what they say,' said Kate darkly. 'But it doesn't always work like that, does it?'

'No system is perfect,' said Paul patiently.

'Is this it?' Harley asked, bringing Kate back to the present.

'Yes,' said Paul. 'This is the crematorium.'

They parked and found the chapel assigned to Andrew Mark Grove.

It was a very efficient procedure. The coffin arrived, and so did the Chaplain. There were a few brief prayers and then the coffin moved slowly through the curtain and disappeared.

Man that is born of a woman hath but a short time to live, and is full of misery.

But he wasn't full of misery, thought Kate. He was full of life. And now he's gone.

'Are they going to set fire to him now?' asked Harley.

'Soon, I think,' said Paul.

'Can we watch?'

'No,' said Kate.

'We're all going home now,' said Paul.

As they walked back to the car, Harley said, 'He were a funny sort of bugger, weren't he? I didn't get what he was on about half the time.'

They were all silent for a moment.

'But I shall miss him,' said Harley.